Also by Ray Hobbs and Publish

Published Elsewhere

WAYS OF GENTLENESS

RAY HOBBS

Wingspan Press

Published in the United States and the United Kingdom by WingSpan Press, Livermore, CA

The WingSpan name, logo and colophon are the trademarks of WingSpan Publishing.

ISBN 978-1-63683-051-3 (pbk.)
ISBN 978-1-63683-959-2 (ebook)

Printed in the United States of America

www.wingspanpress.com

This book is dedicated to the late Albert (Uncle Bert) Marshall, who experienced the worst and blamed the least.

RH

And soul by soul and silently,
Her shining bounds increase;
And her ways are ways of gentleness,
And all her paths are peace.

(From the hymn: 'I Vow to Thee, My Country'.
Words by Sir Cecil Spring Rice, 1859-1918).

As always, I wish to acknowledge the invaluable assistance of my brother Chris in the preparation of this book.

WAYS OF GENTLENESS

1

A Pennine Village
December 1999

Family Matters

Jill picked up the children's overnight bags and said, 'Thank you, Mike. I'm really grateful to you and Helen for having them.'

'It was a pleasure, Jill.' He nodded towards the cottage and said, 'If there's any heavy lifting to be done, give me a shout. Don't go hurting yourself.'

'Thanks, I may just do that.' Turning to the children, she said, 'Liam and Jessica, remember your manners.'

The children thanked their host and followed Jill into the house, where they stared in wonder at the profusion of cardboard boxes. They were moving from a modern, four-bedroom house with the kind of facilities they, like so many children, accepted as normal, into a cottage with three tiny bedrooms and the most basic heating system, but they were excited. She could see it in their faces. 'Let's get your coats off,' she told them, 'and then you can lend a hand.' She unbuttoned Jessica's coat while Liam removed his.

Jessica asked, 'What do you want us to do?'

'I want you to come with me up to your rooms and help me unpack your clothes.' Seeing Liam pick up his bag, she said, 'No, your clean clothes. There's two days' washing in there. I'll deal with that later.' She led them upstairs, where she pointed out the cases and boxes that needed emptying. 'Right, you two, you've each got a chest of drawers. Put socks, underwear and pyjamas in the top drawer, shirts and blouses in the next, and woollies in the bottom two, folded just they are. Then, anything that needs hanging goes into your wardrobes. If you can't reach the rail, leave

3

them on your beds and I'll do it. Okay? I'll be downstairs if you need me.' She knew she'd have to straighten things out after them; at eleven and nine, they were new to moving house, but the task would keep them occupied while she unloaded the kitchen things.

———

Eventually, with dinner out of the way and the dishes washed and dried, Jill put a log on the open fire and sat down. 'Now, tell me what else you've been doing with Auntie Helen and Uncle Mike.' They'd told her quite a lot during dinner, but their new surroundings, the features and layout had proved predictably distracting.

'We went on a canal boat,' said Liam. 'It had a café and everything.'

'Wonderful.'

'And ducks,' said Jessica. 'There were ducks everywhere. They let us feed them.'

Jill listened to the disorganised account of their two-day stay and knew, as she always would, that they'd enjoyed every moment. Helen was one of Jill's oldest friends and she was lucky enough to have married a man who had all the qualities Jill's ex-husband lacked.

Perhaps Liam, being the elder of the two, thought he should show some interest in his mother's fortunes, because he asked, 'What was the funeral like, Mum?'

'These things are never an occasion for jollity, but it wasn't too bad. The only others there, apart from Grandma and I, were some people who used to work with Uncle Maurice, some neighbours, and his solicitor, who was there as executor.'

'What's that?'

'An executor? Someone who makes sure that the terms of the will are carried out properly and according to the wishes of the person who made the will, in this case, Uncle Maurice.'

Jessica, who'd been following the conversation as well as she could, asked, 'Are we going to be rich?'

Jill laughed indulgently. 'No, we're not going to be rich, Jessica. Uncle Maurice left his house and most of his money to the Red Cross. What was left, he divided between Grandma, Auntie Sarah and me.'

'What's the Red Cross?'

Liam tutted and closed his eyes wearily.

'Go on, then, Liam,' said Jill, 'tell Jessica all about the Red Cross.'

'Everybody knows what the Red Cross is. They have a shop in Beckworth High Street.'

'But what do they do with the money from their shops?'

Liam wriggled uncomfortably. 'Something to do with people who are ill.' He added disconcertedly, 'Something like that, anyway.'

'The Red Cross help people anywhere where there's a crisis, whether it's a war, a flood, a famine, an earthquake or a drought. Now you both know, and it was unkind of you to be impatient with Jessica, Liam, especially as you didn't really know the answer yourself.'

Liam looked down at his knees disconcertedly, but Jessica seemed to give the matter no further thought. Instead, she said, 'Uncle Maurice must have been very important.'

'I suppose he was important to his clients. He was an accountant, like the man who advises me on income tax, although he described himself as a management consultant.' Seeing their bafflement all too clearly, she explained. 'He advised people on business management generally.' Then, remembering her own experience of him, she said, 'Actually, he was very much a down-to-earth kind of person. He didn't behave at all importantly. He and Auntie Iris just lived very privately, I suppose.'

'Why?'

'I don't know, Liam. I suppose I knew them better than anyone, but I wouldn't say I knew much about either of them. It's a pity, because I liked them both very much.' She could see them looking puzzled, so she said, 'There are some people who are difficult to get to know, and there are some who make an immediate impression. Uncle Maurice and Auntie Iris were like that. I liked them the first time I met them.' Remembering the pile of personal effects in the back of the car, she said, 'I've got some photos the executor gave me. I'll get them, and then you can see them for yourselves.'

She went out to the car, realising as soon as she reached the doorstep that she should have put a coat on. The cold wind was like a knife, and she was shivering when she returned to the fireside. 'Oh, it's bitter out there,' she said, crouching for a minute in front of the fire to warm herself. It was a floor-level grate set into the original stone fireplace and hearth, with a back boiler for hot water and the recently-installed background central heating but, for the moment, she was just glad of the heat from the log that was now well ablaze.

Jessica asked, 'Is it going to snow?' Her enquiry came with an element of optimism.

'It feels cold enough, but I haven't heard a forecast recently.' She preferred not to think about snow. The Volvo could usually cope with it, but a major Pennine downfall would be a nuisance. Come and squeeze on to the sofa with me, both of you, and you can look at the photos. She opened one of the albums and held it in her lap.

Jessica asked, 'Is that Auntie Iris?' It was a faded, monochrome picture of her as a young woman, no doubt provided by her family, and possibly taken when she qualified as a nurse.

Liam said, 'She was a nurse, wasn't she?'

'Yes, she was an army nurse, apparently. I'm not sure what they called them.'

'She was pretty,' said Jessica, 'but not as pretty as you.'

'Oh, Jessica,' said Jill, giving her a squeeze, 'keep the compliments flowing. My confidence needs all the help it can get.'

In response, Jessica snuggled closer to her.

'That must be Uncle Maurice,' said Liam, pointing to the adjacent photograph. 'He was in the Navy.' After some hurried thought, he asked, 'Was he in the First World War or the Second?'

'The Second World War. The previous one ended in nineteen-eighteen.' It wasn't Liam's fault that he confused the two. It seemed to her that, for whatever reason, History at primary school had been organised deliberately at random, like shuffling a pack of cards. Hopefully, someone somewhere knew what he or she was doing, so that the subject might make more sense at Beckworth High School, where Liam was now.

'That's not a sailor's uniform,' said Jessica.

'He was an officer,' Liam told her. 'They have better uniforms than ordinary sailors.'

'He was certainly an officer,' said Jill, recalling the vicar's eulogy. 'In fact, there's a photo of his ship somewhere.' She shifted another album, a large envelope containing letters, and several individual photographs to find a larger picture of a naval craft secured to a jetty or something of that kind, with a group of officers and ratings in front of it, all in white, tropical uniform. They seemed to be enjoying their work, because they were all smiling. 'That's Uncle Maurice in the middle,' she told them, reaching for her bag, 'and I'll need my glasses to read what it says underneath.' Putting them on, she peered closely and read, 'ML Six-Five-Seven and Ship's Company, Pahang, Malaya, September, nineteen forty-five.'

The next question was predictable, and it came from Jessica. 'Where's Malaya?'

'It's in the Far East.'

'And it's very hot,' said Liam, now recovered from his shame. 'That's why they're all wearing shorts.'

'Yes,' said Jill, 'it must be quite close to the equator. I'm just wondering what "ML" stands for. You can see it painted on the ship's side.'

'You could look it up on the internet,' suggested Liam, 'or I could.'

'We could if the phone was connected.'

'Why isn't it connected?'

'Because it takes time for these things to happen. Actually,' she said, thinking more practically, 'it's just as well, really. I'm worn-out after the move. You two need your sleep, as well, after your hectic two days, and it won't be long before I follow you.' Her eyelids were already feeling heavy.

'Tomorrow's Millennium Eve,' said Liam, 'the last day of the twentieth century. Can we stay up for it?'

'You can try, as it's the only new millennium you'll ever experience, but don't be surprised if you fall asleep and miss it.'

'It's a pity the phone's not connected,' said Liam. 'Computers are going to stop working at midnight tomorrow, and aeroplanes are going to fall out of the sky.'

A look of alarm from Jessica prompted Jill to say, 'Don't talk nonsense, Liam.'

'They said so on the news.'

'That was just the media scare-mongering. Do you really think the airlines would run flights over the Millennium if there was any risk attached? As for the computer, I've taken care of that.'

'How?'

'By doing what I've always done, by living in the past. I set the computer back to nineteen ninety-seven, when it left the factory.'

Liam appeared to absorb that information, and then asked, 'What will you do in three years' time, when it crashes?'

'I'll start saving now for a new one. If I stop your pocket money and use that, I should have enough for a really top-of-the-range model by two thousand and three.'

'That's not fair.'

'It serves you right for frightening Jessica with your silly stories.' More to settle Jessica than to prolong the argument, she said, 'After the Millennium, things will continue much as they are now. People will still need me to care for their dogs and cats while they're away from home, which is just as well, because that's what keeps the roof over your heads and feeds and clothes you.'

'My dad says he pays for everything.'

'I'm not going to get into an argument about that, Liam, particularly at this hour. In fact, it's time you were both in bed. Off you go now, and I'll come up and see you before you go to sleep.'

'It'll be exciting, going to bed in a new bedroom,' said Jessica.

'Not too exciting, I hope, but I know what you mean. Off you go, and I'll see you both in a minute.' She went to the kitchen and opened a bottle of wine. In taking her mother to the funeral and then spending the next day moving into the cottage, she'd earned a drink. It was one of the many things she paid for without any help from Tony.

After a few minutes, she went upstairs and said goodnight to the children, noticing as she entered Liam's room the hastily-crammed and barely-closed drawers. Boys would be boys, but she hoped Liam wasn't going to acquire Tony's worst attributes. Access was restricted to one day a week, and there was surely a limit to the influence the man could wield during one day out of seven. At least, she hoped there was.

She poured herself a glass of wine, resolved to put all thoughts of Tony out of her mind. Instead, she would look at some more of the photographs. The ML-thing still puzzled her. Just going by the men in front of it, it looked quite big, certainly more of a ship than a boat. She wondered how a man trained in accountancy could become captain of even a small warship. Picking up the album they'd been looking at, she turned the pages and found a faded, official letter from the Admiralty, addressed to Lieut. E.M. Warneford, D.S.C., R.N.V.R. It said, *You are to assume command of H.M.M.L. 657....* The rest was obscure officialese, but she imagined "HM" must stand for "Her Majesty's", as in "Her Majesty's Stationery Office". Of course, the country had a king in those days, so it would be *"His* Majesty's". Leafing through the album, she found more pictures of similar craft, and then a newspaper cutting caught her attention. It was from an American newspaper printed in 1941, and the headline read, *The Kids That Hunt U-Boats.* There was a lurid drawing of a sinking submarine and a ship rather like Uncle Maurice's, with *ML* and a number painted in the same place. Beneath the drawing was a glowing account of how volunteer sailors, 'some little more than kids' went out night after night to do battle with the enemy's U-boats. It was stirring writing, but one particular line captured Jill's attention.

They call them motor launches, but make no mistake, these things do the work of warships.

So Uncle Maurice's ship was a motor launch. The news came almost as an anticlimax, but the question was finally answered. She turned two more pages and found a letter from someone representing Queen Alexandra's Imperial Military Nursing Service. It was addressed to Auntie Iris and it read:

Dear Sister Lennox,

I am delighted to be able to welcome you home to Great Britain after your interminable ordeal in Malaya, and I hope you will soon recover fully from the deprivation you have inevitably suffered.

I have read reports of your sterling work whilst an internee, all of which make me extremely proud that, at the time, you were a staff-nurse serving in QAIMNS.

At this stage, Jill remembered hearing long ago that Auntie Iris had been interned by the Japanese. It sounded awful at the time but, if she were honest, she hadn't really given it further thought. Now that something of the scale of brutality perpetrated in those camps was public knowledge, however, the omission and the reminder caused her to feel an awful kind of guilt. On the few occasions when she'd met Auntie Iris, she'd only been conscious of the gentle kindness that had endeared her so strongly to her niece by marriage. She'd never displayed any sign of suffering, but of course she wouldn't. It wasn't a badge to be worn in public. She would have borne her hurt privately and with dignity.

Jill thought of Jessica's innocent observation. Auntie Iris was really quite attractive, as Jill remembered her, with rich, auburn hair and green-hazel eyes. It was a natural comparison for Jessica to make, based only on a black-and-white photograph. Jill's hair was chestnut and her eyes were blue.

She regretted, now, that she hadn't become better acquainted with Auntie Iris and Uncle Maurice. It was too late for that, of course, but it wasn't too late to find out more about them. She wanted to know them better, if only to do their memory proper justice.

2

Pahang, Malaya, September 1945

For Pity's Sake

With their shallow draught, the MLs were ideally suited to searching the rivers and inlets of Malaya, and the process was urgently necessary. The Emperor of Japan had surrendered two weeks previously, but pockets of resistance held by fanatical die-hards were reported to be operating up and down the country. Some had even joined forces with their erstwhile enemy, the Malayan People's Anti-Japanese Army, believing that by working together, they could prevent the British repossessing the colony. Until such dissidents could be persuaded to accept the inevitable, the deadly mopping-up had to continue. From his position on the bridge of ML 657, Maurice Warneford could see that the gun crews were maintaining a ceaseless look-out for enemy activity. He removed his cap and mopped his forehead to stop the perspiration running into his eyes. The bridge thermometer showed a hundred-and-two degrees, and the humidity was stifling.

As the ship approached a wooden landing stage, the port lookout reported a movement in the bushes behind it.

Dudley Keeble, the ML's first lieutenant, asked, 'Shall we give them a burst with the Vickers, sir?'

'No, they could be natives. They may even be Japs wanting to give themselves up.' With the war officially over, the rules of engagement were particularly stringent.

It turned out to be neither of those possibilities, as the figure that stepped on to the landing stage was unquestionably white and, as far as Maurice could tell from her long, auburn hair, female.

11

'Dead slow astern together,' he ordered. 'Turner, take her into the landing.'

'Aye, aye, sir. Dead slow astern together, sir.'

As the ML approached the stage, Maurice ordered, 'Stop both.' The ship ran gently up to the stage, where the woman was standing with a look of bewildered disbelief.

'Hello,' said Maurice. 'Are you all right?'

She made no reply, but blinked several times, as if to convince herself that the ship and its crew were real and that she wasn't hallucinating.

'Make fast,' he ordered the deck crew, 'but gun crews keep a sharp look-out.' He stepped over the side and on to the stage. 'Don't be afraid,' he told the woman. 'I imagine we're on your side. You are British, aren't you?'

'Yes.' She gave a slight convulsion, as if she were about to burst into tears, but collected herself. 'I'm an internee from the camp.' She pointed up river. 'A mile or so that way.'

'Not now, you're not. You know the war's over, don't you? We're only here to search for Japs who don't know when they're beaten.'

'I know.' She did that semi-convulsion again, a sort of stifled sob. 'Someone flew over the camp, dropping notices, telling us to stay put until the Red Cross arrive.'

'You must be from the camp at Kuala Rompin.'

'Yes, I am.'

'It's due to be liberated today.'

Her eyes filled with tears that ran down her cheeks, but it seemed, again, that she was unable to cry.

'Here, take this.' He handed her his clean handkerchief. 'As we seem to be going your way, let me offer you a lift.' Looking at her ragged tunic with the pip on each shoulder, he said, 'You're a nurse, aren't you?'

'A QA, yes. I may be needed back at the camp.'

It made sense. As well as providing what nursing skills she could, she would need to be there when the Red Cross arrived, so that they could carry out a full roll-call and inform next-of-kin. 'In that case,' he said, 'come with us. We'll get you there quicker than on foot. Why did you leave the camp, anyway?' He saw her hesitate, and said, 'It's none of my business. I just wondered, as you'd been advised to stay put.'

'One of the older women wandered off. She was very confused, and I was concerned for her safety, so I went to look for her.'

'Did you find her?'

She nodded and said quietly, 'She was dead. Snakebite.'

'Horrible.' He offered his hand to help her over the ship's counter, but she disregarded it, preferring to board by her own efforts. 'If you follow me, I'll show you to the wardroom. Feel free to use it, and the heads as well.'

Visibly puzzled, she asked, 'What are the "heads", and what's the "wardroom"?'

'I'm sorry. The heads are the lavatory and washing facilities, and the wardroom is what you'll know as the officers' mess. They're both at your disposal.' He led the way down the ladder. As she was wearing trousers, there was no need to warn the crew to keep clear while she made her descent. 'Would you like a cup of tea?'

She looked at him as if he'd offered her vast riches. 'Oh yes, please. I haven't tasted tea since....' Again, her eyes filled with tears.

'Right, I'll organise that. How do you have your tea?'

She closed her eyes for a moment, causing one tear and then another to run down her face. 'I'm trying to remember. Quite weak and without milk or sugar, please.'

'I'll see to it. We only have condensed milk, so it's just as well you don't want it.' He climbed the ladder and asked a rating to brew tea for the passenger.

'It's well seeing I'm with an RNVR crew, sir,' said the Cox'n, relieving Leading Seaman Turner at the wheel. 'Most old sailors would have a dicky-fit if they were ordered to steam with a woman on board.'

'This is an errand of mercy, Cox'n. Superstition has to stand aside.'

'Right enough, sir.'

'Okay, let go the painter.' Leaning over the voice pipe, he ordered, 'Start engines.' As the engines burst into life, he said, 'Half ahead starboard. Steer starboard ten, Cox'n.'

'Starboard ten, sir,' he repeated. 'Ten of starboard wheel on, sir.'

He waited until the ship was in midstream, and ordered, 'Midships.'

'Midships, sir. Wheel's amidships, sir.'

Maurice turned to Dudley and said, 'Take over for a spell, Number One. I'm going below. Let me know when we reach Kuala Rompin.'

'Aye, aye, sir.'

Maurice went down to the wardroom, where he found the passenger drinking tea from an enamel mug.

'I feel as if I've just died and gone to Heaven,' she said weakly.

'Tea can have that effect, Sister, especially in your circumstances. I'm Maurice Warneford, by the way.' He offered his hand.

'How do you do, Lieutenant Warneford. I'm Iris Lennox.'

Now that he had time to look at her properly, he saw that her body was incredibly wasted, and her hair, which was probably quite appealing in normal times, was matted and unkempt. Surprisingly, considering the primitive way of live she must have experienced, her teeth were remarkably white, although he would never dream of mentioning the fact. All in all, though, he felt sorrier for her than he'd ever felt for anyone. 'The rating who brewed you a cup of tea,' he said, 'might have offered you a biscuit, but he evidently didn't. Don't worry, I'll have him court-martialled.' It sounded ridiculous, but it was something to say whilst his thoughts were in turmoil, and he took the lid off a tin of rich tea biscuits to offer her one.

'Thank you, Lieutenant. You're very kind.' Her face convulsed again and, this time, she succeeded in breaking into a succession of heart-rending sobs. 'I'm… sorry. This is….'

'Don't apologise. Here, have another handkerchief. I have a drawerful.' He opened a drawer and took one out for her just as Dudley called down the ladder, 'Kuala Rompin, sir.'

'Okay, Number One, I'm on my way.' He put a consoling hand on the distraught woman's shoulder, but she flinched away from him. 'I'm sorry,' he said. Some people didn't care to be touched, and it was careless of him to forget that, but his actions were dictated by the overwhelming pity he felt for her. It was a new experience, and one in which he found himself less than confident.

Back on the bridge, he took ML 657 into the landing at Kuala Rompin and, when she was secured, he called for two ratings to stand by with Sten sub-machine guns to accompany him ashore. Then, returning to the wardroom, he said, 'We're back at Kuala Rompin, Sister Lennox. Your escort awaits you.'

'Thank you, Lieutenant. You've been very kind.' Clearly embarrassed, she said, 'I must be an awful sight.'

'Not at all, but freshen up by all means before you go ashore.' He pointed her towards the officers' heads, and she took him at his word, seemingly mesmerised at first by the facilities, but then delightedly running water into the hand basin, as if it were a new toy. 'Here's a clean towel,' he said, handing her one from the linen locker. 'There's soap in the dish.'

'This is unbelievable,' she said, surprising him by washing her hands and face without closing the door.

'Take your time.' He closed the door gently behind her and picked up the webbing belt that carried his revolver and holster.

When she emerged from the heads, he said, 'You know, I never asked you if you'd like a cigarette. It's because I don't smoke all that much, but that's no excuse for being a rotten host.'

She smiled for the first time, and said, 'It's a little late now, but thank you for the thought.' She held one hand to her nose, closed her eyes and inhaled deeply, prompting him to ask, 'Are you all right?'

'Yes, thank you. It's the novelty, the scent of toilet soap.'

'It'll soon be an everyday experience,' he assured her.

She followed him up the ladder and over the ship's side.

Leaving Dudley in command, he and the two ratings accompanied her to the camp. It was only a short distance, but she was soon tired, and Maurice could only wonder at the way she'd followed her fellow internee almost as far as the landing stage, when the distance clearly caused her some difficulty in her weakened state. He offered her his arm, but she refused it, preferring to persevere alone.

When they reached the camp, her popularity became apparent when several internees, each as emaciated as her, welcomed her profusely and with obvious relief. They were naturally dismayed to hear of the older woman's death, but their main concern had been for the nurse's safety.

'Thank you so much, Lieutenant,' she said, and it was apparent that a wealth of feeling went into that simple message.

'Not at all. I hope they get you home quickly.' He pushed something into her hand and said, 'In the meantime, take these things with you.'

'I couldn't.'

'They're nothing, just a bit of comfort. Please take them.' He shook her hand and left the compound.

———

The day continued to be one of unreality for Iris and for the others, as the Red Cross officials arrived in the afternoon, and the camp was officially liberated. As the lorry carried the internees away, Iris watched the evil bamboo compound disappear finally from her sight and, after a while, she remembered Maurice's parting gift of biscuits wrapped in a linen napkin, and a leather cigarette case filled with cigarettes. There was also a box of matches. The biscuits had been demolished immediately by hungry internees, but she still had the cigarette case, and she asked, 'Does anyone fancy a smoke?'

Two of them stared at her in surprise, and one asked, 'Do you mean you've got cigarettes? How did you come by them?'

'The same way as I got the biscuits. The naval officer gave me them.' She took the leather case from her tunic pocket and offered it to them. A few minutes later, choking, gasping and coughing helplessly, all three threw their cigarettes out of the lorry. Three-and-a-half years' abstention had left their lungs in no condition to resume the habit and, as one, they resolved never to smoke again, although Iris kept the leather case in her pocket as a reminder of the occasion and of Maurice's generosity.

One of the women said, 'I think he must have taken a fancy to you, Iris.'

'I don't think so.' He'd been the very embodiment of kindness and, at one time, she might have found his slim, dark features and deep, brown eyes appealing. As things were, however, a man was the last thing she needed.

———

Tied up alongside in Kuantan, Maurice and Dudley Keeble sat in the wardroom of their supply ship, enjoying their first drink of the day, which, in that heat, was inevitably beer.

'Just think,' said Dudley, 'the war ended four months ago in Europe, and we're still mopping up after this one.'

'I suppose they're still tying up loose ends in Germany, but think of it this way, Dud,' said Maurice. 'The worst jobs always fall to the most appropriate people.' He opened a tin of Players and offered it to him.

'What happened to your case, Maurice?'

'I gave it to the girl we picked up this morning.' He felt foolish as he said it, and when Dudley made no response, he felt obliged to explain. 'I had to give her something. She's been in that camp three-and-a-half years, living on… "Chinese wedding cake", I imagine, and experiencing all kinds of brutality and deprivation while we've had duty-free cigarettes and subsidised gin, beer and goodness knows what else. It sounds daft, I know, but the Japs had taken everything from her, so I just felt I had to give her something, anything at all.'

'She evidently made quite an impression on you, Maurice.'

He thought about the morning's events, and said, 'Once or twice, when she was overcome at finding us, there were times she almost burst into tears, but couldn't. I think that, after so long, her body had basically forgotten how.'

'How do you work that out?' It was a genuine question from a man well-intentioned but of little imagination.

'I think she got all that out of her system a long time ago, when the horrors were fresh and alarming, and she's been living like an automaton ever since.'

Dudley nodded, not necessarily understanding what he was hearing, but having the good manners not to say so.

'Another thing, Dud, was that she was in a hurry to get back to the camp in case she was needed. I think it takes a special kind of person to live in an animal cage, guarded by the kind of bestial thugs we keep finding in this blasted jungle, and still concern herself with other prisoners' needs.'

There was something else, as well, that he didn't feel inclined to discuss with Dud or, for that matter, with anyone else, although it was the oddest thing. Whenever he thought about Sister Iris Lennox and what she must have suffered, he was conscious of an ache deep inside himself, born of a kind of pity he'd never previously known, because, whilst he'd seen liberated prisoners embarked in ships bound for Australia, and been shocked by their emaciated appearance, he'd never been so close to one.

3

Sympathetic Ears and Kind Words

As Jill had prophesied, life in the new millennium proved no different from that which preceded it. Two weeks on, people still wanted their dogs walked and their cats, rabbits and guineapigs fed and watered. Computers continued to confound and annoy, seemingly unhindered by their inability to recognise the year 2000, and no aeroplane had so far fallen from the sky. The Millennium Dome was now open, for whatever purpose; two praiseworthy souls became the first British women to reach the South Pole and, not to be left out of the headlines, Cherie Blair, the Prime Minister's wife, had been fined for not having a valid train ticket.

On a more personal level, the resumption of internet access at the cottage meant that Jill knew much more than she previously had about Queen Alexandra's Imperial Military Nursing Service and the Fairmile 'B' Type motor launch. She'd even been able to trace, at least broadly, Uncle Maurice's activities since assuming command of his ship. Typically, Liam was impatient to find more detail.

'I can't see the screen, Mum. You're in the way.'

'If you think hard enough, Liam, I'm sure you'll find a polite way to say that. If you're polite enough, you may even persuade me to let you look.'

With studied patience, he delivered the request, 'Please may I have a look?'

'All right, but don't touch anything.' She still hoped he wouldn't turn out like his dad. It was a familiar story after a Sunday spent with him. She went to put the kettle on for a cup of tea before she made a start on dinner.

'Mum?'

'Yes, Liam?'

'Why did they have convoys on the East Coast?'

'Read what it says on the screen and you'll find out.'

Jessica asked, 'What's a convoy?'

'Lots of people travelling together, but the kind Liam's asking about was a lot of cargo ships escorted, or protected, by warships. Uncle Maurice's ship was one of those warships.'

Clearly confused, she said, 'I thought he was in Malaya.'

'He was. When the war in Europe was over, and he was no longer needed to escort convoys down the East Coast, they sent him to Malaya, which is now Malaysia, I think, but don't quote me.' She brought her tea into the sitting room and sat down with it. 'I found some more interesting stuff today,' she said, 'among his personal things. Come and look at these, Liam.' She opened a small flat case and took out several medals. 'The most important one is this,' she said, touching a silver medal with a blue-and-white ribbon. 'It's the Distinguished Service Cross.'

'What's that for?' Liam reached out to touch it.

'Are your hands clean?'

'Fairly.'

'Go and wash them. You don't touch a man's hard-earned medals with grubby hands.'

While Liam was in the bathroom, Jill asked, 'What have you been doing today, Jessica?'

'Maths, Science....' Clearly, those two subjects gave her little pleasure.

'What else?'

'History.'

'Are you still learning about the Romans?' Jill remembered the topic from before Christmas.

'No, local history.'

'As in the Roman Occupation of the local region?'

Jessica thought for a second and said, 'No, it's nothing to do with the Romans.'

'Oh.' She felt silly for asking.

Jessica surprised her by asking, 'Do you need to know history to be a nurse?'

'I doubt it, Jessica.' It seemed to Jill that nurses would perform their duties far better with a clear mind, and confusion seemed to be the aim of those responsible for planning the history curriculum. 'Do you want to be a nurse?'

'Yes, I want to wear a uniform like Auntie Iris's.'

'There is that side to it, Jessica. On the other hand, you have to consider the job itself, caring for people who are ill, or just finding out what's wrong with them. There are lots of other aspects to the job. It's not just about wearing a pretty uniform.'

'Mm.' She seemed to absorb the information, although it was difficult to tell with Jessica. Her thought processes were seldom transparent.

'Right, Mum.' Liam held up his hands to show her.

'You must have washed them pretty thoroughly, Liam.' He'd been gone several minutes.

'I went to the toilet while I was there.'

'After you'd washed your hands?'

'I washed them again afterwards.'

'Good boy. Now you can look at Uncle Maurice's medals.' She opened the case again.

'What's this one for?' He was looking at the medal Jill had left on top of the others.

'The Distinguished Service Cross is "for gallantry during active operations against the enemy at sea." ' Jill had learned that only a few hours earlier. She'd also learned things about the prison camps in the Far East that were better kept from the children's eyes and ears.

———

Liam and Jessica had been in bed almost an hour when her mobile rang. Caller id was still a novelty for Jill, and she was happy to pick up the receiver. 'Hi, Helen.'

'Hi Jill, how's everything?'

'Muddling through, but it's feeling more like home, now I'm getting the hang of everything.'

'It doesn't happen all at once, does it? I must say, I admire you for doing all that single-handed.'

Jill smiled at her friend's assessment. 'Not entirely single-handed,' she said, 'with you looking after the children for me.'

'Yes, I've been meaning to ask you about the funeral. Your uncle, wasn't it? I hope it wasn't too awful.'

'Not awful, exactly. He was eighty-two, so he'd had a fair run, but I was rather fond of them both.'

'When did your auntie die?'

'Four years ago, I think.' Strangely, it seemed fairly recent. 'I've been finding out lots of things about them from some personal effects I brought back from the funeral. One thing I've learned is that he was awarded a medal for gallantry during the war.'

'The war?' Helen sounded surprised. 'Of course, your family are older than most, aren't they?'

'Yes, they are. My mum was the younger of the two, and she had me at the age I am now.'

'Twenty-seven?'

'I wish.' Jill laughed lightly. 'I'm thirty-seven, as you well know.'

'You must have come as a surprise.'

'I gave her a few months' warning, but yes, I wasn't exactly planned.' There was a pause, and Jill imagined there was an additional reason for Helen's phone call. 'Anyway,' she said, confirming that suspicion, 'I know this is a complete change of subject, but I wondered if you'd thought any more about coming back to the studio.' She sounded relieved to have broached the subject, and that was silly, when they'd been friends for years.

'Not recently. I've had a lot going on.'

'Of course you have, but....' She hesitated. 'To be perfectly honest, I'd really appreciate some help.' She added, 'As always, you wouldn't be doing it for nothing.'

'You're the much-qualified expert, Helen, the amateur Latin champion, no less.'

'I know, but you're good. They could learn a lot from you, especially in Ballroom.'

'Flatterer. In any case, I'm out of practice.'

'Not after so short a time, surely. What do you say, Jill? The next beginners' class is on Thursday, as usual.'

'Are you calling me a beginner?'

'Of course not, but it would be a great help if you could lend a hand.'

Jill hesitated. She hadn't danced a step since the break-up with Tony, and she was out of practice, as she'd said, but that was only a hitch and, if she were honest, at odd moments when she hadn't been dealing with the divorce and the move, she really had missed it. 'Okay,' she said, 'if I can get Gemma to look after the kids, I'll come down.'

After Helen had hung up, Jill tried phoning Gemma, the student who usually minded the children, but she had to leave a message on the answerphone. Gemma was pretty good at returning calls, so there was still a chance she'd be available on Thursday.

On Tuesday morning, Jill called, as usual, for Florrie, the smooth-haired fox terrier. She wasn't the friendliest of dogs with her own species, so she had to be walked solo, which was why Jill called for her before the others.

'Now, Florrie,' she said, standing up to escape the frantic licking, 'let's get your check chain on. Florrie, sit. Good girl.' She dropped the chain over Florrie's head and together they left the house. Jill had her own code letters for clients' keys, a safeguard against their falling into other hands and enabling widespread burglary, and she locked the house using the key with the tag marked *LF* for 'Licky Florence'.

They set off up the moor with Jill chatting amiably to her canine companion. 'How do you see me, Florrie? Be as honest as you like. I shan't be offended. The fact is that my husband of thirteen years left me for a grubby bohemian slapper with split ends and a huge arse. Now, what does that say about me? Does it say that I fail in some way to measure up – and I'm using the term metaphorically, you understand – to the slapper in question, or just that it slipped my husband's mind to tell me during the flurry of marriage vows that he prefers his women to be of casual appearance and slipshod ways and, in particular, to be generously-unholstered in the hind quarters?'

Florrie looked up at her frequently, to register the fact that she was listening, but that was, naturally enough, her only response.

'Whether it's one or the other, Florrie, the unpleasant fact remains that he found something in her that I couldn't provide.' She'd pondered the same question repeatedly, sometimes crying herself to sleep, especially in the early stages, but without arriving at a satisfactory conclusion.

———

An hour later, she retraced the path up the moor, this time in the company of Mabel the yellow Labrador, Gwyneth the Dalmatian, Daniel the Springer Spaniel and Joey the Border terrier. Having checked that she was the only human being for miles around, she said, 'Paws up, all those who think Shakespeare was barking up the wrong tree with the Seven Ages of Man. You see, I think he was. Otherwise, why did he concern himself with seven consecutive male manifestations, when a woman could have done at least three of those things and the ironing at the same time?' Her flow was interrupted when she had to bag up one of Daniel's offerings, but she was used to that. 'We women are a remarkable lot, Daniel and Joey,' she continued, 'as Mabel and Gwyneth will bear me out. We can cope with the hurt of betrayal and rejection, and still hide our feelings from the children. We have to, because none of it's their fault. They're just innocent pawns who get moved around the chessboard so that the King can have his way.' Guiltily, she said, 'I know, you've heard it all before. It must be very boring. What else shall we talk about?' She looked from one to another, and was suddenly aware of a man close by. He was wearing walking boots and an anorak that showed signs of frequent use, and he was smiling in a friendly kind of way. At least, she hoped he wasn't laughing at her.

'Good morning,' he said.

'Good morning.' She welcomed the opportunity to let him see that she could communicate with people as well as animals. 'You must think I'm a raving lunatic, talking to the dogs like this.'

'Not in the least. It's a very civilised thing to do, and it's quite an audience you've got there. In fact, you seem to have your hands rather full. I mean literally.'

'Just plying my trade,' she told him. 'I'm a dog walker, cat feeder and garden waterer, among other things.' Now she thought about it, he was so pleasant, she didn't mind if he thought she was loopy. He didn't strike her as being at all judgemental.

'You do an important job. You're an enabler.'

'Am I?' It was news to her.

'Of course you are. You enable people to travel and to get on with their work without worrying about their animals or their gardens. As well as that, you give their dogs much-needed relief.' He added hurriedly, 'I mean from boredom.'

'I suppose so.' As she spoke, she pushed the empty disposal bag she was holding into her pocket.

'I imagine, with all those dogs to care for, you live locally. I only mention it because I haven't seen you around.' He shrugged dismissively. 'Having said that, I don't spend as much time up here as I'd like. I decided I'd earned a day off, for a change.'

He had dark hair and brown eyes, and, whilst not startlingly good-looking in the usual sense, his features seemed to exude goodwill. She asked, 'What do you do?'

'I'm a freelance journalist.'

'Ah.' She was impressed. 'I only moved here a fortnight ago. I used to live in Cullington.'

'Really? I live in Cullington.' He seemed tempted to continue chatting, but Mabel, who was soon bored, was pulling at her lead. 'The dogs are looking restless,' he said, 'so I mustn't keep you. Maybe we'll bump into each other again.'

'I hope so. Goodbye.'

'Goodbye.'

'Now that,' said Jill when he was safely out of earshot, 'is a kind of man that Shakespeare forgot. He's the kind it's pleasant to meet, who does no harm, and who engages in conversation without any ulterior motive.' She moved on, much to the dogs' relief. 'Do I sound terribly jaundiced? Maybe I should change the record, as my dear mum is so fond of telling me.'

It occurred to her that maybe she should. After all, what did she really have to complain about? If she'd had to endure a fraction of what Auntie Iris experienced in the war, she'd have a more than legitimate moan.

4

Loughborough, March, 1946

A Foreign Language

Dr Armitage finished examining Iris and looked away as she buttoned up her blouse. 'You've survived remarkably well, Miss Lennox,' he said.

'I've been very lucky,' she agreed.

'In a sense, I suppose you have.'

'Oh, but I have,' she insisted. 'So many of the patients I've nursed died of malaria, beriberi, blackwater fever, dengue fever, pellagra, dysentery and a long list of other ailments, and all for want of drugs and facilities. I bore a charmed life.'

He raised his eyebrows in mild surprise. 'In all that time, you still saw yourself as a nurse rather than just another internee?'

'Of course, I did. We don't swear an oath as doctors do, but neither do we turn our backs on people who need our help. The doctor who was with us to begin with died of beriberi in 'forty-two, and the medical officer in the men's camp down the road had more than enough to occupy his time and resources, such as they were.'

'I'm sorry, Miss Lennox, that was thoughtless of me. You're quite right, of course.' Changing the subject hurriedly, he asked, 'Have you given any thought to what you're going to do next?'

'No.' It was a simple, unqualified answer.

'I don't suppose you're in a hurry to go back to nursing, although your experience of tropical diseases would be extremely valuable.'

'No, Doctor Armitage, I'm not in a hurry to do anything, really. Since I left Malaya, I've been content to live for the moment. Each meal is a new experience; carpets and upholstered furniture are an unaccustomed luxury, and to ride on a bus is the ultimate freedom. My life is so filled with half-forgotten delights, work can wait, at least until I'm discharged from the QAs.'

'I see. How are you sleeping?'

She smiled at the question. 'I find I can sleep in a bed, now. Until recently, I slept on the floor because I wasn't used to the softness of a mattress.'

'How awful.'

She shrugged the matter aside. 'I'm not alone in that,' she said. 'Most of us spent the passage to Australia and then England sleeping on the steel deck by choice.'

'I see, and I do understand, but I was referring to the quality of your sleep.'

'Of course you were, Doctor. I sleep well enough, thank you. Not surprisingly, I have disturbed nights, but that will probably be a lifelong legacy.'

'I fear so, and I would hesitate to keep prescribing the sedative. Those things are addictive, I'm afraid.' He glanced at his notes again and asked, 'Are your periods back to normal now? That was a concern at one time, I believe.'

'Quite regular, now, thank you, Doctor.'

'I suppose changing circumstances will always disturb these things.'

'One of the medical officers in Australia, a gynaecologist, explained it to me.' Armitage was a doctor, after all, and it seemed only right to enlighten him. 'He said that one of the functions impeded by prolonged starvation is ovulation.'

'I never knew that, but it makes perfect sense.'

'I only discovered it by accident, but it was a welcome development among others that were less well-received.'

'I imagine it was, in those circumstances.'

He really had no idea, but she wasn't prepared to pursue the subject. She said simply, 'Believe me, it was.'

Changing the subject readily, he said, 'And you're gaining weight gradually, the healthiest way to do it, and everything else is quite satisfactory. Yes, you're making excellent progress, Miss Lennox.'

'Thank you, Doctor Armitage.' She stood up and shook his hand.

'Thank you for coming to see me. If you do feel unwell at any time or if you have any concerns about your health, don't hesitate to telephone the surgery.'

'I shan't, Doctor. Goodbye.'

'Goodbye, Miss Lennox.'

Stepping out again into the street, Iris inhaled the fresh, cool air, which was still a welcome novelty after the heat and humidity of the Far East, and walked the short distance home.

Leaving her coat and hat in the hallway, she found her mother in the kitchen, preparing vegetables. It was one of those familiar sights, once forgotten, but now welcomely remembered.

'Let me help,' she said, taking a sharp knife from the cutlery drawer.

'There's no need, dear. I can manage on my own.'

'I've no doubt you can, Mum, but can you imagine what it means to me, to be able to handle fresh, green vegetables again?'

'Oh yes, of course. I'm sorry, dear.' She stood back to let Iris prepare the Brussels sprouts. 'Don't forget to cut a cross in the bottom of each one before you put them into the saucepan.'

'I know.' Iris continued to peel off the outer leaves, scenting the freshness of the inner vegetable as she did so.

'What did Doctor Armitage have to say?'

'He says I'm on the right track. To be honest, I think he was quite embarrassed by the whole examination.'

'Surely not. He brought you into the world.'

'Not that sort of embarrassed. I mean he didn't really know what to say to someone who's just spent three-and-a-half years in an internment camp. He can have no idea of what it was like.' She stopped what she was doing to make her point. 'I mentioned a string of tropical fevers, and I'm sure I was speaking a foreign language as far as he was concerned.'

Her mother looked up at her sharply. 'He should know about them,' she said. 'He's a doctor, after all.' Her simple loyalty as a long-term patient was commendable.

'How many cases of pellagra or blackwater fever do you think he sees in the course of a year, Mum?'

'Oh well, I imagine those things are quite rare.' Almost reluctantly, she asked, 'What *is* blackwater fever?'

'It's a complication of a malarial infection that causes red blood cells to burst in the bloodstream and the bladder. It takes its name from the discoloration of the patient's urine caused by the blood clots.'

Her mother's expression changed from curiosity to one of coy disapproval. 'Not when we're handling food, dear, if you don't mind.'

'You asked me, Mum, so I told you.'

'Well, I think a change of subject is in order. As a matter of fact, I've been meaning to tell you about Ronnie Kerslake. You know he got a commission in the Leicestershire Regiment, don't you? I remember he was rather keen on you at one time, before you both went away. Anyway, he's coming home next month. I thought you'd like to know.'

'Good for him.' Iris was less than excited.

'I know it's been a long time, but… well, you never know.'

'I hope he finds someone who deserves him. Ronnie's a nice boy.'

'Oh.' Her mother was noticeably disappointed.

'Mum, I'm not interested in boys… men, I suppose, by this time.'

'You will be when you've had time to settle down.'

Iris dropped the last sprout into the saucepan and put down the knife she'd been using. 'I don't think I'll ever be interested in men,' she said.

'Really.' Her mother took the saucepan from her. 'Well, you're not going to find a husband if you adopt that attitude.'

'I don't want one.'

Her mother let out a long sigh. 'I know the past few years have been difficult for you,' she said, 'but it's all over, now, and you need to accept that and make an effort to settle down.'

Iris closed her eyes and breathed deeply, urging herself to bring her feelings under control. 'If I told you about some of the things that happened in that camp, you wouldn't believe me, and I'm not going to, anyway. It's enough that I experienced them, without making you suffer as well, but please believe me when I tell you that it's going to take much more than an "effort" on my part to make me "settle down", as you put it.' She opened her eyes again to say, 'I'm going up to my room.' It was better than arguing, and her mother seemed to agree, because she made no response.

Alone in her room, Iris considered the situation. Coming home had been such an exciting event. Everything was going to be just as it was before the war, and the past few years would be just a ghastly and hideous memory. At least, that was the expectation. The reality, however, was a different matter, and it stemmed largely from the fact that no one at home could possibly know what it was like to be held by the Japanese, and Iris suspected she wasn't the only one who found it too difficult and unpleasant to enlighten them. Also, they'd heard a lecture on board ship, in which they were told that the European war had been over for several months and that people at home were trying to look ahead to better times, so returning PoWs and internees were urged not to talk about their experiences, even if they wanted to. All in all, there was a significant hiatus in communication, as well as understanding, between the two, and she couldn't see how it could ever be otherwise.

With those thoughts, she idly picked her way through the boxes of various odds and ends that represented her two, distinct lives, the old and the new. Like most PoWs and internees, she'd made a practice of never throwing anything away that could prove to be remotely useful and, like the 'treasure chest' she'd kept as a little girl, her Pahang box contained items that most people would discard without a second thought, but which nevertheless meant something to her. Three items, however, that were clearly of some recognised purpose were two large, white, men's handkerchiefs bearing the embroidered initial *M*, and laundry-marked *Lt. E. M. Warneford*, and a rather nice leather, or possibly pigskin, cigarette case with *E. M. Warneford, A.C.A.* embossed in gold lettering. The latter was most likely a present, possibly marking Lieutenant Warneford's achievement in becoming a… whatever ACA stood for, because she really had no idea.

Conversation at dinner was easier with Iris's father there. He knew no more about life in captivity than her mother, but he was less inclined to make thoughtless remarks.

'So,' he asked, 'what have you been up to today, Iris?'

'I went to see the doctor. He said I was making steady progress. Apparently, it's healthier to gain weight gradually, rather than quickly, and that's what I'm doing.'

'It would be difficult to do it any other way with rationing as it is,' said her mother grimly.

'This is abundance, compared with what I'm used to,' Iris assured her.

'Well, I'm glad somebody got something right, at least.' She was still chafing after their earlier disagreement.

No doubt sensing tension, her father moved the conversation on, asking, 'And what have you lined up for tomorrow?'

'A hair appointment – my first in four years, so that'll be an occasion – and a visit to the dentist, just for a check-up.'

'It's perhaps as well, although your teeth look pretty good to me.' Smiling at the thought, he said, 'Having said that, I know more about financial health than the dental kind.'

'It's something to be thankful for, Iris,' said her mother, 'that the authorities provided things like toothpaste.'

Once again, Iris closed her eyes and mustered her patience. 'It would surprise me,' she said, 'if the Japanese had ever heard of toothpaste. If you'd seen them, it would probably have surprised you, too. You may as well know that we cleaned our teeth with charcoal. It's not as tasty as Colgate or Gibbs, but it did the job.'

'Charcoal?'

'Yes, we took it from the fire where we cooked our daily ration of rice flour and water. Japanese kindness didn't enter into it. I don't see how it could, when the two constitute a contradiction in terms.'

'I think,' said her father, 'a change of subject is called for.' Seeing that his wife was about to speak, he said quickly, 'No, I insist. I've only become aware, today, in talking to a customer, of some of the hardships Iris may have suffered, and I think we should respect her feelings.'

'Thanks, Dad.' It was welcome news for Iris, although she could only wonder what her father's customer could have told him. 'As a matter of fact, there's something else I'm going to do, tomorrow.'

'Oh yes?'

Thinking of the handkerchiefs and the cigarette case, she asked, 'Do you know what the initials 'ACA' stand for?' There was an Oxford Dictionary in the house, with a glossary of initials, but there was also a chance her father knew the answer.

'ACA,' he said, confirming her guess, 'means that someone is a chartered accountant. Why do you ask?'

'I want to return some property to someone, and thank him properly for the kindness he showed me at a time when I thought kindness had ceased to exist.'

'Of course you must.' He reached across the table and took her hand. 'It's obviously very important to you.'

'You're right, Dad. The only problem is…. Do you know if there's a list, a register, I suppose, of chartered accountants, and some way of contacting them? All I know about him, apart from the fact that he's one of that body, is his name, his rank when I met him in September, and the name, or rather the number, of his boat.'

'I'm sure there is. If you like, I'll ask one of the firms I know to have a look for you.'

'Thanks, Dad, but I'm at a loose end, anyway, and I expect the public library will have a copy – they have lists of most things – so I'll go round there tomorrow and see what I can turn up.' As the thought occurred to her, she said, 'I don't even know if he's been discharged, yet, but it's worth a try.'

5

Tears Before Bedtime

Jill and Helen watched the last of the pupils leave the studio.

'The chap you gave me,' said Jill, 'came in trainers for a dancing lesson.'

'Well, I don't suppose he knew any better. Trainers are so much a part of everyday life, nowadays, it's probably an easy mistake to make, and he wasn't to know they weren't appropriate for dancing. Anyway, I don't think we'll see him again.'

'Something I said?'

'He just told me he doesn't think Ballroom and Latin are for him.' As an afterthought, she said, 'Maybe it was something you said, after all. What did you say to him?'

'Other than the usual things, he asked me if I was married, and I told him I was. I'd have thought it was obvious from the ring, but evidently not.' She put her flat shoes on to drive home and picked up her dancing shoes.

'But you're not married now. Maybe he sensed, somehow, that you were only wearing the ring as camouflage, which you do, don't you?'

'I suppose I do, but I don't think he was so astute. I mean, men aren't intuitive as a rule, are they?'

'I've never thought so. What was he like, really?'

'Well, I got the impression he hadn't come to dance. I taught him the basic waltz box-step, and then, when we started the heel and toe, he wanted to move in close and personal, so I backed off.'

'Yes,' said Helen, switching off the lights, 'we still get those who see the class as a dating agency, although they don't usually make a play for the teachers.' Taking her keys out of her bag, she said, 'I wonder if it's just me they don't fancy.'

'I doubt it. Tonight was the first time for me.'

'Oh well, thanks for tonight, Jill.' After a moment's thought, she asked, 'Would you like to come down on Monday and lend a hand with the Ballroom class?'

'I'll speak to Gemma when I get back and let you know.'

'Thanks, Jill. Where are you parked?'

'Behind you.'

'Good, we can look out for each other.'

———

Jill returned home after dog-walking, the following lunchtime, to see that she had a recorded message. She pushed the button and heard, 'Hi. I'm looking for somebody to look in on my corn snake, and I was given your number. Call me on....'

She had to play the message three times before she was able to make sense of the garbled phone number, which she then dialled.

The phone rang and someone responded with a message that sounded at first as if it were recorded. It also seemed to be devoid of punctuation. 'Roofing Solutions no job too small free estimates given with pleasure Wayne speaking how can we help you?'

'Hello, this is Jill Warneford, the dog minder, returning your phone call this morning.'

The same voice said, 'Great. I just need you to call in once a day and change his water.'

'I'm sorry. In this case, I can't help you. I don't do snakes.'

'Kellogg's perfectly harmless.'

He would be called Kellogg. 'It makes no difference. I don't do snakes.'

'He's not slimy, if that's what worries you.'

'Please listen. I don't touch or even go near snakes, whether they're slimy, scaly, velvety or as rough as sandpaper. Their owners may find them irresistible, but they horrify me. Can you accept that?'

'That's ridiculous. He wouldn't hurt a…. Well, he eats mice, fair enough, but it's nothing personal. Just the diet he's used to, I suppose—'

'I'm putting this phone down now. Please don't call me again.' She pushed the red button and shuddered in retrospect. 'Ugh.'

She'd just started the kettle for coffee when the doorbell sounded, so she went to open it and found her ex-husband on the doorstep. It was clearly the morning for reptiles. 'Hello, Antonio,' she said without sounding at all welcoming. It was one of the names his Italian mother had insisted on calling him, the other being Umberto. He wasn't keen on either.

'You know I can't stand being called that.'

'I know. You prefer to be called "Tony", like that other plausible, egocentric plonker we've got now as Prime Minister. You'd better come in.'

'I thought you'd like Tony Blair,' he said, stepping inside. 'You couldn't stand Maggie Thatcher.'

'It doesn't necessarily follow. What brings you here, or are you setting an example to employees by not making free with the firm's phone? Coffee?'

'Yes, please. Actually, I was out this way, so I thought—'

'You thought you'd have a nosey.'

'This is quite nice,' he said, looking around the room.

'It serves its purpose. My ideal home had to go on the market when my husband, as he was then, buggered off with his latest fancy.'

'Very funny.' He walked over to the photograph of Uncle Maurice's ship and studied it.

'I'll be with you in a minute,' said Jill, going to the kitchen and re-emerging after a couple of minutes with two mugs of coffee. 'It's instant,' she warned him. I keep the real coffee for the important people in my life.'

'Your wit doesn't improve. Who's this in the photo?'

'I'm not familiar with individual members of the crew, but the captain was my Uncle Maurice.'

'Was?'

'He died in November. I went to his funeral just before the New Year.'

'Oh?' Having completed his examination, he turned away from the picture and asked, 'Did he remember you in his will?'

'If he did, it's no concern of yours.'

'I'm not so sure about that. I'm paying you a king's ransom in maintenance.'

'No, you're not. You're paying as little as the law allows, which is why I have to scrape a living looking after other people's animals. However, be that as it may, to what do I owe the dubious pleasure of this visit?'

He shook his head as if in sorrow that his ex-wife should be less than welcoming, and said, 'I've come to ask if you've any objection to my having the kids on Saturday, instead of Sunday, this weekend.' He clapped his hands together once, like a salesman offering a once-in-a-lifetime deal. It was just one of his annoying habits.

'Just this weekend?'

'Yes.'

'Saturday morning is Jessica's ballet class.'

'That's no problem. I'll take her there and pick her up afterwards.'

'If I agree to it....'

'Yes?'

'Do try not to prime Liam with post-divorce propaganda.'

'What on earth do you mean?' Another irritating characteristic was his way of sounding perfectly reasonable when he was being anything but reasonable.

'He told me recently that you pay for everything. It's blatantly untrue, and he can only have heard it from you.'

'I'm under a lot of financial pressure. Things may occasionally be said in his hearing, but that doesn't mean they've been said *to* him.'

'In that case, maybe you should be more guarded when he's within earshot. He's at an impressionable age.'

'All children are at an impressionable age, for goodness' sake.'

'All the more reason why you should exercise care.'

'Oh, this is petty,' he said, putting his mug down and standing up to leave.

'But hardly as petty as your claim that you pay for everything.'

'This is ridiculous. I'll call for the children at...' What time is Jessica's class?'

'Nine o' clock at Beckworth High School.'

'I'll call for them at eight forty-five.'

'Fine. Goodbye, Antonio.' She held the door for him.

He gave her an impatient look and walked out to his car, a September ninety-nine-registered BMW. So much for being under financial pressure. She looked at her watch. It was almost time to give Florrie another walk. It would be good to have civilised company again.

———

Having picked up Jessica and then Liam, Jill told them the news. 'Your dad's coming for you both on Saturday instead of Sunday, this week,' she said.

'We know, and he's bringing us back early so they can get away,' said Liam.

'Early?'

'Five o' clock. They're going to a music festival, and they'll be staying overnight.'

'Thanks for telling me, Liam. I only found out about it this morning, when your dad called. Anyway,' she said, 'it must be the first time he's shown any interest in music.'

Liam seemed bored with the subject already. 'It's Deborah who's keen on it,' he said.

'They shout it in a funny voice,' said Jessica, 'and clap their hands, and they laugh a lot.'

'And they do it all in a silly accent,' said Liam, who was clearly less keen on it than Deborah.

'Ah, folk music,' said Jill. She could see Deborah taking part in that sort of thing, but it tested her imagination to the full to picture Tony at a folk gathering. Somehow, the expensive suits and the new BMW, not to mention his Thatcherite views, didn't seem compatible with navvy work ditties and nationalist protest songs. Maybe he had an alter ego that had been there all along, but without her knowledge.

Jessica interrupted her reverie by asking, 'What about ballet?'

'He'll take you to that. Don't worry, Jessica.'

'Deborah doesn't like ballet.'

That came as no surprise. 'Fair enough. It's not to everyone's taste.'

'She says it's not natural and it's for the "if it" few.'

'I imagine she means the effete few.'

'That's right.'

'As long as you enjoy it, Jessica, it really doesn't matter. In any case, everyone's entitled to an opinion.' She was actually being quite generous, there, and the realisation came almost as a surprise. She thought she must be slipping.

'But she says I shouldn't have to go to ballet. She doesn't understand that I go because I want to.'

'Hm.' Jill turned into the street that was now home, and said, 'Some people only see what they want to see.'

'Yes, they do.' At nine-and-a-half, Jessica could be remarkably astute.

Jill pulled up outside the cottage. 'Right, Liam, homework.'

'Why doesn't Jessica get homework?' He was clearly in a rebellious mood.

'The same reason as you didn't when you were in Year Five.'

'What reason's that?'

'I don't know, but it's most likely the same.'

'You don't argue fair, Mum.' Liam retrieved his school bag, kicking it to vent his feelings.

'Fair*ly*. Most adverbs end in "ly", and I'm allowed to be unfair, which, incidentally, is an adjective. That's why it doesn't end in "ly".'

'Why are you allowed to argue unfair*ly*?'

'Because I'm empowered by the ancient Norman law of *Droits de la Mere*.'

'What?'

'Mother's Rights,' she translated.

As he followed her into the cottage, he asked, 'Can't you ever forget you used to be an English teacher?'

'*Droits de la Mere* is French.'

'There you go again.' Frustrated in argument, he turned to go up to his room.

'Before you go, Liam and Jessica, I made some ginger biscuits last night. Would you like one?' She opened the tin and offered it to them.

'Yes, please.'

'Yes, please.' Suddenly, argument and resentment were forgotten in an ambience of ginger-flavoured self-indulgence.

38

'Jessica,' said Jill, 'come with me and I'll show you what I've discovered.'

'Why not me?' Liam was poised with one foot on the bottom stair.

'What I'm going to show Jessica will still be here when you've finished your homework.' It was unlikely to be of any interest to him, but she might easily have turned up something else by then. She switched on the computer and clicked on dial-up. Eventually, she was able to call up the website she'd found that morning, and said, 'This tells you all about Queen Alexandra's Royal Army Nursing Corps, as it's now called.'

Jessica assimilated the information in her usual, deadpan way and asked, 'What was it called before?'

'Until nineteen forty-nine, it was called Queen Alexandra's Imperial Military Nursing Service, but I suppose, with the empire disappearing rapidly down the plughole, they thought they'd better give the service a new name unconnected with it.'

'Deborah says the word "empire" should be taken out of the dictionary and never used again.'

'That would make history even harder to understand.' After a little thought, she said, 'Maybe that's the idea, and Deborah's working on the same principle as the National Curriculum Council, that if they make history sufficiently inaccessible, no one will remember anything, and the embarrassing bits will be lost among the rest.'

'Do you think so, Mum?'

'No, darling, I'm just being silly. Now, let's find out about these army nurses.'

———

There was a bundle of letters, all addressed by hand to Miss Iris Lennox, presumably Auntie Iris's maiden name, and tied up with a white hair ribbon. Jill looked further, but the only letters addressed to Uncle Maurice were of the business kind. It made a kind of sense. A woman was much more likely than a man to keep personal letters. She was stereotyping, she knew, but stereotypes had been ordering her life for the past two years, and the mindset had become firmly established.

There were other letters addressed to her, but those in the bundle were all addressed in Uncle Maurice's precise handwriting, which made them the most interesting, and, looking at their postmarks, she found that they were arranged in chronological order. She hesitated before opening the first, experiencing guilt on more than one level. Even though her aunt and uncle were no longer alive, it seemed an intrusion into their privacy. Worse than that, though, and quite incredibly, at thirty-seven, she felt like a child prying into an exclusive, grown-up world. She thought about that for several minutes before reflecting that her curiosity was born of affection and deep respect. With that thought in mind, she opened the envelope and began reading.

His form of address struck her as excessively formal, but she read on.

Dear Sister Lennox,

I was more than delighted to receive your telephone call and letter, and it's very thoughtful of you to want to return the handkerchiefs and cigarette case, but there's really no need. I have no shortage of handkerchiefs, and the cigarette case was a gift to you. To be perfectly honest, it's of no use to me, as I gave up smoking when I re-entered civilian life and found that cigarettes were in such short supply. If it helps to remind you of the change in your fortunes, as I suspect it does, please think of it as your own. I gave the case as well as the cigarettes and the biscuits to you because they were the only comfort I could offer. It was little more than a gesture, but it was all I had available, so please enjoy it.

I've thought about you often since our meeting on the Rompin River, when I was deeply concerned about your health, so I'm delighted to hear that you're on the road to recovery. I hope it continues. As you know, I was discharged from the Navy only a month ago. The search for entrenched enemy troops and war criminals kept us active for some time, but now, thankfully, I've fired my last shot in anger and returned to civilisation, all of which gives me an idea. Now that we're both home, having met in less than ideal circumstances, do you think we might meet again and bring each other up to date with our fortunes? Loughborough is a relatively short journey from Newark, so it would seem a shame not to. I'd be happy to travel down for the day, if you're agreeable. Are you on the telephone? That would make things easier.

Please let me know. You'll find my home number and address at the head of this letter.
  Yours most sincerely,
  Maurice Warneford.

The letter posed one important question. At least, it seemed important to Jill, who wanted to know every detail. Just how had she found his address and phone number? Could he have given them to her when they met? She dismissed the idea immediately. It wasn't the kind of thing people did, in those days, on a first, or even second, meeting. Possibly, she got his address from the Admiralty, although that was unlikely. She couldn't imagine them divulging personal details to just anyone. She would give the matter some thought, that and something he'd said about the cigarette case. He'd wanted to give her some comfort, and it was the only thing he could think of. He'd called it 'a poor offering', but if it was all he had, it was a wonderful gesture. Just the fact that he wanted to give her some comfort made it so. He was obviously and uncomfortably conscious of her... what? Her state of health, of course, and the dreadful life she'd been leading. That made sense. She opened the box again to take out the pigskin cigarette case and, suddenly, holding it in her hands, she found herself blinking back tears at the thought of Auntie Iris's distress and Uncle Maurice's spontaneous kindness. It *was* spontaneous. She knew that from the letter, and there was something else that was important. It demonstrated that such men existed, and that knowledge was beyond rubies.

6

A Temporary Difficulty

Iris had no idea what to expect. She'd offered to meet Maurice at the station, but he'd told her he was making his own way to Loughborough. She wasn't sure what he meant by that, petrol rationing being as stringent as it was. She could only wait and see.

The answer was revealed shortly before ten o' clock, when she heard the deep, growling beat of a powerful motorcycle outside the house. She went to the door to welcome its rider. 'Hello, Maurice.'

'Hello, Iris.' They'd already agreed to brush formality aside. Maurice removed his gauntlets to shake her hand and, wary though she was, nowadays, in the company of men, she found his large, warm hand reassuring.

'Come inside.' She led the way to the sitting room, where her mother was waiting with barely-concealed curiosity. 'Mum, this is Mr Warneford. He was Lieutenant Warneford when we met.'

'How do you do, Mrs Lennox?'

'How do you do, Mr Warneford? Iris tells me you were very kind to her when you met in Malaya, although the circumstances remain a mystery to me.'

'Oh, that was nothing. It was after the Japanese surrender. We were searching the river for pockets of resistance when we found Iris alone and, we thought, vulnerable. We only escorted her back to the camp.'

'You did much more than that,' protested Iris.

With her query presumably answered, Mrs Lennox asked, 'Would

42

you like some tea after your journey, Mr Warneford? I'm afraid I haven't been able to find any coffee for some time now.'

'Tea would be very welcome, thank you, Mrs Lennox.' When she'd left the room, he said, 'I can't tell you how relieved I am to see you looking so well, Iris.'

'Thank you. I weighed less than five stones when we met, so you must have been alarmed.'

Suddenly, he was embarrassed. 'I mean, please don't think I'm making a personal observation. It's just that you look generally healthier in every way.'

'Don't worry, Maurice. At fifty-three pounds, I was skin and bone, and I was well aware of it. I've gained twenty pounds since then, and I've still some way to go, but I'm getting there.'

'I remember feeling completely helpless at the time.'

'I know, but you cared, and that meant a great deal to me.' She smiled and said, 'The biscuits were very welcome, too. You were the toast of Kuala Rompin Women's Internment Camp, if only in water.'

'It was little enough, and I'd like to redress the balance. Will you let me take you to lunch?'

'If it's just between friends, yes, please, I'd like that.'

'Good.' It seemed that he had another question that needed to be addressed. He said, 'That's a very charming dress, but would you be happier in trousers, as we'll be using my motorbike?'

She laughed. 'It would be easier. I'll change before we go.'

'Where are you going?' The question came from her mother, who carried a tea tray into the room, placing it on an occasional table.

'Maurice and I are going out to lunch.'

'Oh, that's nice. You'll be able to get to know each other properly. How do you have your tea, Mr Warneford?'

'With milk, but no sugar, thank you, Mrs Lennox.'

She poured the tea and added milk. 'Iris tells us you're a chartered accountant.'

'Yes, I'm afraid it's a family tradition. I work for my father's firm.'

Iris asked, 'Would you rather be doing something else?'

'In retrospect, I'd probably have chosen something different, but most people would say that, and accountancy is a secure job at a difficult time. I have to be thankful for that, I suppose.'

'That's what I keep telling Iris, that she should count her blessings, now that she's home again.'

'I imagine that's easier said than done, Mrs Lennox.'

'Not if she puts her mind to it.'

Iris winced, conscious that Maurice was aware of her discomfiture. 'Yes,' she said, 'you wouldn't think I was twenty-seven, would you?'

———

In the restaurant of the Royal Clarence Hotel, Iris felt able to talk more freely. 'Until I put her right, only last week, she imagined that the Japs provided us with every requisite, including toothpaste.'

'That's quite a thought. I shouldn't ask, because it's a very personal matter, but how did you manage to keep your teeth so beautifully white and healthy?'

'Charcoal and ashes. It was all we had.'

'Remarkable.' Realising that they'd strayed into the very subject she would doubtless prefer to avoid, he said quickly, 'I'm sorry. I'm sure there are pleasanter things we can talk about.'

'I'm always ready to do that.'

'Of course.' He thought quickly before asking, 'What are you going to do next?'

'Oddly enough, I received a letter, this week, inviting me to an interview for the post of Matron at Linden Manor Preparatory School. It's not far from here, although I'd have to live in, not that it would be such a bad thing.'

'Wouldn't it?'

'You had a taste of the way things stand at home. It can't go on much longer without ending in a major row.'

'Fair enough. You know best.'

'Not according to my mother.' She took a sip of wine and, seeing him pick up the bottle, said, 'No more for me, thanks. After four years without alcohol, my metabolism struggles to cope with it.' Returning to the subject of her mother, she said, 'Apparently, I need to make an effort, now, to settle down after my unpleasant experience. She has no idea what it was really like, and I'm not inclined to enlighten her. My dad knows more than she does, but he's reluctant to share it with her.'

'I realise it's difficult for you to talk about it.'

'You're absolutely right.'

'So, changing the subject....'

'Feel free.'

'I've been wondering. When I asked you to join me for lunch, you said something like "as between friends", and I wondered what you meant.'

'Oh, dear.' She hesitated. 'This is going to sound awful.'

'Forget I asked. I've no wish to embarrass you.'

'No, in all fairness, I should explain.'

'Only if you want to.'

She considered what she was about to say, conscious that, with her chance remark, she was probably about to offend the person who least deserved it. 'When you invited me to lunch, it was simply a friendly gesture on your part. I'd no call to say what I did.'

'If you had a concern, you had every right to voice it. Were you worried that I might see this as something more than a friendly meeting?'

She nodded dumbly. 'I didn't want to lead you on,' she said miserably.

'Point taken. You haven't, so there's no harm done.'

She looked down at her empty plate, wondering what to say next. Because of her clumsiness, their meeting, which should have been a happy occasion, had become awkward and difficult.

'Iris?'

She looked up slowly. 'Yes?'

'Look me straight in the eye and tell me everything's fine. I'm not offended – there's no reason why I should be – and there's absolutely no need for you to feel awkward.' He reached forward to put his hand on hers, but she withdrew it. He apologised immediately. 'I'm sorry, that was thoughtless of me.'

Suddenly, she hated herself. 'No,' she said, 'it's all right.' She reached out to touch his hand. 'It really is, Maurice.'

'I was wrong to raise the subject,' he said, nevertheless feeling her hand tighten around his, 'because I seem to have touched on something very personal.'

Again, she hesitated. He'd offered her a way out of the unpleasant situation she'd created, and she had to be careful, now, how she expressed her feelings. 'I'm not… at ease… generally, in male company,' she said. 'Having said that, not all men are as sensitive as you. Also, it's wrong of me to shun the entire male population because of the barbaric behaviour of a few, but I really can't help it.'

'That's understood, and I respect your feelings.'

He was smiling and, before she realised it, so was she. 'It was good of you to make this journey,' she said awkwardly. 'I'm sorry I've made it so difficult.'

'I wanted to see you restored to health, to know you were all right, and I haven't found it remotely difficult.'

'But now you know that I'm neurotic and terrified of men, how do you feel?'

'Considering your experience, I'm not at all surprised. Your physical health is obviously improved, but the rest is bound to take longer. To answer your question, I'm glad I came.'

'Are you really?'

'I wouldn't have said it if I hadn't meant it.'

The waitress came to collect their plates. She asked, 'Can I interest you in the dessert menu?'

Maurice looked across at Iris and lifted his eyebrows. 'You've still some way to go,' he reminded her.

'You're too good,' she said. 'Yes, please.'

When the waitress was gone, Iris asked, 'If you hadn't trained to be an accountant, what would you have considered?'

'Medicine, I suppose. Dentistry, perhaps. Anything to do with people. Figures are lifeless, soulless things.'

'And you're a "people" kind of person. I know that now.'

The waitress returned with the menu, and they made their choice.

When they'd given their order, he asked, 'When's your interview at the prep school?'

She looked surprised. 'It's next Thursday afternoon, the fourteenth. Why do you ask?'

'So that I can keep my fingers crossed for you.'

She laughed gently. 'You're unbelievable.' As the thought occurred to her, she asked, 'Did you go to boarding school?'

Affecting a Nottinghamshire working-class accent, he said, 'No, me duck, t' grammar school were good enough fer me.' He was pleased to see that his silliness obviously amused her.

'You know,' she said, 'this is the first time I've laughed in more than four years.'

'In that case, you've some time to make up. You should practise regularly.'

'You make me laugh, and you're going to be miles away.'

'Well, now you know that my interest in you is reassuringly platonic, let's meet again. It should at least be good for a laugh.' As an afterthought, he said, 'You could wear that rather fetching dress again, and we could travel by bus.'

'Do you really want to see me again?' She sounded incredulous.

'Of course I do.'

'No strings?'

He peered around her hands and shoulders, and said, 'None that I can see.'

'All right, let's meet again, and I'll try not to be difficult.'

'Be as difficult as you like. I can cope with it.' Seeing the waitress out of the corner of his eye, he said, 'Ah, here comes the duff.'

'The what?'

'The pudding. I occasionally forget myself and slip into the argot of Jolly Jack the sailor.'

'Of course.' In the light of everything else, she'd given little thought to his wartime experience. 'Do you miss the Navy at all?'

'Some aspects of it. The East Coast was quite hectic, so I only miss the quiet bits. I'm a gentle soul, really.'

'I know.'

'Now,' said Maurice when the waitress had gone, 'enjoy that apple tart and cream, and let it build you up.'

Laughing again, she said, 'It's funny when you think that so many women are trying hard to lose weight, and I'm struggling to do the opposite.'

'Yes, it beats me how they manage to put it on with rationing the way it is, but don't lose heart. You'll get up to your fighting weight eventually.'

That reminded her of something. 'You know,' she said, 'before the war, I enjoyed swimming. All the time I was in Malaya, I dreamt of being able to swim in the local pool. I used to imagine the water, cool and welcoming…. It was something to hold on to, but then, when I came home, I realised it was impossible.'

'Why?'

'Because I couldn't possibly wear my bathing costume.'

'I imagine it wouldn't have been the perfect fit it had been.'

'Worse than that. What would I have looked like? With my emaciated figure, I could have given Olive Oyl a run for her money.' On reflection, she said, 'I probably still could.'

'If you don't mind my saying so, six months have made a significant difference. I'll tell you what. I enjoy swimming, too, so let's go together, and then, if anyone looks sideways at you, they'll have Popeye to deal with.'

'I may hold you to that.'

'You'd better bring a can of spinach, just in case.'

———

Later, when she changed out of her trousers and back into her dress to join her parents for dinner, she remembered that Maurice had been very complimentary about it. It was difficult to fault him, even if she'd wanted to. In taking his leave of her, he'd been content to shake her hand, but she'd defied her inhibition by inclining her head and accepting a kiss on her cheek. It was something she hadn't foreseen; it had even taken her by surprise, but it had been a day of surprises.

Naturally, her mother lost no time in pursuing her passion for matchmaking, and the subject arose at dinner.

'Mr Warneford is a very pleasant young man,' she told her husband. 'He's a chartered accountant.'

'And platonic friend,' insisted Iris.

'Oh, not that again.' Her mother gave her a weary look. 'You're twenty-seven, Iris. Time is running out.'

'My youthful appeal hath all too short a lease,' she agreed. 'Not only that, but my child-bearing days are also heading for the hills.

Quite soon, they'll disappear over the horizon, and then maybe… who knows? I may get a bit of peace.'

'I can feel a change of subject coming on,' said her father. 'Tell me about the job you've applied for.' He was a practised diplomat.

7

Tail-Wagging and Nagging

Jill's last call before picking up the children was Maggie. Unlocking the back door, she smiled at the picture on the outside wall, of a snarling Dobermann, and its message, *Go on, break in and make his day!* She imagined that such signs referred exclusively to male dogs. A great many people imagined the male to be the more menacing of the two. How little they knew.

She responded to the barking from within by calling through the letterbox, 'It's all right, Maggie. It's only Jill.'

Maggie welcomed her into the service room, which was where she lived when both owners were out for the day, and waited excitedly for her to slip the check collar over her head. 'Good girl, come on, then.' She led her outside, locking the door as she went. The key was labelled with the code, *SM*, which stood for 'Soft Maggie.' She was extremely amenable, and the only reason Jill didn't walk her with the Four was that, for some unknown reason, Mabel, the yellow Labrador, was afraid of her. Maybe she'd had a unpleasant experience with a Dobermann. She couldn't imagine that dogs were remotely capable of dealing in stereotypes, so that was the likeliest reason. Other than that, she simply had no way of knowing.

As they walked up to the moor, she remembered the time she'd left her teaching post to spend more time writing, and less in coping with the whims of politicians and bureaucrats. With Tony's business doing well, it had been an easy decision to make. The dog-walking came later, when she realised that sitting in front of a computer for long periods did little for her physical and mental health. More recently, of course, it had become a financial necessity.

It was walking Maggie that reminded her of that time, and particularly of Tony's typically ill-thought-out remark that she was taking a personal risk in walking 'alone' on the moors. She looked down affectionately at Maggie and reckoned it would take a particularly dim-witted assailant to waylay a woman walking a Dobermann or, for that matter, any of the other dogs she took on to the moor.

By association, she was reminded of one of Uncle Maurice's letters to Auntie Iris. He was congratulating her on her appointment as Matron at a boys' preparatory school. He seemed to agree with her that she would have little to fear in a school for boys aged between eight and twelve, and that the masters would be, in all probability, a quiet and sober lot. It was interesting, although it seemed, like the other letters she'd read, to raise questions as well as answering them.

They walked for about half-an-hour, after which she looked at her watch and realised it was time to take Maggie home and pick up the children. 'Home, Maggie.' They turned and made their way down the side of the moor.

Once home, Jill washed up Maggie's water bowl and refilled it. Then, after a farewell stroke and a hug, she left the house and drove to Jessica's school.

———

'Mum, this car smells of dogs.' Jessica delivered her observation almost as Jill fastened her into her seat.

'Well, that's not really surprising, darling. At a rough count, ten dogs must have ridden in it today, although not all at the same time, but they all said the same thing.'

'What?' From Jessica's tone, it was clear she knew it was a wind-up.

'They all said, "This car smells of people".'

'You're daft, Mum.' Even so, she was smiling.

'What have you been doing today?'

'Art.'

'Is that all?'

'Of course not. We did everything else, but we only get one quick art lesson a week, now. It's to make room for Science.'

'That's scandalous.' She meant it, too.

'What does "scandalous" mean?'

' "Shameful", "disgraceful". That sort of thing.'

'We have to do SATs, next year. That's disgraceful, too.'

'I agree.'

'Who's to blame?'

Jill had to think about that. It wasn't right to inflict her prejudice on a nine-year-old child, or was it a prejudice? She'd asked a question, to which there was basically only one answer. 'The politicians. They all like to interfere, regardless of outlook.' Happily, they'd reached Beckworth High School, and Liam was waiting outside the gates. With any luck, the subject could be laid to rest. He opened the front passenger door and got in, dropping his bag at his feet and looking thoughtful.

Jill asked, 'Are you trying to remember the words, Liam?'

'What words?'

'Something along the lines of, "Hello, Mum. Hello, Jessica." I know a kiss is out of the question with so many of your peers around you, but a polite greeting would be nice.'

'Hello, Mum. Hello, Jessica.'

'Hello, Liam.'

'Hello, Liam. Mum, what are peers?'

'In one sense, they're members of the House of Lords, although, in another sense, they're people like you. Your peers are the people you know at school.'

Her explanation brought forth no response from Jessica, but Liam evidently considered that an explanation of his behaviour was necessary. 'I was thinking,' he said. 'That's why I didn't say anything. I can't think and talk at the same time.'

Jill nodded. 'It calls for a degree of co-ordination, doesn't it?' After a moment's thought, she said, 'Or maybe they're mutually exclusive, like swimming and weeing in the sea.'

'Oh, Mum!'

Via the driving mirror, Jill could see that Jessica was also looking embarrassed. She had to stop embarrassing her children, even though it was fun. 'What were you thinking about, Liam?'

'Mm?'

'When you got into the car,' she prompted.

'Oh. I'd been talking to Mrs Kirby.'

'What does she do?'

'She teaches music. There are others, but she's the one who teaches us.'

'Good. What were you talking about, or was it a private thing?' It was always a possibility.

'Of course not. I asked her if she liked folk music. You know, the stuff Dad and Deborah like.'

'What did she say?'

'She said that she doesn't care for it, but it's important to remember that people should be allowed to do what they enjoy, just as long as they're not hurting anyone else.'

That sounded reasonable. 'I agree with her. Mrs Kirby is evidently a fair-minded person.'

'Well, it hurts me when Deborah shouts it all over the house, and my dad joins in.' He added, 'He couldn't carry a tune in a bucket, even supposing there was a tune to carry.'

'That's true, but where on earth did you hear that expression?'

'You said it, once, when he was singing in the shower.'

'Oh, dear.' She needed to be more careful when the children were around.

'Mum?' The word had a pensive sound to it. Clearly, Jessica was about to change the subject.

'Yes, Jessica?'

'Are you going out tonight?'

'Yes, as it happens. Why do you ask?'

'You went out last Thursday, and you used to go out on Mondays, and Gemma used to come.'

'Quite right, Jessica. Gemma's coming tonight while I help Auntie Helen with her dancing class.'

'Yay!'

'I never realised I was so unpopular. Would you like me to go out every night?'

'Of course not. It's just good when Gemma comes.'

'Okay, I can live with that. What do you like about Gemma?'

'She's fun.'

'Yes,' said Liam, whose agreement was welcome, if unexpected.

'Mum,' said Liam, 'this car smells of dogs.'

'This is where we came in, Jessica.'

———

'We have a new member, tonight, Jill,' said Helen. 'He's not a beginner, but he wants to brush up on his Ballroom. I thought you'd like to take him next door.' Turning to where a group of students were chatting together, she called, 'Steve?'

One of them detached himself from the group and joined Helen and Jill. 'Hello,' he said. 'Forgive me. I didn't recognise you at first without your dogs.'

Realisation came, and Jill said, 'The man on the moor, of course.'

'Steve.' He offered his hand.

'Jill. I'm glad to meet you again.'

'Well, you two seem to know each other already,' said Helen, 'so I'll leave you to get on.'

Still smiling at the coincidence, Jill asked, 'Would you like to come this way?'

'Of course.'

She opened the door of the next room and switched on the light. 'Okay,' she said, 'I gather you want to brush up on your technique. Where would you like to start?'

'I don't know. You're the teacher.'

'In that case, what's your favourite Ballroom dance?'

'It has to be the foxtrot.'

'Mine too. Let's go straight into it. With no music, I'll count us in, okay?'

'That's fine by me.' He took her in hold, and she counted, 'One, two, three, four....'

After a while, she said, 'Steve, you're a fraud.'

'What *do* you mean?' He was smiling.

'You want to improve your foxtrot, but there isn't an awful lot wrong with it.'

'I'm sure you can still help me improve. I mean, no one's perfect.'

'I didn't say you were perfect. For one thing, you need to go forward on your heel, and not with your foot parallel to the floor, as if you're skating.'

'There,' he said, like someone who has just won a major argument, 'I said I was in need of correction.'

'You're actually quite good, Steve.' She hesitated and asked, 'Do you prefer to be called that, and not....'

'I prefer "Steve", if you don't mind.'

'Noted.'

'There are quite a lot of Stephens about,' he explained, 'but there are many more Steves, and I decided a long time ago that I preferred to be one of a crowd.'

'All right, Steve—' She stopped abruptly.

'What's the matter?'

'Listen.' Through the wall, she could hear, 'I'll Never Let You Go.'

'Not bad,' he commented.

'Not bad at all, so let's take advantage of it.'

He took her in hold again, and they danced to the rest of the track.

'You're improving,' she told him as the strains died away. 'You'll soon get used to moving forward on your heel.'

'I just need someone to nag me.'

'I can't believe I just heard a man say that,' she said, laughing.

'It's true, Jill. My wife and I used to dance quite often, and she was forever nagging me about my slipshod ways.' He must have sensed that she was unsure what to say, because he explained quite matter-of-factly, 'She died six years ago.'

'I'm so sorry, Steve.'

'You're very kind, but it passed the hurting stage some time ago. I'm just conscious that I need to be nagged about my foxtrot now and again.'

'I'm sure I'm a poor substitute, but I have to mention that you're becoming a little hunched. Try to hold your head up more, so that it's in a straight line with your back. That's better.'

The voice of Anthony Newley came again from the next room.

'They're playing our song,' said Steve.

'Okay, let's dance, but remember what I've told you.'

'It's difficult, Jill. You'll just have to keep nagging.'

'I'll start shouting if you don't behave yourself. It was probably my temper that caused my husband to think again.' Now that she'd mentioned it, she wondered why she had. It certainly hadn't been her intention.

He went forward confidently on his heel and danced with an improved posture. At the end of the number, he asked, 'Do you ever dance just for fun, Jill, or only when you're teaching?'

'That's a good question. I used to enjoy dancing, and I've only recently come back to teaching it.' Smiling, she said, 'I used to nag my husband, who, admittedly, isn't a natural dancer.'

'Have you given up trying to improve him?'

'You could say that. Anyway,' she said, keen to move the conversation away from personal matters, 'shall we have a look at your waltz, always provided Helen's finished with the foxtrot?' Another helping of Anthony Newley would present a problem, but Helen obliged, as if by telepathy, with a recording of 'Who's Taking You Home Tonight?'

'Wasn't that convenient?'

'It was,' she agreed, joining him in a waltz.

As she drove home, she wondered again about Uncle Maurice's letter. In particular, his agreement with Auntie Iris about the security offered by a boys' prep school puzzled her, unless they were referring to it as a cushioned retreat from the hubbub of normal life after her incarceration in Malaya. She thought, although not for the first time, how pleasant it would be to share her ideas with someone, a sounding board, in fact. There was no obvious candidate, however; Tony was gone, not that he would have been much use, and Helen's interests were rooted very firmly in the present. No, she had nothing more helpful than her own intuition, and the realisation was quite discomforting.

8

A New Resolution

Maurice left his changing cubicle and looked around for Iris. He couldn't see her immediately, but bathing caps made most women anonymous, and he was sure she'd find him, so he walked down to the deep end and dived in from the pool side. He continued underwater, breaking surface about halfway along the pool and swimming to the shallow end. As he did so, he remembered Iris telling him how she'd dreamt of entering the cool water of the swimming pool and, after his comparatively brief time in the heat and humidity of the Far East, he could sympathise with her. It was a fleeting thought that came to an abrupt close when he heard her voice beside him.

'Isn't it wonderful, Maurice?'

'Isn't it just?' It was really very ordinary in his experience, but he knew how special it was for her. She looked very happy, and her fears about her appearance were quite groundless. She was slender, but not unnaturally so.

'It's my first time here since before the war, and the place hasn't changed at all.'

'I'm glad.' He meant it, having once revisited a childhood haunt and experienced the dissonance between memory and reacquaintance.

'I'll see you at the deep end,' she said with childlike enthusiasm. Then, without waiting for a response, she struck out in a very respectable front crawl. She'd clearly been a capable swimmer, and would be again when her muscles had time to redevelop.

He set off after her, reaching the end as she did and finding her clinging to the glazed earthenware trough.

'I'm as weak as a kitten,' she confessed, unaccountably surprised.

'It's not all that surprising, but you'll improve.'

'I mustn't overdo it.'

'No, but I'm here in case you do.'

She looked at him oddly.

'If you get into difficulties,' he explained, 'I'll pull you out.' Making light of the possibility, he grinned and said, 'I have a certificate for life-saving.'

'So have I,' she said, 'but it wouldn't be much use to me now.'

'Get your strength and your breath back before you do anything else,' he advised her, 'and then, when you feel you've done as much as you can, we'll call it a day.'

'I'm an awful let-down.'

'Don't be daft. You're an out-of-practice swimmer who's bound to improve with the right approach.'

Surveying the length of the pool, as if for the first time, she asked, 'Could you bear to do a gentle breast stroke with me to the shallow end?'

'It'll be a pleasure. Are you sure you're ready for it?'

'I'll be all right.' She sounded fairly confident.

'Go on the inside, and then you can grab the rail if you need to.' He waited for her to start, and then followed her, watching her all the way until they reached the far end.

'I'm so sorry,' she said, standing on the floor of the pool. 'I've done as much as I can.'

'All right, let's get out. Do you need a hand?'

'No, thanks, I'll manage.' She started up the wooden steps and then faltered as she felt the full weight of her body, now unsupported by water.

'Take it easy. I've got you.' He led her up the steps before lowering her on to the concrete side. 'Just sit there until you're ready to go and change.'

Someone asked, 'What do you two think you're doing?'

Maurice turned his head and saw that the question had come from a fully-dressed man, most likely the pool superintendent. 'I'm supporting someone who's weakened by almost four years of starvation and malnutrition. What did you think I was doing?'

'We have to be careful,' said the man. 'People get up to all sorts of things in this place.'

'Do they, now? Do you know what you need to do?'

'What?' The man eyed him suspiciously.

'Each time one of those unpleasant little ideas of yours occurs to you, you need to have a cold shower.' He pointed towards the shower cubicle. 'It'll cure you in no time.'

'I'm only doing my job,' said the man resentfully.

'Well, here's something else you can do. Have you got a female colleague?'

'Yes. Why?'

'Because this lady is going to need some help in reaching the changing cubicles, and if I try to help her to that side of the pool, you're bound to accuse me of something unpleasant.'

'I'll go and get her.'

Maurice took a seat beside Iris and waited.

'Good for you,' she said.

'He just needed to be put straight, that's all.'

'I can't believe that people "get up to all sorts of things" in a place as public as this,' she said.

He smiled gently and said, 'And I don't even know what he was talking about.'

The superintendent arrived with his colleague, who asked, 'What's the problem, duck?'

'This lady needs help to get to her changing cubicle,' Maurice told her. 'If I'm allowed to help her to her feet without this man sending for the police, maybe you'll be good enough to help her there.'

''Course I will. Heave her up, then.' She waited until Iris was on her feet, and said, 'Come on, duck. Let's get you to your cubicle.'

Maurice gave the superintendent a despairing look whilst shaking his head, and went to change, wondering as he did, just what 'sorts of things' people did get up to in the swimming pool.

He was waiting by the exit when the female superintendent arrived with Iris, who looked a little embarrassed.

'I'm all right, really,' she said, 'but thank you for your help.'

'That's all right, duck. Your fella's here now, so he'll take care of you.'

When they were alone, Maurice said, 'I don't know about you, but whenever I've been swimming, I feel hungry. If such a thing can be found in these straitened times, would you care to join me in a sticky tea?'

She laughed weakly. 'You're a tonic, Maurice, you really are.'

'Where do you suggest?'

'There's a nice teashop in the town centre. You can park outside it.'

'Okay, if you feel strong enough to ride pillion, we'll go there.'

'Of course I do. You mustn't fuss.' She waited for him to take his place on the saddle, and then climbed up behind him. Satisfied that she was secure, he started the engine and headed for the town centre, noticing as he did that, unlike the first time they'd ridden together, she held his waist, rather than the strap between their saddles.

They rode into the town centre, where, responding to a tap on his shoulder and Iris's pointing finger, he pulled into the side of the street and switched off the engine.

'It doesn't look very busy for a Saturday,' she said.

'Let's go in and find out.'

When they enquired, they were shown to a table beside the window, where they studied the menu.

He asked, 'Shall we have the set tea?'

'You're determined to fatten me up, aren't you?'

'It's a sacred trust,' he told her seriously, 'albeit self-imposed.'

'Okay, let's have the set tea.'

'You don't look very happy about it.'

She sighed. 'I'm just disappointed.'

'That your return to the swimming pool was less than you'd hoped?'

'That,' she agreed, 'and that I put you to a lot of trouble, and all for the sake of ten or fifteen minutes in the pool.'

'You're wrong on both counts,' he said, pausing when the waitress came to take their order. 'We'd both like the set tea, please. What teas have you?'

With an air of apology that was probably routine by that time, the waitress said, 'The only tea we can get is English Breakfast, sir'.

'That being the case, let's have a pot of the English Breakfast.'

'Very good, sir.'

When they were alone again, Iris asked, 'What made you say I was wrong?'

'Firstly, you didn't put me to any trouble. Secondly, our time in the pool was incidental. I came to spend time with a friend. Am I allowed to call you a friend?'

'Of course.'

'Good, because that's what I did. Believe me, if I ever go to any trouble, I make sure everyone knows about it.'

She appeared to study him briefly before saying, 'You make light of almost everything. I say, "almost", because you really gave that superintendent what-for.'

'He asked for it by insulting both of us. He was lucky I didn't chuck him into the pool.' As they were on the subject, he felt he should explain his actions. 'I'm sorry I had to manhandle you,' he said, 'but it was preferable to letting you fall back into the water, as I'm sure you'll agree.'

'I can't disagree—' Suddenly, she shuddered.

'What is it, Iris?'

'The man who's just come in.' She narrowed her eyes and looked away.

Maurice glanced over his shoulder. 'Change places with me.'

'Are you sure?'

'Absolutely.' He stood up and pushed his chair back to let her in.

When they were seated again, he asked, 'Do you know him?'

'No, he's a complete stranger. It's just… He gave me the horrors, just for a moment.'

'Are you all right now?'

'Yes, thank you. I'm sorry, it's the most awful thing.'

'I know.' The man was dark-haired, he had a swarthy complexion, and a carefully-cultivated moustache that stopped an inch short of a sparse beard. His only western feature was his eyes. He'd just divested himself of his coat, which he'd worn over his shoulders without troubling the sleeves. With a theatre in close proximity, Maurice guessed he was an actor, but whatever his calling, he must have presented a sight that triggered a chilling association for Iris.

'I woke up last night in the middle of a nightmare,' she told him. 'The noise I made even woke my mother, who's a sound sleeper. Naturally, she reminded me that everything was all right, now. My dad was more sympathetic, but it left me thinking. Everything isn't all right. I thought I'd left the horrors behind in Malaya, but they followed me home, and that's why I have nightmares and I freeze when I see someone who looks even vaguely oriental, like that man who came in just now.'

'It's perfectly understandable.'

'But more than irritating for you, I'm afraid.'

Their hands were inches apart on the table. He asked, 'Do you mind if I hold your hand?'

'No, I don't. Not now.' She moved her hand forward and let him take it, feeling the warmth and security she'd felt when he shook hands with her on his previous visit.

One of my little foibles,' he told her, 'is that, when I have to discuss something very serious, I find it easier if I have physical contact. Does that sound absurd?'

'No, and certainly not compared with my strange fancies.'

'I don't find them at all strange or irritating. I only know a little of what you experienced in Malaya, but it doesn't surprise me at all that you react as you do in certain circumstances.' He squeezed her hand reassuringly.

She said quietly, 'You're more understanding than I deserve, Maurice.'

He shook his head very definitely. 'Deserving has absolutely nothing to do with it. I don't know any of the details, I just try to understand.'

The waitress arrived with their order, but Iris left her hand in Maurice's while she unloaded the contents of the trolley on to their table.

'Thank you,' he said.

'If you need anything else, just ask.'

'We will.'

The waitress went to the bewhiskered man's table and spoke to him. Maurice heard him say in a resounding voice, 'The set tea, please, my dear, and a pot of Earl Grey, if you will.' He was clearly an actor, and Maurice was perversely glad the teashop had only English Breakfast tea. He squeezed Iris's hand and winked.

She asked, 'Shall I pour?'

'If you will. I'm a hopeless pourer.'

'Can we talk about you for a change?'

'If you find me interesting enough. Frankly, it would surprise me.'

'Oh, but I do.' She was insistent. 'Tell me how you enjoy yourself when you're not working.'

'I rather think this is where you're going to lose interest in me. The fact is, I play cricket. At least, I did before the war, and the club have agreed to have me back, so I'll be playing in the coming season.'

'I like cricket. I played it at school.'

'Really? What were you, bat or a bowler?'

'There you go again,' she said impatiently, 'talking about me when I want to know more about you.'

'I'm sorry. I bowl right-arm leg breaks, I usually bat at number three or four, and I'm delighted that you enjoy cricket.'

'I bowled right-arm medium pace, I batted low in the order, and I wasn't very good.'

'Everyone has to begin somewhere,' he assured her quickly, realising that the thespian with the facial adornment was coming to their table.

'I say, old man, I'm sorry to interrupt you, but, quite incredibly, the waitress tells me they have no Earl Grey. I just wondered what you were drinking.'

'She was telling the truth,' said Maurice, squeezing Iris's hand to reassure her. 'You'll just have to settle for English Breakfast, as we did. We can only blame that well-known pair Rationing and Austerity.'

'Ah, so it's true, then.'

'Every word,' confirmed Maurice.

'I've been living abroad, so all this is new to me. Sorry to have disturbed you, old chap.'

'Think nothing of it.' He just wanted the man to go, and was rewarded a moment later. 'It's all right, Iris,' he said, 'he's gone.'

Her face was white. 'I'm sorry,' she whispered.

'You really need to stop apologising, at least, to me.'

'I'll try. It's not easy.'

A stray thought occurred to him, and he asked, 'Do you know today's date?'

She frowned. 'Not off-hand. Is it important?'

'Vitally important. It's the twenty-third of March, and you know what that means.'

'Do I?'

'You should. It means that, one week from tomorrow will be the thirty-first of March, a time for a clean sheet and a fresh start, when old ways are discarded, and new resolutions abound.'

Shaking her head at his silliness, she asked, 'Aren't you confusing it with the first of January?'

'Not for one moment. Being an accountant, I live by the financial year. It's so popular that even the Revenue get in on the act six days later. Now, my suggestion is that you make a new financial year's resolution to stop apologising to me whenever a reminder of your horrible time in Malaya causes you to react. Is that a lot to ask?'

'It probably is,' she said, laughing, 'but it's such a silly idea, it rather appeals to me, so I'll give it a try.

Later, as she sat down with her parents to eat, her father asked her how her day had been.

'Very pleasant indeed, thank you. I swam in the pool for the first time since I left for the Far East, and I managed two lengths before I was exhausted, but it was a start.'

'A good start, I'd say.'

'Thanks, Dad.'

Her mother said anxiously, 'You need to be very careful, Iris.'

'I was in no danger, Mum. I had my personal lifesaver on hand all the time.'

'Mr Warneford?'

'The same.'

'He seems to be a responsible young man.'

'He is, Mum.' Then, side-tracking what she suspected might be another attempt on her mother's part to challenge her unmarried status, she asked, 'Dad, have you ever thought of the new financial year as a time for breaking with the past and making new resolutions?'

He considered the question and smiled broadly. 'I confess, I haven't thought of it until now, Iris, but it's as good a time as any to challenge our habits. It might even be thought of as a safety net, a chance to revive New Year resolutions that have fallen by the wayside. You know, I may just float the idea at the bank on Monday. It should surprise a few people who might benefit from that kind of reappraisal.'

Left behind, as usual, by the conversation, her mother asked, 'What on earth are you two talking about?'

'Just an idea, Mum, put to me by that responsible young man Mr Warneford.'

Like so many of Maurice's ideas, it was a good one. He was, as her mother had said, responsible, as well as being understanding, unusually accommodating, and a great deal of fun. The more she saw of him, the more she liked him, but she had to control her feelings for him. That must be her first resolution, because anything deeper than a close friendship was out of the question.

9

A New Perspective

Jill saw Steve again at the dance school over the next few weeks. On the second occasion, a married couple joined her Ballroom class, and then another couple turned up a week later, so the atmosphere continued to be friendly, but without the intimacy of her first class with Steve. It was still necessary, in the absence of a partner, for her to dance with him, but he was very civilised about it, and she was grateful for that.

She also saw him again on the moor when she was walking Maggie. He naturally stopped to speak to her whilst maintaining a shrewd distance between Maggie and himself.

'She's very friendly,' Jill assured him. 'If you were aggressive towards me, she'd have you in a flash. Otherwise, there's no problem.'

'Is she yours?'

'No, but I'm one of her favourite people, so she'd protect me.'

'Good for her. What's her name?'

'Maggie.'

'Is there a connection?'

Jill nodded. 'She's only two, but her name was an act of political nostalgia on her master's part. Otherwise, apart from stumping up the money for her, he's had little to do with her. Fortunately, her mistress trained her, and she's an infinitely more responsible person than her husband.'

'Dobermanns get bad press, don't they?'

'Only because of irresponsible owners. Like Rottweilers and

German shepherds, they're bred to be guard dogs, so they're not ideal pets for beginners.' Sensing that the conversation was rather one-sided, she asked, 'Is this your favourite place for walking?'

'When I'm at home, yes. I sometimes find myself agonising over a passage I'm writing, so I spend a bit of time on the moor. When I return to the piece I'm working on, it usually falls into place. I don't know how it works, but I'm glad it does.'

'It makes perfect sense,' she said, thinking about her current preoccupation. 'I'm trying to unravel a mystery, myself, but I think it's going to call for more than a walk on the moor.'

'Why don't we walk together? That way, some of my peculiar facility might prove infectious. You never know.'

'All right. I've got ten minutes before I have to take Maggie home and pick up my children from school.' They set off together.

'Would you like to tell me about your mystery, Jill?'

'All right. I'm trying to find out more about an auntie and uncle I never knew all that well. At least, I didn't know them as well as I'd have liked. My uncle died in December, which is what triggered my quest, but all I have to go on is a bundle of letters from him to her, written in the early stages of their relationship, and what little my mother can tell me.' She explained the unusual circumstances of their meeting on the river in Malaya.

'That sounds like a fascinating project. 'Where are you currently hung-up?'

'Well, apparently, she took a job, shortly after she came home to England, as matron in an independent prep school for boys, but it was very short-lived. She was only there a few weeks.'

'Do you know why?'

'I haven't a clue.' She stopped to remove a glove and search one of her pockets for the letter. 'Here it is,' she said, opening it and finding the appropriate paragraph. 'He says, "What rotten luck. For what it's worth, though, I'm sure you did the right thing in resigning. Frankly, I think it was a pernicious practice, and I'm a hundred percent with you. Honestly, Iris, you've seen too much of that kind of thing. Also, you mustn't think you're letting anyone down. It's going to take more than a well-meaning matron to change things." Then, he goes on to arrange another meeting with her.' Feeling that she'd been going rather too quickly, she said, 'I should explain that he was living in Newark, and her home was in Loughborough.'

'And this was happening shortly after the war?'

'Nineteen forty-six, yes.'

He was thoughtful for a spell, and then he said, 'You're not dealing with someone whose reactions would necessarily be what you or I would consider normal. The poor woman would have lived in hell for three years or more.' By way of explanation, he said, 'Some time ago, I did a lot of work on Japanese war crimes....' He stopped briefly in mid-thought and asked, 'Where was the internment camp?'

'I can't remember, but he mentions the place in one of his early letters. I'll have another look and let you know.'

'It's not bound to throw any more light on the mystery, but you never know.' Delving into an inside pocket, he took out a card and gave it to her. 'Here's my phone number and email address.'

'Thank you. I'll try not to phone you. I know how irritating that can be when you're trying to work, but I'll email the name of the camp to you when I find it.' Looking at her watch, she said, 'It's time to take Maggie home, now.'

'Okay, I'll walk down the moor with you as far as my car.'

'Are you happy, now, that Maggie won't bite you?'

'Oh, yes. I'm wary of any dog until it's vouched for. I've nothing against them, you understand. I rather like them, but I don't take kindly to being bitten.'

'No one can argue with that.'

They walked to the main road at the bottom of the moor, where they took their leave of each other, she heading for Maggie's home, and he to his VW Golf parked at the side of the road, but not before he'd repeated his offer of help. So far, she found it impossible to fault him, but she was still inclined to be wary.

When Liam got into the car, Jessica said, 'You had games today.'

'How do you know?'

'Your face is all dirty.'

Jill laughed. 'It is, too. When we get home, you can have a shower, but leave your football kit out so that I can wash it.'

Jessica said, 'He always forgets.'

'That's true,' said Jill, but you're not perfect. If I take the trouble to wash and iron your clothes, you might at least put them away tidily.'

When they were home, Jill repeated her standing rule about homework before television. Liam seemed to think that if he challenged it often enough she would relent, and that was never going to happen.

'Dad lets us watch telly.'

'You don't have homework on Sundays,' she reminded him. 'That's because I insist on your doing it on Friday, before you watch television.'

'That's not fair.'

'If you think that, Liam, you should try shouldering a mum's workload and responsibilities. You'd probably find that as unfair as I do.'

'Deborah's house is mucky,' said Jessica. 'She doesn't do half of what you do.'

'Well said, my little champion. Now, you sit down and read while Liam has a shower, puts his muddy kit in the washing basket and does his homework.' While all that was happening, she would make herself a cup of tea and look for the name of the internment camp that Auntie Iris was in.

When the children were in bed, she went to the computer and wrote an email.

Good evening, Steve,
The internment camp was at Kuala Rompin, Pahang, Malaya. I'm afraid that's as much as I know, except that she was there from the Japanese invasion of Singapore, so I hope that's useful.
Kind regards,
Jill.

Having done that, she shut down the computer, satisfied that if he did find out anything interesting he would doubtless let her know on Monday at the class.

Her mobile rang at a little after nine-thirty. She imagined it would be either an enquiry about dog care or a cancellation.

'Hello. No task too great, no dog too small. Jill speaking. How can I help you?'

'Hello, Jill, it's Steve. I got your email.'

'Oh, good. I didn't mean to disturb you at this time.'

'It's no trouble, honestly. I've been having a look at my notes. Did you know there were two camps at Kuala Rompin?'

'No, I didn't.' She was actually surprised that he'd found even one.

'It was normal practice for the Japanese to keep men and women in separate camps, although the two at Kuala Rompin came under the command of a Colonel Seiji Nakamura, who was tried for war crimes and hanged in nineteen forty-six.'

'Charming.' She poured herself a glass of wine as a distraction.

'The Japanese always maintained that they didn't make war on women and children, which sounds noble enough, but it was basically meaningless, as they had other ways of making their lives unbearable. About the only concession they made was to spare them the heavy manual labour they forced male prisoners to do. You'll have heard about that, I imagine?'

'Very generally, I must confess.'

'The best-known example was the Burma-Siam Railway, that was constructed by Allied prisoners-of-war, and they say that one man died for each sleeper that was laid. It amounted to about twenty-five thousand.'

'Horrible.' Inadequate though her imagination was, she was conscious that her voice was little more than a whisper.

'I shan't dwell on it, but I did mention this afternoon that your aunt must have endured three-and-a-half years of hell in that place, coping with near-starvation and no medical supplies.'

'It all sounds so... inhuman.' There were no doubt more appropriate ways to describe it, but she was struggling to comprehend the enormity of what she'd heard.

'It was, but many of its perpetrators were tried and punished after the war.'

'I can accept that, but all the trials in the world couldn't undo the harm those people had done.'

'I absolutely agree, Jill.'

'What I really don't understand is that my auntie was such a kindly person. I first met her long after the war – I wasn't born until nineteen sixty-two – but, even so, I'd have expected her to be full of anger and resentment against the Japanese.'

'So would I, and I should mention that it wasn't just the Japanese. They used the lowest grade of troops as camp guards, and that included a great many Koreans, who were unbelievably primitive.'

'You obviously did a lot of research, Steve.'

'I did, and I found it quite harrowing, as I'm sure you do, so I shan't go on about it.'

'I'm grateful to you for that, as well as for what you've told me.' He'd given her a great deal to think about.

'You're welcome to any help I can give you. I just hope I haven't horrified you too much.'

'Don't worry about that.' In spite of herself, she laughed as she said, 'I'm just pouring myself a drink.'

'That sounds like a good idea. I may do the same.'

As the question occurred to her, she asked, 'How did you find my mobile number?' She knew she hadn't given it to him.

'I looked in the local paper and found your advertisement. "No Task Too Great, No Dog Too Small". I liked that.'

'Thanks. It works for me.'

'Good.' There was a pause, and he said, 'I almost forgot to tell you that I've given some thought to the letter you read this afternoon.'

'Oh yes?'

'About your aunt's resignation from the prep school.'

'Right.'

'Well, the only "pernicious practice" I can think of that might have been common to her experience in Malaya and a boys' prep school of the time was corporal punishment.'

'That certainly makes sense.' She was surprised it hadn't occurred to her already. 'They only got around to banning it in independent schools two years ago. Good thinking, Steve.'

'Yes, I imagine that, with her experience, she would abhor violence, especially against vulnerable children.'

'I suppose all children are vulnerable. That's been my experience, anyway.'

'As a parent?'

'And as a teacher. That's what I did until five years ago.'

'I see. I shan't pry.'

'Yes, I think you got that one just right.'

'Only too pleased to oblige. Is there anything else I can help you with?'

She laughed good-naturedly. 'No, thanks. I've taken too much of your time already.'

'Not at all. I've done as much as I'm going to, today, so my time is yours, if you need it.'

'You're more than generous— There is one thing.'

'Name that thing.'

'Okay. In a previous letter, he congratulated her on her appointment at the school, and agreed with her that she would feel safe enough in a prep school. I found that strange, and I wondered if maybe it was because she needed the enclosed security of the place after being pitchforked into the wide world again.'

'It's possible. I shouldn't be surprised, as well, if she turned out to be uncomfortable in the company of men.'

'Because she'd spent so long in a women's camp?'

'Maybe "uncomfortable" is too much of a euphemism. I'm thinking of the kind of man she knew there, and I'm surprised that she ever wanted to go near a man again.'

10

A Home Truth and a Confidence

The regime at Linden Manor Preparatory School was quasi-military, a feature Iris found disturbing, as the boys' ages ranged from eight to twelve, making the rigid ethos seem inappropriate, at least. Her duties so far, however, had been undemanding. She'd been called upon several times to render first aid, and she was required to administer prescribed medication. In addition, some of the boys suffered from asthma, and one had epilepsy, which called for a watchful eye. Otherwise, she was alerted frequently to cases of bed-wetting, which were common. On such occasions, she had to run a bath for the boy in question, change his bedding, and provide him with clean pyjamas. In each case, she tried to be reassuring, knowing as she did, that bed-wetting was usually caused by anxiety. The boys appreciated her understanding, unlike the housemasters, one of whom had already told her she was pandering to the weak and self-indulgent. Fortunately, she could handle criticism and even present a cogent and forceful argument when she felt it was necessary, but she found herself on one occasion in a situation with which she was completely unable to cope.

It became apparent that Bramwell Minor, so-called because he was the younger of the Bramwell brothers currently on the school roll, had been awarded three demerits during the current week, thus incurring a summons to the Headmaster's study that Friday afternoon. It seemed to Iris that it was a particularly cruel system, as a boy could be given all three demerits on Monday morning, and have to wait a whole week to be punished, but she was apparently alone in that conviction.

She had just entered the sanatorium when Bramwell Minor's housemaster marched the ten-year-old offender along the corridor, and past her door, to the Headmaster's study, and she watched in dismay as they paused outside the door, the master gripping the wretched Bramwell's collar against the unlikely event of an escape attempt. He rapped on the oak panel and, on receipt of a stern invitation, entered the study.

It was at this point that a chilling and terrifying event took place. Startlingly and with no warning of which Iris was aware, the corridor with its doorways and oak-panelled walls appeared to be absorbed into a haze before being snatched away, and she found herself transplanted inexplicably into a distant, yet horrifyingly familiar, setting. The air was hot and humid and, where she'd been aware of masters in worn academic gowns, their places were taken by soldiers wearing the grey-green uniform she'd come to fear and loathe. An officer loosened his long, *shin gunto* sword in its scabbard and took a step closer to the two men now forced into a kneeling position before him....

She opened her eyes and she was once again outside the sanatorium, immediately conscious of the perspiration dripping from her forehead; in fact, she was perspiring all over. She could feel it prickling, cold and wet beneath her clothes. Her mouth was devoid of moisture, her heart was thudding rapidly and violently, and it took all her strength for her to reach the nearest bed, where she sank on to the mattress with her head bowed between her knees. She began to sob helplessly.

———

She was largely recovered by suppertime, when she sat at the lower staff table in the refectory, wondering how these men could contemplate acts of violence against the small boys she saw before her, and she had to force herself to think of other things in order to keep her heightened emotions under control. Meanwhile, Bramwell Minor was nowhere to be seen.

It was a little after eight when she was alerted by a knocking on her door, and she went to open it, expecting to be informed of a bed-wetting incident. Instead, the expression on the boy's face suggested an emergency of a more dramatic nature.

'Matron,' he said, 'can you come to the third-form dorm, please?'

'What's the matter, Fenner?' She found the practice of addressing young boys by surname cold and unfriendly, but it was nevertheless expected of her.

'It's Bramwell Minor, Matron....'

He was obviously struggling to put the problem into words. Maybe it was embarrassing. At all events, she picked up her emergency bag and followed Fenner to the dormitory.

When she opened the door, she found a group of boys clustered around one bed. They backed away when they heard the door open and close, and she saw that the occupant of the bed was lying face downward. A closer look revealed that he was Bramwell Minor and that he was in acute distress.

She crouched beside him and asked, 'What is it?' She knew already, but she felt that a sympathetic enquiry wouldn't be out of place.

His distress and, to some extent, the muffling effect of his pillow, made him less than coherent, but one of the others explained, 'It's his... behind, Matron.' There was no sniggering, as there might have been in different circumstances. It seemed they were equally shocked by his condition.

'Let me have a look, Bramwell.' She could see from the loose waistband that his pyjama trousers were unfastened, and she lowered them as gently as she could, being in no doubt as to the nature of the problem, although it was the extent of it, once it lay revealed, that shocked her more. 'Oh, Bramwell,' she said softly, 'you poor little mite.' Reaching for her bag, she took out a bottle of witch hazel balm and a wad of cotton wool. 'This is going to feel cold, but it'll take away the stinging.' She soaked the cotton wool with witch hazel and dabbed it gently on to each livid weal while her patient sobbed into his pillow. As she stroked his shoulder compassionately and covered him again, she advised him to continue to lie face downward. 'Call me again if he needs me,' she told the others.

The next morning, after Prayers, she knocked on the Headmaster's door and waited for his usual gruff response. When it came, she pushed open the door, wondering how a clergyman could be so forbidding.

'Good morning, Matron,' he said. 'What brings you to my study?'

'Good morning, Doctor Ballantyne. Last evening, I was called to attend Bramwell Minor after he'd received a most severe flogging.'

'So the punishment was not without effect.' The words seemed to proceed from within his large, bushy beard, without discernible movement of his lips, an impression that served to accentuate his remoteness.

Iris contained her anger and continued. 'The child was in great pain and distress. He was unable to lie comfortably, and was therefore denied sleep.'

'He should perhaps have considered that when he earned the demerits that led to his punishment.'

'He's not yet eleven years old, Doctor Ballantyne.' She felt that the information must surely be meaningful to him in some way.

The Headmaster nodded in formal agreement. 'He's at an age when he must learn to understand the consequences of his actions.'

'But did he really deserve to be beaten so severely?'

'Obviously, Matron, for the punishment to have taken place.' Looking up at the large wall clock, he said, 'Unless you have another matter to bring before me, I must insist that you excuse me, as more pressing matters demand my attention.'

'Doctor Ballantyne, I was in Singapore when the colony was surrendered to the Japanese, and I was interned by them until liberation in nineteen forty-five.'

'A most distressing experience, I imagine, Matron, but I fail to see how that is any of my business.'

Iris breathed deeply and went on. 'Cruelty, sadism and bestiality are everyone's business, Headmaster, and particularly when, like you, they claim to serve a loving and merciful God.'

'How dare you!' For the first time, he was angry, and Iris could only imagine the fear he must inspire in the children under his tutelage. She, on the other hand, felt no such fright, having experienced far worse.

'Far be it from me to defend my captors, but they did have the excuse that, beneath a thin veneer of civilisation, they were emerging from a feudal and barbaric existence. You, Doctor Ballantyne, have no such excuse. Your treatment of Bramwell Minor was vile, brutal and sadistic. In that one act alone, you demonstrated beyond reasonable argument that you are a disgrace to the Church you represent and the religion you claim to follow.' She blinked rapidly to dispel the tears of anger that threatened to undermine her dignity.

The Headmaster was shaking with scarcely-controlled fury, and it was with some difficulty that he formulated his next sentence. 'In all my years in the clergy and as a schoolmaster, I have never been subjected to such calumny or downright insulting behaviour. Clearly, you have no place in this school—'

'Let me save you the effort, Doctor Ballantyne,' she said. 'You'll receive my written resignation later today.'

Several days later, Maurice parked outside Iris's home.

'This is rather splendid,' she said as he climbed out of the Hillman Minx.

'Hello, Iris,' he said, kissing her lightly on the cheek. 'My father insisted I sold the Panther and used this instead. He says it creates a better impression with clients.'

'I'm sure he's right.'

'And,' he said, holding up an index finger for emphasis, 'it means you can wear one of your rather fetching frocks instead of being restricted to trousers.' He added hurriedly, 'Not that you don't look equally enchanting in trousers. It just gives you a choice, and I'm all for variety.'

'You're priceless,' she said, laughing at his nonsense. 'Come inside. My mum's out shopping.'

'I'm sure she doesn't bite.'

'No, she's worse than that.' She looked down at her trousers, chosen for the occasion, and asked, 'Would you prefer me to wear a dress?'

'That's entirely up to you. You'd be just as welcome in oilskins, seaboots and a sou'wester.'

'I'll change into a dress. Would you like a cup of tea while you're waiting?'

Affecting dismay, he said, 'You're not going to be that long, are you?'

'Of course not. I just thought I'd offer it as a courtesy.'

'That's very kind of you, thank you, but I'll just wait with barely-suppressed excitement.'

'You say the daftest things.' Serious again, she asked, 'What are we going to do?'

'I suggest a light-but-lazy lunch, and then we can have a run out to somewhere where there's open countryside.'

'I'm not objecting, but what made you think of that?'

'It would be an opportunity to sit still, take a deep breath and relax.'

'Okay.' She seemed happy with that suggestion. 'I'll be back in a minute.' She ran upstairs to change out of her trousers.

While she was gone, her mother arrived home, so Maurice naturally offered to relieve her of her shopping.

'Thank you, Mr Warneford, but there's very little, as you can see.' Looking around, she asked, 'Where's Iris?'

'She's upstairs, changing.'

'How odd.' Then, distracted, she asked, 'Was that your car I saw outside?'

'Yes, my father put his foot down and made me forsake the Panther for something more genteelly appropriate.'

'It's rather nice.'

'Thank you.'

In another abrupt change of subject, she said, 'I'm surprised Iris didn't offer you a cup of tea while she changed.'

'She did, Mrs Lennox, but I declined her offer. Incidentally, I'm taking her to lunch.'

'Oh.' She sounded pleased rather than surprised.

'And speaking as a humble male,' he said as Iris came into the room, now wearing the dress he'd seen on his first visit, 'I think that's the perfect choice.'

'Thank you.'

They took their leave of Mrs Lennox and went out to the car.

'She's still nagging me because I left the job at the school,' said Iris.

'She knows hardly anything of the circumstances, but she's never been one to let that prevent her from sitting in judgement.'

'The main thing is that you know you were in the right.'

'It was uncanny,' she said. 'I've never been as bold as that. I told him he was a disgrace to the priesthood and a few more things besides.'

'You were absolutely right, Iris, and having right on your side always helps.' He swung into the main road and asked, 'Shall we go to the restaurant we used the first time?'

'Why not? It was good.' She added, 'By the way, I'm going to try not to be a casualty today.'

'You've never been a casualty, but I know what you mean.'

'Something very strange happened, though. I'll tell you about it, and then I shan't mention it again.' As he pulled in beside the restaurant, she said, 'I'll tell you when we're at the table.'

A waitress showed them to a table and gave them each a menu. Iris gave it a look, made her decision, and said, 'It was the strangest thing and it was quite awful. It happened when I saw the boy being taken to the Headmaster's study.' She hesitated.

He waited for her to go on.

'Can you imagine having a nightmare about something you've experienced, but when you're wide awake?'

'Yes, but tell me about it.'

'It was as if suddenly I was back at Kuala Rompin. I could see everything quite clearly, the guards and everything. Two men had tried to escape, and the Japs brought us to the men's camp to witness their execution.'

'Look, if it upsets you, don't talk about it.'

'It's all right,' she said definitely. 'It's not one of my favourite memories, but I'm not going to get upset. I'm determined about that.' She braced herself to go on. 'Anyway, my nightmare – or call it what you will – ended before the horrible part, thank goodness, but I found myself in a state of panic. I was perspiring all over and my pulse rate was breaking all records, but above all, I was terrified. It was as if the nightmare was following me around, just waiting to happen again when I least expected it.'

The waitress came to their table and asked if they were ready to order, which they did. When she was gone, Maurice said, 'The same thing happens to my uncle, not so often nowadays, but it was a big problem at first. He had a bad time in the first war, being buried alive at one time, and the nightmare came home with him. The awful thing is that he's always refused to see a doctor.'

'I can't see what good it would do. I mean, they can't wave a magic wand so that it never happened, can they?'

'No, but I wouldn't rule it out. Seeing a doctor, I mean, not waving a wand.'

'Oh, well.' She smiled and said, 'Right, I've told you, and now it's out of the way.'

'You must never feel that you can't talk to me about... anything at all.'

'I don't. It's my choice.' She seemed uneasy about his assurance, as if he were assuming greater importance in her life than she was prepared to allow. Of course, it was possible he was imagining it. He tried to dismiss the idea.

The weather was so mild that, once they were out of the town, Maurice parked at the roadside, and they got out to walk.

'A bit of fresh air and exercise will do us both a power of good,' said Maurice, 'but let me know when you feel you've walked far enough.'

'I'm hardier than you think,' she said, laughing, 'but these heels aren't ideal for walking great distances.'

'I'm sorry. It never occurred to me, but we won't go far.'

They'd walked a quarter of a mile or so, when Iris said, 'The one good thing that's come out of my experience at the school is that it's helped me decide what I want to do with my life.'

'Some good had to come of it.'

'I suppose so.'

'Well, don't keep me in suspense.'

'Don't rush me.'

'All right, the floor is yours, and you can hold my hand, if it helps.'

She smiled. 'I don't need to do that. It's your support, if you remember. 'It came to me when I was caring for those little scraps.'

'Privileged little scraps, it has to be said.'

'That's true, but there's something cruelly ironic about privilege when parents send their children to a place like that to be treated in such a Dickensian way. Anyway, my major decision was to go back into nursing, but a different kind of nursing from that which I've known.' She stopped momentarily.

'I'm riveted, Iris. Do go on.'

'I believe there's a children's hospital in Nottingham. Isn't that right?'

'I believe so.'

'That's what I'm going to do,' she announced. 'What those children at the school needed instead of regimentation and brutality was their parents' love. I shall never have children of my own, so I'll care for other people's children instead.'

Maurice stopped walking, causing her to stop, too. He said, 'I think that's probably the most noble thing I've ever heard, but tell me one thing, I mean, as long as it's not terribly private. Why will you never have children of your own?'

She hesitated, as if gathering her nerve before saying, 'I really have no intention of getting married, sooner, later or, in fact, ever.'

He started walking again, disturbed by her revelation. 'Is it because of the thing you told me about? That you feel uncomfortable with men?'

'Yes, exactly. It goes without saying that marriage involves the ultimate intimacy between two people, and that's something I can never allow. It's why I told you earlier that you and I could never be more than friends.'

He found himself temporarily without an answer, although it seemed that no response was expected of him, because Iris broke the silence. 'You can't imagine what it was like, trying to nurse sick internees with no drugs or medical facilities. They suffered from a long list of tropical diseases, you see.' She smiled faintly and said, 'I told you I wasn't going to talk about it, didn't I?'

'Don't worry.'

'Where was I? I know. There was a young girl with beriberi. She was swollen almost out of recognition by body fluid.' She stopped again and said, 'I hope this isn't too soon after lunch, Maurice.'

'No.' He gave her hand a squeeze.

'It's caused by shortage of thiamine, otherwise known as vitamin B One. Polished rice and rice flour, which formed our staple diet, are particularly lacking in vitamins. Anyway, I went to the officer who was second-in-command to the Commandant, to plead with him for some vitamin tablets, because I knew the Japs had access to them as well as other medical supplies. His name was Captain Hayashi, and he seemed to have a soft spot for me. At least, that was what I thought. My hair colouring, you see, was so unusual in his experience that he found me fascinating.'

'Iris,' he protested, 'you don't have to tell me this.'

'Some memories are so difficult to put into words, I prefer as a rule not even to try, but on this occasion I will, and then you'll know the whole story as well as the reason why I can never contemplate a close relationship with you or anyone else, in spite of all your kindness and the fact that I've grown so fond of you. The fact is that, instead of giving me the vitamin tablets I needed, he offered them in exchange for... favours... and when I refused him, he took me by force.' She paused, possibly trying to shake off the memory, before saying, 'It wasn't just once. It happened on three separate occasions.'

He'd suspected something of the kind, but the news still came like a body-blow. 'Oh, Iris,' he said eventually, 'what a ghastly thing to happen to you.' He wanted very badly to hold her, although he'd no idea why. It was just a reflex, and one that he had to suppress, because that was the last thing she would want. Then, realising there was nothing he could say or do, he simply remained uncomfortably silent.

She asked, 'Can we go back to the car, now?'

'Of course.' He turned with her.

'You see, all the signs are that you do want more from me than just friendship, and I can't keep you hanging on like this.'

'What do you want to do?' He thought he knew already.

'I don't *want* to do this,' she said, 'and I don't want to hurt you.' She brushed a tear aside. 'In fact, it's because I don't want to hurt you that I think it will be by far the best thing if we stop seeing each other now, before we become even more involved.'

11

February 2000

'...Before the Swallow Dares'

It was pot luck that Saint Valentine's Day fell on a Monday. As proprietress of the dancing school, Helen made a big thing of it, but Jill was relieved and grateful to find that Steve, who showed signs, however subtly, of being attracted to her, and who knew, by that time, that she was single, refrained from making any overture. On the following Monday, however, he was less guarded.

'Jill,' he said, 'I don't know if I've mentioned the fact that I'm a member of the Wool Exchange Club.'

'No, I don't think you have. It sounds very... exclusive.' She disliked the word, "posh". In any case, she couldn't think of anything else to say, and she'd always regarded the Exchange Club as a select gathering, like the Freemasons, except with mixed membership. Mischievously, she recalled that Tony had found it particularly exclusive.

'Not really, but it's a marvellous thing. They have a real dance band that plays the classics from the nineteen-thirties, and the atmosphere's second to none. We used to go there regularly, but I haven't been recently, of course.' He was obviously leading up to a proposition, and his next sentence confirmed it. 'The thing is, next month, they're having a Daffodil Ball in support of the Marie Curie foundation. It's on the eighteenth, which is the nearest Saturday to the twenty-first, the first day of spring, and I wonder if you'd consider coming as my guest.' He added hurriedly, 'Absolutely no strings attached, I assure you.'

Jill thought quickly. Her first inclination was to make an excuse, or even to tell him candidly that she wasn't ready even for a casual date, but that would be churlish. He'd gone out of his way to help her with the Uncle Maurice thing, and he was the most inoffensive man she'd known in a long time. Also, he exuded honesty, so that when he said "no strings", she believed him. 'You know,' she said, 'I'd like that very much. Thank you, I'll look forward to it.'

'You'll enjoy it, I know.' It was clear that he, too, was looking forward to the event.

'What will everyone be wearing?'

'Ah.' It seemed the question had taken him by surprise. 'As it's a ball, rather than one of the regular, monthly dance nights, the dress code is full evening dress.' He asked awkwardly, 'Will a long ballgown be a problem?'

'It shouldn't be.' It would involve a Saturday afternoon in Ilkley and an expensive sweetener for the children. Beyond that, however, it was unlikely to be a problem.

———

'Why are we going to Ilkley, Mum?' The question came from Liam.

'So that I can buy a dress and so that you can have a treat.' The fun way to go clothes shopping was with a friend, but Jill was reduced to doing it the hard way.

Liam seemed to have missed the latter part of the sentence, because he asked, 'Why do you have to go to Ilkley to buy a dress?'

'Because people in Ilkley wear beautiful, expensive dresses, and then they grow tired of them and give them to charity shops.'

'Are we going to a *charity shop*?' He made it sound like a jumble sale.

'Unless you're very lucky, we may go to several before I find what I'm looking for.'

'Why do you have to go to charity shops?'

'Because I have two little mouths to feed and two little bodies to clothe – the expensive way, I might add. I only buy my clothes from charity shops, not yours. If it helps, it's unlikely any of your friends from school will see us, so they don't need to know that your poor old mum's fallen on hard times.'

84

Jessica asked, 'What sort of dress are you looking for, Mum?'

At last, a civilised question. 'A ballgown, Jessica.'

'Are you going to a ball?'

'Yes, just like Cinderella, except that she wore glass slippers, whereas I have to make do with a pair of shoes I bought about three months ago. That's if I can find a dress to match them.'

Jessica seemed to ponder that information before asking, 'Aren't you supposed to buy the shoes to match the dress?'

'That's the way it's usually done, Jessica, but in Lone Parent Land, the rules are often bent by those "made tame to fortune's blows".'

'Who said that?' The challenge came, as usual, from Liam.

'A chap called Edgar in *King Lear*. At least, he said some of it.' She turned into Brooke Street Carpark and found a place surprisingly quickly. Then, having paid and displayed, she took the children in search of a ballgown.

———

When they reached the British Heart Foundation, Liam said in a tone laden with suffering, 'This is the fourth shop you've tried. I've been counting them.'

'This is just what we need, isn't it, Jessica? A mathematician with a low boredom threshold. Let's have a look in the window first.' She studied the showcased dresses and then peered between them. 'A-ha. Let's go inside.'

Once inside the shop, she made straight for the Empire-style, silk-chiffon lilac gown she'd seen. 'It's gorgeous,' she said with mounting excitement, 'and it's on the size ten rail. Oh, my beating heart.'

An assistant asked, 'Would you like to try it on?'

'Yes, please.' She took the gown from the rail, saying, 'Liam and Jessica, don't touch anything. In fact, don't even breathe.'

Inside the curtained changing cubicle, she doffed her jeans, jumper and shirt, and stepped into the gown. So far, so good. She left the cubicle and asked the assistant, 'Would you be kind enough to hook me up?'

'Of course.' The assistant did the necessary and left her to view the result in a full-length mirror.

'Oh, it's my lucky day,' she said, turning one way and then the other, and standing on tiptoe to replicate the effect of high heels. 'It's absolutely perfect.'

'It looks lovely on you,' said the assistant. Then, turning to Liam, whose bored features told their own story, she asked, 'Don't you think your mum looks beautiful?'

Liam's cheeks grew red, but he remained silent.

'He's on the brink of adolescence,' explained Jill.

The assistant nodded sympathetically. 'Embarrassment lies around every corner. My boys were the same.'

'I think you look really beautiful,' said Jessica.

Jill crouched and kissed her. 'Thank you, my little morale booster.' Then, for the sake of fairness, she kissed Liam, making him squirm. 'I know the words were on the tip of your tongue, Liam. You just couldn't bring yourself to say them, could you?'

———

Liam had recovered his composure by the time they arrived at Betty's, and, as they queued for a table, he even joined Jessica in reading the 1930s advertisements that lined the entrance to the Tea Room. The Betty's treat compensated for the frustration and boredom that had preceded it, whereas Jessica regarded it as an exciting finale to an afternoon of new and stimulating experiences. For her part, Jill was simply delighted to have found the perfect ballgown, which, in her reluctance to allow it out of her sight, she hung temporarily from the picture rail in the sitting room. It was still there, although purely by oversight on Jill's part, when Tony called for the children the next morning. It was the first thing he noticed.

'Someone's been extravagant,' he remarked.

'Whereas someone else really hasn't a clue about these things, which is why he's talking, as usual, through his fundamental orifice.'

He ignored the riposte, but said instead, 'You must be going somewhere special.'

'If you have to know, I'm going to a ball at the Wool Exchange.'

His look of surprise was immediately gratifying. 'And just how have you managed that?'

'I was invited. What did you imagine?'

'I suppose that kind of thing impresses some people.'

'Of course,' she said, feigning sudden recollection, 'they wouldn't let you in, would they?'

'It wasn't a case of that,' he said huffily. 'I just didn't see the need for the long wait and the ridiculous vetting process.'

'I suppose it was the same with the golf club,' she said, recalling similar frustration.

'I'm not prepared to talk to you when you're in this vindictive mood. In any case, it's time we left. Where are the children?'

Jill called upstairs, 'Liam and Jessica, you're dad's in a hurry to leave.' She was rewarded when Liam came down, followed by Jessica.

'We went to Betty's yesterday,' Jessica told him excitedly.

'If you can afford that kind of thing, I'm obviously paying you far too much in maintenance.'

'Not according to the settlement you signed,' said Jill.

Moving towards the door, he said, 'Come on, children, I think we'll leave before this conversation descends any further.'

'*Pas devant les enfants*,' she reminded him sweetly.

When they were gone, she phoned her mother. A hiatus in Uncle Maurice's letters was puzzling her. It would be very much easier if she had Auntie Iris's letters as well, but there was no sign of them, and her mother was the only alternative source she had.

The phone rang several times before her mother picked it up.

'Hello.'

'Mum, it's Jill.'

'Hello, love, I was upstairs when you rang. I was about to run a bath.'

'I'm sorry. Should I phone you later?'

'No, that's all right. It'll keep.'

It was quite early. The task of getting the children ready and her conversation with Tony had caused her to forget the fact. 'It's not terribly important.' She decided to be truthful. 'Well, it is, really.'

'Go on, dear.'

'It's about Uncle Maurice and Auntie Iris.'

Her mother sighed. 'I saw very little of them, as you know, so I don't know how helpful I can be.'

'Well, all I have to go on is some letters from him to her, so I'd be grateful for any help at all.'

Again, there was an audible sigh, and her mother asked, 'Why is it so important to you? They chose to keep themselves apart from the family, so they probably had a good reason for it, even though they never saw fit to divulge it.'

'I got on with them particularly well, Mum. I visited them several times when I was at university, I was very fond of them, and they were family, so it is important, really.'

'To say he was my brother, he wasn't in a hurry to keep in touch with me. Anyway, what do you want to know?'

'They'd been exchanging letters in nineteen forty-six, and they'd apparently been seeing each other as well, but then, suddenly, the letters seemed to dry up for several months, and then, when they started again, they made no mention of the break or why had taken place.'

'Strange.' She seemed to be pondering the subject; at least, she was quiet for a spell, and Jill was about to speak again, when she heard her mother say, 'You know, I'd completely forgotten, but talking about it just now brought it back to me. It was just after the war – I think you told me that – and I remember asking Maurice about her because he'd been using his precious petrol ration to visit her in Leicester, or somewhere like that.'

'Loughborough.'

'Yes, that's right. You seem to know more about it than I do. Anyway, he seemed quite despondent, and he told me he wouldn't be seeing her again, and that it wasn't her fault.... No, I tell a lie. I believe he said it was neither her fault nor his. I think he blamed circumstances, whatever they were, but I really can't be certain. It was a long time ago, more than fifty years, in fact, and the memory can play tricks.'

'Even so, Mum, that's a great help.'

'It's no trouble.' She dismissed Jill's thanks seemingly without a thought, but then she asked, 'Did you say you visited them when you were at university?'

'Yes, a few times. They were always very welcoming.'

'Strange. It was almost as if, having taken up with Iris, he wanted to shut the family out altogether, but apparently not.'

'I never felt excluded, Mum.'

'Oh well, there are things we'll never know.'

'I'm rather afraid so. Certainly, the closer I look into it, the more questions it raises.'

'I imagine it will.' Clearly, her mother had lost interest in the matter, a fact she demonstrated with her next question. 'How are you settling down at the cottage?'

'Everything's fine. The children have accepted it almost without complaint. Jessica hardly ever complains – for a nine-year-old, she's remarkably philosophical – but adolescence is catching up with Liam, and it's not cool to accept things too readily.'

'Oh dear. I suppose they're with Tony and that awful woman today.'

'It's a regular Sunday thing.' Suddenly, she smiled as she remembered the gown and Tony's reaction to it, and she decided to share the fun with her mother. 'Tony arrived this morning to collect the children, and he saw a ballgown I bought yesterday at the Heart Foundation—'

'Really, Jill, do you have to buy your clothes from those places?' She was almost as disapproving as Liam.

'Now that I'm a lone parent, yes, I do. Anyway, it's the most beautiful gown. It's lilac and silk-chiffon, but the point is that Tony started complaining, as usual, that he must be paying me too much—'

'That's ridiculous.'

'I know, but the thing that really upset him was that I've been invited to a ball at one of the places he couldn't get into.'

'Where's that, dear?'

'The Wool Exchange Club.'

'Oh? Who's invited you there?'

'One of the pupils at Helen's dance class. I'm doing a bit of teaching again.'

'Good, it would be a shame to let your ability go to waste, but tell me more about this man. What's he like?'

Jill had been well acquainted from girlhood with her mother's penchant for matchmaking, and she was quick to dispel any ideas she might have. 'I hardly know him,' she said. 'All I can tell you is that he's a widower, he's very polite and friendly, he's a freelance journalist and he's also quite a good dancer.'

'He sounds promising. How old is he?'

'I don't know, Mum. I'd put him at about forty, but honestly, don't get excited, because I'm really not ready for a grand romance, or even a little one, for that matter.' Almost to herself, she said, 'I don't suppose he is, really.'

'You don't suppose he is what, dear?'

'Ready for romance. The thing we're going to is called a Daffodil Ball, and you know what Shakespeare had to say in *A Winter's Tale* about daffodils.'

'You know I don't. What did he say?'

' "Daffodils, that come before the swallow dares, and take the winds of March with beauty." It's just possible that he's as hesitant as I am.'

12

April 1946

Starch and Cricket Whites

The woman who appeared in the oak doorway was small in stature, but she carried with her a perceptible aura of authority. Her uniform was immaculate, and her small cap was pressed and starched with perfect precision.

'You must be Miss Lennox,' she said, peering at Iris through circular, horn-rimmed glasses.

'Yes, Matron.'

'Well, come into my office.'

Iris followed her into a large room darkened, in spite of a large sash window, by a preponderance of mahogany furniture. Its overall impression was one of severity.

'Take a seat, Miss Lennox.' Matron indicated a Windsor hoop-back chair, and Iris accepted her invitation.

'Now, Miss Lennox,' said Matron, referring to a document on her desk, 'I've read your references from the nursing service and from Dr Armitage, and I have to say that I'm most impressed. I gather you were interned for the duration of the war in the Far East. Were you the only nurse in your camp?'

'Initially, there were two of us, Matron, but the other nurse died within a few weeks of our internment.'

'Oh?'

'She caught malaria, which developed into blackwater fever.'

'I'm not familiar with blackwater fever, Miss Lennox. Perhaps you would enlighten me.'

Iris remembered explaining the condition to her mother. She hoped her potential superior would be more appreciative. 'Blackwater fever is a complication of malaria, in which red blood cells burst in the bloodstream and the bladder. Its name is a reference to the discoloration of the patient's urine, caused by the blood clots. It was quite common.'

'Had you no remedy, no way of halting the malaria at an earlier stage? I believe quinine is the usual treatment.'

'None whatsoever, Matron. The Japanese refused us all medication. They took the line that their need was greater than ours.'

Matron closed her eyes for a moment, possibly digesting the information, before she said, 'You must feel extremely vengeful towards the Japanese, Miss Lennox, although no one can blame you.'

Iris answered truthfully, 'Certain individuals would have tested the mercy of a saint, but I bear no ill-will towards the race in general. I prefer to leave recrimination to the authorities, although it seems to me that the only purpose the death penalty serves is that of exacting revenge, itself an ignoble motive.' She had heard, only that week, that Captain Akira Hayashi had been tried on a number of counts, including the public beheading of the two prisoners who had tried to escape. He and several others had been hanged in a prison in Tokyo, but the news had given Iris no satisfaction, despite her personal suffering at his hands.

'I'm most surprised to hear it.'

'There's no secret, Matron. As in any situation, we each react as individuals according to our psychological identity. There are those victims who become obsessed with vengeance, some even become mentally unstable; in fact, I knew several who did. However, I believe that hatred and brutality have no greater adversary than love for our fellow human beings, and that is why I want to return to nursing. If that sounds banal, Matron, I offer no apology, because it is my genuine, personal conviction.'

'Remarkable.' Matron blinked and then consulted Iris's application again. 'I see that you were employed for… a matter of only weeks, it seems, as Matron at Linden Manor Preparatory School, and that you chose not to offer the Headmaster there as a referee. Why is that?'

'I left of my own accord, resolved never to set foot in such a place again, Matron.'

'Oh?'

I should explain that I was called to the dormitory to attend a ten-year-old boy who was in great pain and distress, having suffered a severe flogging that afternoon. When I examined his lacerated posterior, I found it difficult to believe that a civilised man could inflict such savagery on a small boy, and that was what I told the Headmaster the next morning, when I tendered my resignation. You can imagine, Matron, that a reference from him would have done my cause no good at all.'

'I'm sure, Miss Lennox, just as I'm sure, in that particular case, you were absolutely in the right.' She gathered up the documents in what seemed a final gesture, and said, 'In Queen Alexandra's Imperial Military Nursing Service, you enjoyed the title 'Sister', I see.'

'Yes, Matron. I received promotion on my return to Britain.'

'Quite. I see, also, that some considerable time has elapsed since you had any appreciable experience of nursing children.'

'Beyond the demands of camp life, when children suffered the same diseases as the adult internees, that is true, Matron, but I am a willing student.'

'I'm sure you are, Miss Lennox.' She unscrewed the cap of her fountain pen, saying, 'I'm offering you the post of Staff Nurse in this hospital. I'm also going to give you a reading list, and I shall expect to find you conversant with each item on it.' She signed her name on an official form, favoured Iris with a rare, fleeting smile and said, 'Your appointment will be confirmed by letter.'

As Iris left the hospital, she thought how wonderful it would have been to share her news with Maurice, but that was out of the question. She didn't even suppose he would want to hear from her. It was the greatest tragedy that she felt unable to join him in the kind of relationship he wanted, when, at the same time, she needed quite desperately his remarkable sensitivity, understanding and, above all, his friendship.

———

Twenty miles away, in Newark-on-Trent, Maurice was advising a client.

'There's absolutely nothing wrong with a director borrowing money from his company,' he said, 'providing the other directors agree to it, which they do. The Inspector of Taxes sees nothing wrong with it, either, as long as he can help himself to the tax on it.'

'What bloody tax?' Mr Staveley was a plain-speaking man.

'It's the law, Mr Staveley. The Revenue will charge you income tax on the loan until such time as you repay it. It's known as benefit-in-kind, and the taxman will be on to it in a flash.'

The disgruntled client sighed heavily. 'In that case,' he said, 'I suppose I'll have to repay it.' He drummed with his fingers on the desktop and said irritably, 'I thought it was your job to save me income tax.'

'I've just told you how to avoid one tax bill. Be fair, Mr Staveley.'

'I really don't know. We fought a war against dictators, only to be dictated to by bloody politicians and tax gatherers. It's worse now than it was before the war, with these buggers in charge.'

Maurice had to steer the conversation in a positive direction. 'Repay the loan, Mr Staveley, and that'll reduce the tax you have to pay on it.'

'Aye, a tax bill saved is one in the eye for Hugh bloody Dalton.' Almost in the same breath, he asked, 'Are you playing on Sunday, Maurice?'

'Yes, if I can remember how.'

'You'll remember, all right.'

'I haven't played since before the war.'

'Aye well, the same can be said of all of us.'

With the topic changed safely to cricket, Maurice could allow another ten minutes before going to see his next client.

———

A little over an hour after leaving the hospital, Iris walked into the house, surprising her mother.

'Back so soon,' she said. 'You were quick.'

'It wasn't an advertised post, so I was the only one being interviewed.'

'Oh, I see. How do you feel it went?'

'It couldn't have gone better, Mum. I'll get a letter in the post, confirming the appointment, and then I'll know when I can start.'

Her mother's surprise was reward in itself. 'You know already?'

'Yes, there was no competition, so Matron was able to tell me at my interview.'

'Well done, Iris.' Her mother gave her a rare hug. Then, when she'd properly digested the news, she said, 'There's a regular train service, as well.'

'Don't get carried away, Mum. I shan't be living at home.'

'Why ever not when it's only a short train ride away?'

Once again, she was obliged to describe something her mother had never experienced. 'There'll be times when I'll come off night duty fit for nothing but to fall into bed. Believe me, I've done it many times. No, it'll be much easier if I live at the nurses' home.'

'Well, if your mind's made up.' Clearly, she was disappointed.

'It's the only way it'll work, Mum, and I'll get time off occasionally to come home.'

'Oh well, it's better than nothing.' She filled the kettle and lit the gas under it. 'What kind of questions did she ask you?'

'They were mainly about Malaya.'

'Really?'

'She asked me about Linden Court as well.'

Her mother grimaced. 'I was afraid of that.'

'She said she had no doubt I was in the right.'

'Good heavens.'

'Yes, I'm not the only person who deplores brutality against helpless children.'

Her mother was characteristically dismissive. 'You do exaggerate, Iris,' she said.

'Do I?' Having experienced the elation at being offered the job she most wanted, she now felt her temper rising. 'You didn't see the horrible, red weals on his bottom, or the pain he was still suffering, hours after the flogging. Don't tell me I exaggerate, when you don't know the extent of it!'

'Well, it's just like the way you go on about the internment camp.'

By this time, Iris was very angry. 'Apart from the fact that I don't "go on" about it – in fact, I mention it very rarely – yes, it's just like that. I know the truth, and you haven't a clue!'

'Don't tell me I haven't a clue, Iris—'

'Why not? It's true. You weren't there when they refused us medication, or when they marched us to the men's camp to watch two men being beheaded. You weren't there when one of the Jap officers....' She stopped short of describing her experience with Captain Hayashi. It was better if her mother didn't know that. 'You didn't see any of that, did you? So how can you accuse me of exaggerating?' She stopped when she saw the tears in her mother's eyes. 'I'm sorry, Mum,' she said, 'but it's better I leave it at that. You don't want to know any more.' She opened her arms to her and they held each other, both crying for their different reasons. There were times when Iris preferred not to talk about her experiences, and there were other times when she missed being able to write to Maurice, sometimes to speak to him on the telephone, but most of all, to talk face to face. He was the only person she could talk to openly about such things, but now it was impossible for her to do that, because of something else she found impossible.

Now in his own flat, Maurice took out his cricket whites, half-afraid they might no longer fit him. Seven years was a long time. Almost resigned to the worst, he removed his trousers and pulled on the flannels to find that.... Wonder of wonders, if anything, they were a trifle loose round the waist. Hooray for rationing, and he'd never thought he would say that. Delighted, he took them off, folded them, and picked up his boots to whiten them. In an age when so many things had changed, his cricket flannels had not forsaken him.

Iris had forsaken him, although that was unfair, so he banished the thought immediately. It wasn't her fault any more than it was his. He thought about it as he poured Blanco whitener on to a sponge and applied it to one of his cricket boots. Considering Iris's experience in Malaya, and it still horrified him to think of it, he could forgive her for everything, even supposing there were anything to forgive. She hadn't wronged him. Far from it, she'd acted in his interest.

He cursed when a drop of Blanco hit the linoleum, and he was thankful he was in his own place. His mother would have gone mad if he'd done it at home. Using part of the sponge that wasn't covered in Blanco, he crouched to wipe the lino clean, reminded all too clearly of the expert way his shared steward in the depot ship used to prepare his tropical shoes, and without ever spilling a drop of whitener.

By association, he recalled meeting Iris for the first time, at the landing stage at Kuala Rompin. Almost immediately, he checked himself. Thinking about her did no good at all. She was lost to him, another casualty of the war.

13

March 2000

A Little Insanity

Jill was in the bathroom when Steve arrived, but she heard Gemma answer the door and was surprised to learn from the fragment of conversation she overheard that she and Steve were already acquainted.

She picked up her evening bag and hurried downstairs. 'Steve,' she said, 'I'm sorry to keep you waiting. If you haven't already been introduced, this is Jessica and this one is Liam.'

'How do you do?' Jessica offered her hand formally.

'I'm delighted to meet you, Jessica, and you, Liam.' He shook his hand, too.

'I've only just arrived,' he said in answer to her apology, but somewhat distracted, captivated as he was by her appearance. 'You look sensational, Jill.'

'Incredible.' Gemma lent her agreement quite spontaneously.

'Thank you, both. That was quite a reception. Now, Gemma, help yourself to whatever you fancy from the kitchen.'

'Oh, temptation,' she murmured. Then, more sensibly, she said, 'I suppose your mobile will be switched off?'

For a moment, Jill was thrown. 'I hadn't thought of that, Gemma.'

'Have you something to write on? I have the Club's number here,' said Steve, taking his mobile from his coat pocket. 'There's always someone on duty to take calls.'

Jill picked up the pen and pad she used for shopping lists, and took down the number as he read it. 'Thank you, Steve,' she said. 'That was good thinking.'

'Okay,' said Gemma, putting the slip with the number on it beside the landline phone, 'Have a great time, both of you.'

'Thank you.' Jill bent to kiss the children, who'd been studying Steve discreetly. They seemed fascinated by his white bow-tie and silk scarf. 'I'll see you both in the morning. 'Bye, Gemma.'

''Bye, Jill. 'Bye, Steve.'

As they walked out to Steve's car, she asked, 'How do you know Gemma?'

'She's one of my brightest students. I work part-time at the university.'

'Ah.' She sat in the passenger seat, gathering her voluminous skirts. It was one explanation that hadn't occurred to her.

'That really is a beautiful gown,' he said as he got into the driving seat. 'Very fitting, really.'

'You're very kind.' She noticed his tailcoat hanging from the offside hook. 'It really is full evening dress, I see.'

'The Exchange Club are old-fashioned, delightfully so, in my opinion. I think it's good to preserve the values that give us pleasure and do no one any harm.'

'I agree.'

'Good. What do you know about the Exchange Club?'

'Nothing beyond the fact that my ex-husband found it so difficult to join that he gave up on it.' She still smiled at Tony's reaction at seeing the ballgown.

'Yes, they don't decide in a hurry.'

'And he's not exactly a model of patience.'

He made no comment. Instead, he said, 'Just to put you in the picture, the regular dances and occasional balls began only ten years ago, when Frank Morrison, the bandleader, started the band from scratch with a collection of elderly, rejected musicians, some of whom had played during what they tend to call the "Golden Age", the nineteen-thirties.'

'How marvellous, but you said they'd been rejected. What was that about?'

He turned into Bradford Road before replying. 'They'd been members of the Cullington Orchestra, but some of the younger end formed a breakaway orchestra, excluding the older players, thus emerging "leaner and fitter", if I dare borrow a particularly unsympathetic phrase of the time. According to Frank, the old boys were desolated; the orchestra had existed since nineteen-twenty, I believe, but then Frank, who has the ability to see further than most men, had the brainwave of forming a dance band.'

'What a brilliant thing to do. Presumably, as he's still around, he's younger than the original musicians?'

'Frank's fifty,' he confirmed. 'I know that because we share the same birthday, except that I was born ten years later than him.' He turned into Westgate and then into Albion Street and the carpark of the Wool Exchange Club.

He opened her door and offered her his hand, saying, 'Don't be put off by the grandiose surroundings on the ground floor. It's been like that since time immemorial, but the fun takes place on the first floor, in the ballroom.'

Having donned his tailcoat and overcoat, he led her to the members' entrance, where he showed their tickets and took her to the cloakroom.

Looking around her at the marble pillars, she said, 'I see what you mean about the ground floor. It's all very imposing.'

'It was built in the seventeenth century by men of substance for their peers and successors,' he told her.

When they'd deposited their coats, he took her to the wide, marble staircase lined with portraits of prominent clothiers of the past two hundred years. 'Some of these people would never have approved of the goings-on upstairs,' he said, 'but who cares?'

They reached the first floor, where they could hear the sounds of people enjoying themselves and, when they reached the entrance to the ballroom, Jill was instantly captivated by the style and mood of the place. 'It's frozen in time,' she said, 'Art Deco, just perfect.'

'I'm glad you like it,' he said, acknowledging a look of recognition from a tall, attractive woman of about their age.

She came over and said with obvious feeling, 'Steve, it's so good to see you again.'

They exchanged greetings, and Steve said, 'Sarah, this is Jill Warneford, a good friend as well as my dancing teacher. Jill, meet Sarah Morrison, whose husband Frank is in charge of the proceedings.'

'They shook hands, and Jill said, 'He might have left out the dancing teacher bit. There's nothing like raising expectations, is there?'

'We're all here to enjoy ourselves,' Sarah told her, 'no more than that, but because you're a new face, and because this is the first time I've seen Steve in far too long a time, why don't you both join us at our table? It has it's advantages, you know. One is that we get steward service while the others have to help themselves.'

'That's very kind of you, Sarah,' said Steve, looking at Jill for her reaction. 'We'd love to. Thank you.'

Looking through the crowd, Sarah said, 'Here comes the main man. Frank, come and say, "Hello" again to Steve and meet Jill. They're going to join us at our table.'

A powerfully-built man with greying hair came to Sarah's side. 'Steve,' he said, 'it's been far too long, and it's all the better to see you again. How are you?'

'I'm well, thanks, Frank. I'd like you to meet Jill.'

'Delighted,' said Frank, shaking her hand, 'and you're all the more welcome for bringing Steve back into the fold. What are you both drinking?'

Seeing that the focus was on her, Jill asked, 'Would dry white wine be in order?'

'That's a good idea,' said Steve.

'Splendid. Four minds in perfect unison.' Frank signalled one of the stewards, who made his way towards them. 'Two bottles of the Club Chablis and four glasses, Dave, please.'

'Right you are, Frank.'

Sarah emerged from a brief conversation with Steve and Jill to say, 'Jill teaches at Helen Rawlinson's School of Dancing, Frank. That's how she and Steve met.'

'And what a perfect way to meet.'

Jill let that go uncorrected. The evening was about dancing, after all, not dog-walking.

'I'll have to leave you for a short spell,' said Frank, getting up, 'just to get things under way, and then I'll come down and join you again.'

'We'll hear the band's signature number,' Sarah told them as he left for the band room, 'and probably a first quickstep or a foxtrot, and then he'll hand over for a while to Geoff on piano.'

Jill asked, 'Do any of the original musicians still play?'

'I'm afraid not. The two oldest, Hutch and Norman, are both eighty-five, now. As Hutch's granddaughter, I have inside knowledge, you understand. They turn up occasionally, to listen and advise; at least, that's what they call it, but they've both admitted, now they're in their ninth decade, that they're short of wind.'

There was a hush as the musicians made their way to the platform. Then, when they were all settled, Frank made his entrance, gave a downbeat, and the band began 'The Sun Has Got His Hat On' to the enthusiastic applause of the members. It was the briefest of introductions and, as the last note faded, Frank spoke into the microphone. 'Good evening, everyone, and welcome to this special occasion at the Wool Exchange Club. Spring is here, so let's celebrate the fact with a quickstep that says it all: "Spread a Little Happiness".'

Sarah turned to Jill and Steve, and said, 'Off you go, you two. Frank will be down in a few minutes.'

Still captivated by the sounds the band were making, Jill followed Steve on to the floor, and they joined the line of dance. 'This is wonderful,' she said. 'I still can't believe it.'

'I knew you'd enjoy it.'

After a minute or so, she said, 'We've neglected the quickstep so far, haven't we?'

'Am I so awful?'

'Of course not. You're quite good, really.'

'I have to confess, it's not my favourite dance.'

They continued without speaking until Jill said, 'The foxtrot's your favourite, isn't it? I remember asking you.'

'It is, but I'm fond of the waltz, as well.'

'I'm keen on both of them, too.'

'Have you a favourite waltz?'

She had to think about that. 'Yes,' she said, 'but it's one that's not likely to be played here.'

'Why not?'

'Because it's from the fifties. It's "True Love". Do you know it?'

'Bing Crosby and Grace Kelly? Who doesn't know it?'

She laughed gently. 'Lots of people, but I'm glad you and I speak the same language.'

The number ended, and Frank introduced the pianist, who was going to take over for a spell. Jill and Steve returned to the table to find the wine poured ready for them, and Sarah ready to compliment them.

'You two looked so natural,' she said.

'Thank you,' said Steve, surprised.

'The quickstep isn't his favourite dance, apparently,' confided Jill.

'No one would have known.'

'No one would have known what?' Frank took his place beside Sarah.

'That the quickstep isn't one of Steve's favourites, and there he was, quickstepping in the manner born. I think it's all down to having the right teacher.'

'Except I haven't worked on his quickstep.'

'Ah, but he was dancing with you, Jill,' said Frank, 'and that makes all the difference.'

She laughed lightly. 'If you say so, Frank.' Suddenly, a bell rang in the recesses of her memory, and she said, 'Forgive my ignorance, but are you the Frank Morrison who writes film music? I'm thinking of *Yellow Violets*.'

'Guilty on both counts.'

'Oh, but I loved that score.'

'Thank you, I'm glad you enjoyed it.'

'I did, and it means so much more to me, now that I've met the composer.'

'That's a huge compliment, Jill. Thank you.'

The pianist announced *Stay As Sweet As You Are*, causing Sarah to reach for Frank's hand. Simultaneously, Steve whispered in Jill's ear, and they, too, got up to dance.

'This is a beautiful song,' murmured Jill.

'A classic foxtrot,' agreed Steve.

'I hope I didn't go overboard about Frank's music.'

'Not in the least. He's brilliant, but he's also very modest.'

They danced to the end without speaking, such was the power of the music to concentrate the emotions.

Geoff announced 'By The Sleepy Lagoon', and Frank said, 'After this dance, Sarah and I will have to leave you for a couple of numbers, but may I ask Jill for this one, Steve?'

'By all means, Frank. Sarah, may I have the pleasure?'

'Of course.'

Frank led Jill on to the floor and they danced to Eric Coates' timeless waltz.

'I hope we'll see you here regularly, now that you've had a taste of what it's about,' said Frank.

'I really can't say. As you know, I'm here as Steve's guest and because it's a special night.'

'Quite.' Clearly, he was reluctant to address the obvious question, and she was grateful for that. 'He's popped in a few times over the past few years, but he's never found the heart to make it a regular thing, so it's particularly good to see him tonight and, of course, to see you for the first time.'

'Do you mean, since he lost his wife?' She had to ask.

'You know about that, then. Yes.'

'He's a lovely chap, and I appreciate your concern for him, Frank, but you must understand that he and I are friends, no more than that.'

'Thanks for telling me that, Jill. It makes it easier to avoid awkwardness.'

The number came to its end, and Frank took Jill back to the table, as Geoff announced, 'We're about to hear a special number, ladies and gentlemen. It's special because the band first performed it in nineteen-ninety, when everything was new, and I'm just waiting for Frank to come up and relieve me, because it's only right that he should be in front for this one, and that the vocal refrain should be provided, as it was then, by his lovely wife Sarah.'

The two appeared on stage to an eager welcome.

'Thank you, Geoff,' said Frank, taking the stick. 'In case you haven't already guessed, it's going to be a foxtrot, and it's the Rogers and Hart classic, "Blue Moon". Are you ready, Sarah?'

'Yes, darling.'

There was renewed applause at that intimate exchange, because the couple were popular with the members and, as the applause receded, the number began.

Jill knew the song, having danced to it and taught with it, but now she was hearing it afresh, as she was hearing everything that night, although the song had particular meaning because of the special bond

Ray Hobbs

between Sarah and Frank that must have been evident to everyone in the ballroom.

When it was over, they stayed for the quickstep 'I'll Never Say Never Again, Again', which was apparently another of Sarah's standards, and which proved equally popular. After that, Frank handed over to Geoff again and he and Sarah returned to their table.

'That was beautiful, Sarah,' said Jill, seconded readily by Steve.

'Thank you. Those two songs mean a great deal to Frank and me, but I try not to hog the limelight. It's just unfortunate that we're currently short of vocalists, and particularly, a male one. We had an excellent singer at first, one of my students, but we couldn't hold on to him forever.'

'Dan had a fling with my daughter Kate, who also played with us,' said Frank, 'but their careers have taken them elsewhere.' He patted Sarah's hand and said, 'Until we find someone, it's down to Sarah and me, and we don't do a bad job, do we, darling?'

'I think you're both superb,' said Jill.

'You can come again,' Frank told her, standing up. 'I now have to address the multitude.' He walked into the centre of the ballroom to speak to the members and their guests about the Marie Curie Charity, the reason for the ball. As he did so, Jill saw Sarah reach for Steve's hand and, in a simple but eloquent gesture, smile and gave it a pat.

Geoff made another announcement, one that took Jill entirely by surprise. 'Here's a change to the original programme, ladies and gentlemen. It featured in the film *High Society*, and you won't be surprised to hear that it's the waltz 'True Love'.'

Frank smiled broadly at Jill and Steve. 'I think we'd all like to dance to that,' he said.

'What a surprise,' said Jill, taking to the floor with Steve.

'I mentioned it to Frank, and he slipped it into the programme. Every so often, they have a special request night, but he included it tonight as a favour.'

'It was very kind of him, and of you, too. Thank you, Steve.'

'It was no trouble.'

They danced the rest of the number without speaking, simply enjoying the music and the gentle, insistent pulse of the waltz.

Jill had another opportunity to dance with Frank, as well as to thank

105

him properly for 'True Love'. 'I appreciate that it's not part of your normal repertoire,' she said.

'No, but it's a glorious number by a great songwriter, and we're here to entertain. As well as that, it's good to be able to welcome you and Steve, Jill.'

'You're very kind, Frank. I get the impression that Steve's been missed.'

'He has. He's such a genuine, decent, likeable chap that his loss was felt by a great many. I've been fortunate in that I've never experienced that, myself. My earlier marriage broke up because we were basically incompatible. My ex-wife went on to find someone else, but then, so did I.' He smiled and said, 'And I've never looked back.'

'My marriage failed simply because my ex-husband found someone else.' As she spoke, she surprised herself. It wasn't the kind of information she would normally impart to someone she'd just met.

'We all make mistakes,' he said, 'and your ex-husband certainly did. Did he dance, by the way?'

'Yes, badly.'

Frank shook his head sorrowfully. 'Never trust a man who doesn't dance well,' he said. 'If a man can't control his feet, what can he control?'

Laughing, she said, 'I've never thought about it that way.'

'You should. When you want to rid yourself of the hurt, just think of him stumbling with both left feet round the dance floor.'

'Thank you for that. I will.' She laughed again as the picture came to her and, before long, the number ended.

Frank returned to the band for the remainder of the evening, which closed perfectly, from Jill's point of view, with 'Goodnight, Sweetheart.' She and Steve took their leave of their host and hostess and walked to Steve's car.

'It's quite unbelievable,' said Jill when they were in their seats.

'What's unbelievable?'

'Too such lovely people, and the wonderful time I've had. Thank you, Steve.'

'The pleasure really was mine. It's that sort of place, you see.'

Only half-understanding, she asked, 'Wasn't it difficult, going back after all that time?'

'No, it wasn't at all difficult,' he said, pulling out of the carpark and into Albion Street. The welcome was as warm and genuine as ever, and your company made a huge difference as well.'

'Really?'

'Absolutely.'

'If I helped at all, however unintentionally, I'm glad, but what did you mean about the Wool Exchange being "that sort of place"?' It was important for her to know.

'Only that I only ever think of it as a place of good feeling. In fact, it probably sounds fanciful, but I think it's also a place of healing.'

'I don't think that's at all fanciful. It's a place where people's enjoyment is profound, and that alone has a healing quality. Don't you think so?'

'I do.'

The idea appealed to her. 'Do you know of any instances?'

'A few. You can see the best example in Frank and Sarah, because it was the band and the Exchange Club that did it for them. They were both suffering when they met, they got off completely on the wrong foot, but the ballroom worked its magic, and they came together.'

' "Dance is a little insanity that does us all good." '

'I'm afraid you'll have to help me with that one.'

'Edward Demby,' she prompted.

'Of course. The man who campaigned for racial tolerance before it even had a name.'

'The same.' Thoughts of a healed rift reminded Jill, by association, of her current brainteaser.

'A penny for them,' he said, 'or are you almost asleep?' They were just entering the street that led to Jill's cottage.

'Not yet. I'm sorry, I was thinking about my aunt and uncle. They were estranged for a while, and I can't say for certain why that was.'

'We must have a chat about it, and see if we can arrive at an explanation.' He pulled up outside the cottage. 'I'll let you out and see you to the door,' he said.

14

June 1946

A Surprise Spectator

Maurice left the Inland Revenue office in Nottingham, and was about to cross the road via the zebra crossing, when, having looked right, he looked left and found himself face to face with Iris. Surprised, he raised his hat and said, 'Iris, hello. How are you?'

'I'm well, thank you, Maurice, and you?'

'Robust as ever. You're looking well.'

An angry voice behind him demanded, 'Are you going to cross the road or not?'

'All in good time,' said Maurice, turning to face him. 'In the meantime, be my guest, in spite of your boorish manners.'

For a moment, the impatient man seemed to consider challenging him, but thought better of it and pushed past him instead, stepping on to the crossing and causing the traffic to halt abruptly.

Maurice shook his head disapprovingly. 'Life's too short for that kind of thing,' he said, wondering inwardly quite what to say. Eventually, he settled for, 'Where are you heading? Perhaps I can offer you a lift.'

'Oh, I don't want to put you to any trouble, Maurice. I've just been doing some shopping, and I'm on my way back to the nurses' home.'

'In that case, let me drive you there. Better still, if you've nothing pressing, we could have a cup of tea, and then I'll drive you home. There's a teashop round the corner.'

She opened her mouth to speak and, for a moment, he imagined she might make an excuse and go on her way, but then she said, 'That would be nice. Let's do that.'

Transferring his briefcase to his right hand, he gave her his arm and led her to Mason's Teashop, where he opened the door for her to go before him.

'You mentioned the nurses' home,' he said, 'so, evidently, you got the job you wanted.'

'Yes, I did.'

'Congratulations.'

'Thank you.'

A waitress pointed them to a table, where they sat down. Maurice handed Iris the menu and asked, 'Is it going well?'

'I love it, I really do.' For the first time, she seemed almost to relax. 'I suppose every job has its less-appealing side, but, taken all round, it's the perfect job for me.'

'In that case, I'm delighted.'

There was no mistaking the shame in her eyes as she said, 'You're also very generous, Maurice.'

'Am I?'

'I treated you badly.'

'Oh, nonsense. You didn't treat me badly at all.' He looked up as the waitress came to them, and asked her, 'What teas have you?'

'Only English Breakfast, I'm afraid, sir.'

'My favourite, as it happens. What are you going to eat, Iris?'

'Nothing, thank you.'

'Really? Be a devil and join me in a toasted teacake, at least.'

She allowed a smile and said, 'All right, seeing as you insist.'

'Which I do.' Turning again to the waitress, he said, 'Two toasted teacakes, please, and a pot of my favourite tea.'

'Very good, sir.' Then, looking at his tie, she said, 'Maybe I should say, "Aye, aye, sir".'

'Oh, are you an ex-Wren?'

'Yes, sir.'

'Well, I'm glad to meet you.'

'The pleasure's mine, sir.'

Amused by the conversation, Iris asked, 'What is your tie?'

'It's the RNVR Officers' Tie, the Royal Naval Volunteer Reserve, that is, sometimes known as the "Wavy Navy" or just "Really Not Very Reliable". I suppose it depends on your point of view.'

Smiling, she said, 'You haven't changed at all.'

'In three months? I hope not.'

'I meant....' Clearly, she found it difficult to say.

'Whatever you meant, if it causes you embarrassment, you don't have to tell me.'

'I meant, I thought that if I saw you again, you'd be angry and resentful, but I should have realised you'd never be like that.'

'I tend to chew the carpet in private, I'll admit, but I have to say that, face to face, I do try to be civilised.'

She looked uncomfortable again. 'You know,' she said, 'when you're being silly, like this, I realise how much I miss you.'

There was evidently something to be gained by being silly. 'Let me tell you what you've really missed,' he told her. 'Last Sunday, I took four wickets for twenty-eight runs. It was good, bearing in mind the fact that we leggies tend to be a shade on the expensive side, necessarily, of course.'

'Well bowled, but I was trying to be serious.'

'You should never be serious on an empty stomach, but here come the teacakes. They should help.'

She laughed. 'You're impossible.'

The waitress served the teacakes and returned with the tea things.

'Thank you so much,' he said.

'It really is a pleasure, sir.' She gave him a friendly smile as she left.

Iris lifted the teapot lid to examine the tea.

'Feel free to give it a stir,' suggested Maurice. 'I'm no purist.'

She stirred the tea and poured it, handing Maurice his. 'It's my day off,' she said, 'but shouldn't you be at work?'

'I'm the senior partner's pampered son, and he doesn't know how long my visit to the Revenue took. For all he knows, I might still be waiting for them to receipt the documents I delivered, signing and countersigning it in duplicate, triplicate or quadruplicate in four different colours of ink. Don't worry, my time is yours.'

'I was trying to say earlier that I've missed being able to talk to you, even on the telephone. Writing to you was better than nothing, but to cut myself off from you altogether left me with absolutely no one to confide in.' With a straight look, she asked, 'Am I being too selfish for words?'

'No, you're not, but your grammar is deplorable. I imagine you meant to say, "No one in whom I could confide." Had my old English master been here, he would have had a seizure on the spot.' With no change in his expression, he said, 'For what it's worth, I've missed you as well, although I'm delighted to see you in better health.'

'I've put twelve pounds on,' she told him.

'You're to be congratulated as well as admired.'

'Thank you.'

Changing the subject, he asked, 'How did the hospital people view your hurried exit from the school?'

'When I explained it, Matron was very understanding. She agreed that I was in the right.'

'Good for her. What else did she ask you?'

'Oddly enough, she asked me about tropical diseases. She asked me about Malaya and was surprised that I didn't feel vengeful towards the Japanese.'

'I have to confess, so am I.' He'd wondered about it frequently.

'As I explained to her, we all react in our different ways, and my way is to leave the business of reparation and punishment to the authorities. I can't see how repaying hatefulness and brutality in their own coin will ever solve anything.'

'What do you suggest as an alternative?'

'I think we should concentrate on showing compassion and concern for the rest of the human race, thereby setting an example. Surely, that's better than revenge.' She paused, as if waiting for him to speak, and then asked, 'Does that sound impossibly trite?'

'It doesn't sound at all trite. It sounds like lots of praiseworthy, noble and high-minded things I can't even find the words for, but I'm more than impressed.'

'Did you mean to say,' she asked mischievously, ' "For which I can't even find the words"?'

'*Touché*. I thought I'd feed you that one, just to keep the scores level.'

'I don't believe you. Would you like some more tea?' She picked up the teapot and strainer.

'Yes, please.'

She refilled his cup. 'Are you playing next Sunday?'

'Yes. Why do you ask?'

'It's my next day off,' she said thoughtfully. 'Whereabouts are you playing?'

'Northcoate. It's very posh, hence the "e" on the end.'

'Maurice,' she said quite seriously, 'given that nothing has changed, could you bear us to start meeting again?'

'I think so. I confess, I've been… if not wholly discomfited, I've certainly not been comfited, or anything else that's sugar-coated.'

'But you know I can never be more to you than a friend.'

'Yes, I know that.'

She thought for a moment. 'Even so, Northcoate is quite difficult to get to, and please don't correct my grammar.'

'Don't worry, I'll come to the nurses' home and collect you.'

'You make me sound like a parcel.'

'I know, but it's more grammatical than telling you I'll pick you up.'

'I suppose it is. Her features finally relaxed, and she said, 'I'm ever so glad we bumped into each other this afternoon.'

'So am I. Anyway, tell me about your new job, now that you're Sister Lennox again.'

'Staff-Nurse Lennox, now.'

'Shameful. What do your patients call you?'

'Just "Nurse," but they often put a great deal of love into that one word.'

'What kind of thing do they come in for?'

'You name it and we do it. A little boy came in yesterday to be circumcised.'

'He'll have to grit his teeth, but he'll find it's worth it in the end.'

She aimed a slap on his wrist. 'Don't be awful. When the anaesthetic wore off, the poor little thing felt ever so sore.'

'I expect the little boy felt sore as well.'

'You're impossible.' Even so, she was laughing. 'He told me it was the worst day of his whole life.'

'It would be.'

'He's only six. Mind you, it's the only life he's ever known.'

Maurice squirmed. 'Joking apart, I feel for the poor little chap. I was a mere infant when they did me, and that was a good thing, because it's surprising what you can forget at that age.'

'I suppose it is.' She looked like someone wanting to change the subject, which wasn't surprising. In the circumstances, there were probably easier topics than the history of his private appendage. 'You told me about your bowling figures last Sunday,' she said finally, 'but how did you fare with the bat?'

'More tea, Iris?'

'No, thank you, and don't change the subject. Be brave and tell me what you made with the bat.'

'Less than twenty,' he mumbled.

'How many less than twenty?' She held him in what, had the exchange been more serious, might have been an intimidating stare.

'Twenty,' he whispered.

'You were out for a duck,' she said triumphantly.

'Don't tell everyone, Iris,' he whispered. 'The waitress thinks I'm a war hero.'

'So do I,' she told him indulgently. 'You're the officer who came and found me.'

'And now,' he said, looking at his watch, 'I'll have to take you home.'

'Yes, don't get into trouble on my account.'

He caught the waitress's eye, and she came over. 'I'd like the bill, please.'

'I'll bring it for you, sir.' She took a slip of paper from the bench beside the cash register and brought it to him on a plate. He placed the money on top of the bill, saying, 'That's right.'

'Thank you, sir.' She looked at the money on the plate and repeated her thanks.'

'You're welcome. Carry on.'

'Aye... Yes, sir. Goodbye, sir. Goodbye, Miss.'

As they left the teashop, Iris said, 'I thought she was going to dance a hornpipe for you.'

'Are you familiar with the hornpipe? I'm afraid they never taught us that at *King Alfred*.'

'Yes, I was in a school production of *Ruddigore*.'

'What did you do?' He was fascinated already.

'I had an important part. I was Mad Margaret.'

'How marvellous. I wish I'd seen that. Anyway,' he said, offering her his arm, 'I'll ask the waitress for a hornpipe next time we go there.'

They walked to the zebra crossing, and Iris said, 'Somehow, I expected you to wear morning dress and a bowler hat, like my dad.'

'What does your dad do?'

'He's a bank manager.'

They waited on the crossing for the traffic to stop, and then crossed the road.

'Bank managers are important people,' he said. 'We only wear fancy dress when we have to give evidence in court.'

'Why do you have to go to court?'

'It doesn't happen very often, but we have to feed information to the tax lawyers who represent our clients when they're in dispute with the Revenue.'

'That sounds scary.'

'Never mind,' he said, leading her to his car, 'at least, you'll know an accountant if you need one.' He opened the passenger door for her.

Starting the engine, he asked, 'Where's the nurses' home? I've only a vague idea of where the hospital is.'

'Chestnut Grove, off Mansfield Road. It's not far; in fact, I could easily walk there.'

'Not on your Nelly. Now that I've found you again, I'm not going to let you escape so easily.' He pulled out and joined the traffic heading in the general direction of Mansfield Road. 'If I call for you at, say, twelve o' clock on Sunday, I'll take you to lunch before we go on to Northcoate.'

'You're spoiling me again, Maurice.'

'When I meet a girl lost in the Malayan jungle, I see to it that she wants for nothing.'

'And it happens frequently, I imagine.'

'It's pretty routine,' he confirmed.

'I wasn't lost, by the way, and it's left at the next turning.'

'Thank you.'

Ray Hobbs

'That big cedar,' she said, pointing out the landmark, 'is at the entrance to the nurses' home.'

He drew into the side of the road and parked. 'Do you mean to tell me,' he asked, 'that I could have left you to find your own way back to the internment camp?'

'Yes, but I'm glad you didn't. Thank you for the tea and the lift. You can't imagine how pleased I am that we met.' She inclined her head for him to kiss her.

'I'll see you on Sunday,' he said, kissing her cheek.

''Bye.' She picked up her bag and got out of the car.

''Bye.' He watched her go, longing to take her in his arms, but knowing it would spoil everything.

15

Wise Words

Jill had caught glimpses of Jessica's new class teacher, Miss Howlett, as she emerged to welcome each parent into her classroom. She was very young, possibly no older than her mid-twenties, and she had a busy, authoritative manner. Whether that was her normal bearing or one she adopted only on parent evenings was impossible to say. Her predecessor was now on maternity leave, and Jill smiled as she recalled Jessica asking her if pregnant teachers were sent 'on holiday' when they could no longer squeeze between their students' desks. It was a sensible, practical question.

Eventually, Miss Howlett reappeared to ask, 'Is Mrs Barstow here?'

Jill stood up and went to her door. When they were inside the classroom, she said, 'I'm Jessica Barstow's mum, but I reverted several months ago to my maiden name, which is Warneford.'

'Oh, I see. Take a seat, Ms Warneford.'

'Thank you.' She noticed, incidentally, that Miss Howlett had been a little heavy-handed with her make-up. It was as well she wasn't required to teach that.

'Jessica's strength seems to lie in the literary area,' said Miss Howlett, viewing the document before her with evident concern. 'Maths, on the other hand, is somewhat of an issue.'

Jill did her best to conceal the jarring she felt when someone misused the word 'somewhat' in place of 'something'. Also, Miss Howlett should have been aware that the concern, rather than the subject, was the issue. However, she simply said, 'It runs in the family,

Miss Howlett. I could never get maths to add up, either; in fact, it was only through hard work and determination that I passed "O" Level.'

Miss Howlett explained patiently, 'It has nothing to do with heredity, Ms... Warneford. There's no reason why any child should regard mathematics as a closed door.'

Jill remembered hearing that in her teaching days. It was meaningless then, and nothing had changed. She asked, 'Why not? Because Chris Woodhead says so? You're on dangerous ground if you follow his edicts too literally. As I recall, he advocated carnal liaisons between male teachers and sixth-form girls, on the grounds that he'd tried it and he could recommend it. If you ask me, the attraction was that a young girl would lack the experience to recognise his shortcomings.' She added, 'If you'll allow the expression.'

Miss Howlett ignored both the pun and the latter argument, preferring to address the immediate challenge. 'It's an accepted principle, Ms Warneford. In this case, the Chief Inspector is simply the public mouthpiece.'

'That's one way to describe him,' agreed Jill, 'but look, we could argue about this until doomsday. I'd really like to ask you about the way History is being taught.'

Cautiously relieved, Miss Howlett asked, 'What would you like to know, Ms Warneford?'

'I'd like to know how children can be expected to develop any sense of historical sequence, when topics and periods are chosen seemingly at random, so that the task of arranging them in some form of meaningful order makes the solution of Rubik's Cube look like a nursery task.'

Miss Howlett leaned forward, placing her fingertips together in what she possibly saw as the requisite pose when enlightening an obtuse parent. 'History is no longer taught as a sequence of events,' she explained patiently.

'I think that's basically what I just said.'

Miss Howlett continued with studied patience. 'What the National Curriculum is doing is giving children the tools they need to analyse historical data, rather than presenting them with a list of meaningless facts.' She smiled benevolently. 'It's a new concept, so it's possibly a little difficult for you to appreciate.'

'As concepts go, Miss Howlett, it's as old as history itself. I imagine you're old enough to remember "O" Level, when we learned sequential, historical facts that were anything but meaningless. After that, we went on to "A" Level, when we began to analyse those facts, and some of us continued to do the same at university. I certainly did, and I wouldn't have stood an earthly if I'd been through the half-hearted, ill-conceived, mystifying, haphazard, self-defeating rigmarole that the National Curriculum Council chooses to call History.'

Miss Howlett's hands parted. Temporarily at a loss for an answer to Jill's assertive assessment, she asked, 'Are you saying you studied History at university?'

'English and Modern History,' confirmed Jill.

'But Jessica told me you looked after people's dogs.'

'That's right, and I don't need a degree for that, so don't worry, I shan't argue with you about it.' Suddenly, she felt sorry for the hapless teacher. 'Look,' she said, 'the important thing I've learned this evening about Jessica is that she's extremely literate, but failing to impress in maths. I've known that since the end of Year Two, which only bears out what I've always thought about the effectiveness of the National Curriculum, so I'll leave it there and let a few more parents have their say. I hope they won't be as difficult as I've been.' She extended her hand. 'Thank you for your patience, Miss Howlett, and good night.'

———

Jill had another reason for keeping her appointment with Miss Howlett quite short, and that was that she had to be at the dancing school by six-thirty. In the event, she arrived a few minutes later, apologising to Helen and her pupils. She was surprised to see that Steve wasn't among them, but she had to wait until the end of the evening session to learn the reason for his absence.

'He's away until tomorrow,' Helen told her. 'He's working on a piece about the jewellery business and he's staying overnight in London.' Wrinkling her nose in affected regret, she said, 'I asked him if he'd be bringing back any free samples, but he said it was unlikely.'

'You'd have been surprised if he'd said he might.'

'True, but you're holding out on me, Jill.' Impatiently, she said, 'Tell me about Saturday.'

'What do you want to know?'

'Everything.'

'Well, I met Frank and Sarah Morrison. Lovely people. Of course, you know them, don't you?'

'Yes, go on.' She was almost exasperated in her eagerness for detail.

'The whole evening was perfect, the band, the music and the ballroom, which you know, of course.'

Articulating each word carefully, as if to a child, Helen asked, 'How did it go with Steve?'

Jill took pity on her. 'Look, Helen, don't expect too much. I'm not ready to start another relationship, and I'm not sure he is, either.'

'He likes you a lot.' Helen could be like a schoolgirl at times.

'And I like him – as a friend – but, with divorce a recent and bruising memory and two troubled children to consider, I'm really not interested, Helen.'

'Are the children still affected by the break-up?'

'They're bound to be. They're only just getting used to Sunday access, and I know they're not keen on Deborah, which isn't entirely surprising as she'd try the forbearance of a saint, but it's nevertheless something I have to consider.'

'Tony must have been out of his mind, leaving you for a frump like her.'

'It's something no one will ever understand.' Jill picked up her dancing shoes as a hint. She had to get back to let Gemma go home. 'I have to picture Tony staggering around a dance floor,' she said.

'That's not difficult. He has two left feet and he's bloody hopeless. Anyway, who's told you that?'

'Frank.'

'There,' said Helen triumphantly, 'that means he's convinced you're better off with Steve.'

Jill laughed. 'It doesn't mean a thing, and I must go.'

She arrived home to find Gemma working at the computer.

'Hi, Jill,' she said, 'did you have a good night?'

'Quite good, thanks.'

'Steve wouldn't be there, of course. He's in London.'

Suddenly, everyone wanted to talk about Steve. 'How do you know?'

'He told us he wouldn't be at uni tomorrow.'

'It would be a long way for him to go, Gemma.' The influence of *Neighbours* and *Home and Away* on young viewers was slow to fade.

'Erinsborough, I know. I've heard all the jokes.' She saved her work and took out the floppy disc. Then, looking at the money Jill had put on the desk, she said, 'That's too much, Jill.'

'Take it anyway. I feel guilty at taking up so much of your time. I wonder, sometimes, if you have any life of your own.'

'I'm between fellas, Jill, and it's surprising how much work I can get through as a singleton.' She added, 'What's more, I can work here more easily than I can at home, because it's quieter.'

'There is that, I suppose.' It was a shame as well as a surprise. Gemma was quite attractive, with friendly, blue eyes and long, fair hair that enhanced her clear complexion. She was also good fun. Unless taste had become a thing of the past with young men, someone was missing a treat.

'Anyway, how was Saturday night? I didn't have time to ask you when you got in.'

'Yes, that's what I mean about taking so much of your time.' She really didn't want a long conversation like the one she'd just had with Helen, so she said, 'I had a lovely time in excellent company, but please don't start matchmaking, Gemma. It's far too soon for me even to consider it, and I don't think Steve's completely over his tragedy, either.'

Gemma shook her head dismissively. 'He's doing okay, and you'd be a numpty to lose him, Jill. He's a rarity, a really lovely fella. Take it from me, you'd be second time lucky.'

'Spoken with all the wisdom and expert knowledge of your twenty years.'

'That's right.' It must have seemed obvious to Gemma.

Jill saw Steve on the moor two afternoons later and, once again, it was while she was walking Maggie. For a man who'd complained that he didn't get out as often as he would like, he was spending rather a lot of time out of doors.

'Hello, Steve.'

'Hello, Jill. Hello, Maggie. Are you really trying to wag your tail, or is it a trick of the light?'

'She knows from the tone of my voice and yours that you're no threat,' Jill told him. 'Also, I've told her about Saturday evening, and she's most impressed. How was the trip to Hatton Garden?'

'Not bad. I suppose Helen told you. It's not the most riveting topic for an article, I have to say, although I suppose it depends on how you feel about fabulous jewellery. Shall we walk?'

'Mm.' She and Maggie walked beside him. 'I've never been close enough to any priceless examples to decide quite how I feel about it. I can probably take it or leave it.'

'That's a healthy attitude, Jill. When these people, the dealers and manufacturers, talk about the beauty of a stone or a piece of jewellery, I'm impressed. I'm much less impressed by talk of breath-taking prices, which, I suppose, are what the business is really about.'

'Huge sums of money are meaningless to most of us,' said Jill. 'Don't you agree, Maggie?'

Hearing her name, Maggie looked up at Jill, who stroked her cropped ears and spoke to her. 'You're a gem yourself, Maggie, and a priceless one at that.'

'You love your dogs, don't you?'

'Yes, I do. They've never done me any harm, and they're excellent company.' As the thought occurred to her, she said, 'Good company is worth riches, isn't it? Like Saturday night. After the events of the past year, there was so much good feeling in that ballroom, I could feel it buoying me up.'

'It always had that property, although I have to confess it was something I'd forgotten for a while.' They walked a few steps further, and he said, 'I stayed away from the ballroom at first, as a means of self-preservation, and that, believe it or not, became a habit. As habits go, it was quite meaningless, but I still found it a difficult one to break, so you see, Saturday evening was good for me, too.'

'I'm glad.'

'And I'm sorry,' he said, visibly embarrassed. 'I don't make a practice of parading my feelings. I'm afraid it rather came upon me.'

'There's no need to apologise. We're all human, and you've suffered more than most.'

'Even so.' He was clearly ready to change the subject, but he surprised her with his next question. 'How long have you been on your own, Jill?'

She had no need to think about her answer. She was unlikely to forget the date. 'A little over a year,' she told him. 'Ever one for the grand gesture, and without a thought for the practicalities, my husband offered to pay for the divorce on the grounds of adultery. He's just complained ever since the decree was granted, because he's required to support the children. I don't think he'd bargained for that.'

'It seems fairly obvious, even to me.'

'Have you any children?'

'No.'

It was a simple, unqualified reply, and she had no intention of pursuing it. Instead, she said, 'It's not as if my ex-husband is in reduced circumstances, either. He's a partner in Wilkinson's Estate Agents.'

'In that case, I shan't feel sorry for him.'

'Very wise. Altruism is wasted on some people.' She stopped, and Steve and Maggie both stopped and waited for her to go on. 'At least, I thought so until recently.'

Maggie sniffed at the ground, having lost interest, but Steve asked, 'What happened recently to change your mind, Jill?'

'It was something I read in one of my uncle's letters. You were kind enough to help me with them on one occasion, if you remember.'

'I remember it vividly, and I'd be happy to do so again.'

'You're too kind. It's a reference he made to her surprisingly forgiving attitude towards the Japanese nation, despite the way they'd treated her. He mentioned it in his first letter after the mysterious interval. It was dated three months after the previous letter.'

'I remember your telling me about the break.'

'Of course. Believe it or not, after that, she actually went to a cricket match to watch him play.' Her tone suggested that she would certainly hesitate before following her aunt's example.

'Romance has been known to blossom at such events. What did he say about her attitude towards the Japanese?'

'He said he was still trying to come to terms with her forbearing point of view. He admitted that he could only feel outraged on her behalf, and said that his inclination was to favour retribution of the harshest kind – I think he'd be referring to the death penalty at the time – but that he admired her stance. He also said that it helped him understand her wish to return to nursing.'

'And did she?'

'Yes.' Jill remembered that quite clearly. 'She'd retired by the time I visited them in Newark, and her hospital, the old Children's Hospital in Nottingham, had recently closed. I'm talking about the late seventies, when it was most likely absorbed into the General Hospital.'

'She sounds like a remarkable person.'

'I'd certainly call her that.'

'I think, also,' he said, 'that, having suffered at the hands of the Japanese, she had to go one way or the other. It's not unknown. She could have become bitter and resentful, even vengeful, or....'

'Or what?'

'I believe the psychologists call it "sublimation", the re-direction of an anti-social urge into a force for good. That's one possibility. Another, of course, is that it was simply in her nature, that she was incapable of anything but kindness.'

Jill stopped again. 'It's time to retrace out footsteps,' she said. 'I hope you'll stay with us, because I'm very interested in what you're saying.'

'Of course I will.'

'I certainly remember her as a very kindly person; in fact, that's my chief impression of her. I remember being so affected by her passing that I made a special effort to go to her funeral, although I confess I remember very little about it.'

'How long ago was it?'

'About four years.' She considered that and said, 'Yes, it was in the early summer of 'ninety-six, not so long ago, but my experience of it was confused by the misery of losing someone who'd made a surprisingly deep impression on me within a very short time.'

———

When the children were in bed, Jill took out the collection of belongings she'd brought home from Newark, and searched it for a copy of the order of service for Auntie Iris's funeral. It was the kind of thing people often kept, so she was hopeful.

After much sifting and several distractions, she was rewarded, and she sat down to read about the funeral she'd attended almost ten years earlier.

Naturally, it gave the name of the church, St Agnes's, and the officiant, the Revd Martin Rowe, information that was interesting in its way, but she opened it to find out more. There were two hymns, both apparently chosen by Auntie Iris: 'Dear Lord and Father of Mankind' and, surprisingly, 'I Vow to Thee, My Country'. She would doubtless have her own reasons for choosing that. There was possibly a connection with her service as an army nurse, but Jill had no way of knowing, so she read on. There was a tribute from Uncle Maurice, and she remembered feeling desperately sorry for him at the time, although he delivered it with great dignity.

The prayers and liturgical items were what most people would expect at a funeral, and they naturally told her nothing about Auntie Iris as an individual, and she was about to put the order of service back in the pile, when she spotted something on the back that looked like a quotation. She examined it more closely and read:

Iris's Maxim

'Hatred and brutality have no more powerful an adversary than love for our fellow human beings.'

16

Mascot to Foxtrot

With the cedar tree for a landmark, the Nurses Home was easy to find, and Maurice went straight to reception, where a woman of forbidding countenance sat importantly behind a desk.

'Yes?'

It was a positive start, at least. 'Good morning. I arranged to meet Staff-Nurse Lennox here at eleven-thirty.'

'Is she expecting you?'

'Yes, that was the arrangement.'

'All right. Wait over there.' She nodded her head in the direction of two wooden chairs that stood beside the entrance.

'Thank you.' He thought someone should be polite, and he was about to take a seat, as requested, when Iris came downstairs in a summer frock. Sensibly, she carried a cardigan.

'Hello, Maurice.'

'Hello, Iris. What a perfectly charming frock.'

'Thank you.' Smiling at the compliment, she bent at the reception desk to sign herself out.

'Do you have to be back by any particular time?'

'Eleven o' clock is the regulation time. We're not likely to be so late, are we?'

He was aware of the receptionist's eyes shuttling between them as they spoke. 'I thought I'd take you to dinner after the match. That's if you don't mind us stopping off at my place so that I can make myself respectable, now that you know I am respectable, if you see what I mean.'

'I'm not sure I'm properly dressed for eating out,' she said, looking down at her lightweight frock.

'Your ensemble is what the well-dressed woman is wearing today,' he assured her, 'suitable for restaurant, yacht, park, promenade and members' enclosure.'

She laughed. 'If you insist.'

'Which I do, but lunch awaits, so shall we take our leave?' He beamed at the receptionist, who looked at him uncertainly before rearranging the signing-out book and pen.

'Goodbye, Miss Diggle,' said Iris.

'Yes, er, goodbye, Miss Diggle.'

'Goodbye.'

As they left the building, Maurice asked, 'Is her name really Miss Diggle?'

'Yes, it rather suits her, don't you think?'

'More than "Miss Tickle", certainly.' Laughing, he opened the car door for her, saying, 'I can put the roof up again if you prefer to ride without the draught.'

'No. Thank you, it would be a shame on such a lovely day. Where are we going to eat?'

'The Grand, just round the corner from here. It sounds grander than it is, I assure you.'

'I believe you.'

He drove literally around the corner into Mansfield Road and then into the carpark of the Grand Hotel.

When they were seated at their table, Iris said, 'We seem to spend all our time talking to each other across a table.'

'Very civilised, too, but we've never been to a cricket match together. That really is breaking with habit.'

'And it's equally civilised,' she said. 'By the way, I see you're wearing that tie again.'

He squinted downward, as if to remind himself. 'My RNVR tie? It's the only one I have.'

'You do talk nonsense.'

'I'll tell you what. We'll go shopping sometime soon, and you can choose a new one for me, then I'll be able to take this one to the dry cleaners.' Looking over her shoulder, he said, 'Here comes the waitress. More decisions.'

They chatted throughout lunch, and Maurice was careful to keep the conversation light. He was sure Iris knew exactly what he was doing, but he couldn't help that. He simply accepted that women were more intuitive than men, and that it was a cross he had to bear.

After lunch, they went out to the car and set off for Northcoate Cricket Club.

'What's the betting,' he asked, 'you turn out to be my lucky mascot? I'm feeling lucky enough to take lots of wickets for not very many, and then go on to make a pile of runs, or *vice versa*, depending on the toss and the winning captain's preference.'

'That's quite a responsibility, Maurice.'

'On both of us.' It pleased him to see her laughing at his silliness. She needed some laughter in her life. 'Tell me about the hospital,' he said, casting around for a harmless topic. 'It seems odd to have a separate hospital for children.'

'I don't know so much about odd,' she said, 'but it arose out of necessity.'

'I'm all ears.'

'It was founded in eighteen sixty-nine by public subscription. It was prompted by the appalling infant mortality rate, and its aim was to provide hospital care for the children of the poor, under the age of ten.'

'I imagine that was the most vulnerable age group.' It hadn't occurred to him until then.

'That's right. You see, Maurice, you can be serious when you try.'

'I wouldn't dream of joking about something of that kind.'

'I know you wouldn't.'

He watched her pull the brim of her hat down, and said, 'I can easily put the roof up if the wind's a problem.'

'It's not a problem, Maurice, but I have to wear a wide-brimmed hat on a day like this, with my colouring.'

'Do you burn easily?'

'Too easily. It was always a problem in Malaya.' She laughed. 'It's a problem for all redheads.'

'I'd call your hair dark auburn, and I think it's exquisite.'

'It's never been called that before.'

'It has now, and it's a genuine compliment.'

'In that case, thank you.'

They passed the sign that told them they were entering the village of Northcoate, and Maurice turned down the lane that led to the cricket ground.

'We're in good time,' he told her, 'so I'll introduce you to everyone before I change.'

Northcoate's captain won the toss and elected to field, so Maurice took his place at the front of the pavilion, waiting tactfully until the opening batsmen were in the middle before padding up to go in at number three. He was particularly pleased that Iris's offer to help with tea had been readily accepted. It seemed to him that she could only benefit from interacting with as many people as possible in normal life. Only that way could she begin to accept that she was properly home with nothing to fear. His reasoning was based solely on his experience of his uncle, whose lapses into the delirium caused by shellshock had become gradually and mercifully fewer over time.

After one over, he concluded that Northcoate's new opening bowler was a useful acquisition, an impression he shared with Cyril, West Stoke's captain, who sat beside him.

'That lad's too good,' said Cyril. 'We'll have to watch him.'

He was proved right in the third over, when one of the opening batsmen played at a seemingly innocent delivery and was caught at third slip. The umpire wasted no time in raising the finger of dismissal.

'Right, Maurice,' said Cyril, 'no heroics, just stay there as long as you can.'

Maurice walked out to the middle, offering a sympathetic word to the man he was replacing. He nodded a friendly greeting to Bill Staveley, his client and now his batting partner, at the other end. He was allowed to call Mr Staveley 'Bill' when they were playing cricket. Once at the crease, he spoke to the umpire. 'Middle and leg, please.'

The umpire helped him adjust and, assured that he was ready, nodded to the triumphant bowler to complete his over.

Maurice saw out the over, content to play defensively until he was surer of his opponent. That left Bill Staveley to face the other bowler, which he did quite capably, taking two twos, and then a single off the last ball, which meant that he must face the danger man again. The first ball was a wide, a gift to West Stoke, and Bill played his next for two. It did nothing for the bowler's temper, a fact that became obvious when he ran up to bowl his next delivery. His venom was wasted, however, as Bill played it for another two runs. It seemed he had the bowler weighed up, taking two more runs off his fourth delivery, but the next was short-pitched, rocketing off the uneven wicket and rising above waist height to hit Bill's elbow with a sickening crack that Maurice heard quite plainly.

Bill was naturally moved to profanity, nursing his injured elbow so that Maurice was prompted to run down the wicket and ask, 'Do you want someone to look at that, Bill?'

His response was unrepeatable, so Maurice waved to the pavilion with his bat to alert Cyril to the fact that he had an injured man. 'Come on, Bill,' he said, 'you can't finish the innings with that elbow. You'll have to retire hurt.' He took Bill's bat from him and walked with him to the pavilion, where Iris and another woman were waiting.

'Come and sit here,' said Cyril, making room for him on the bench.

Iris removed his glove and eased up his sleeve. Turning to the woman beside her, she asked, 'Can you find me a triangular bandage and a safety pin, please?'

'I'm sure I can.'

'You need to go to hospital,' she told Bill, whose face was white with pain. 'The bone may only be chipped, but it needs to be examined and X-rayed. I'm going to put your arm in a sling to immobilise it. It's all I can do for now.'

'Thanks, duck. I'm obliged to you.' Turning to Maurice, he said weakly, 'I'm glad you brought this lass, Maurice, but will you get out there an' put that bowler in his place?'

Maurice and Cyril walked out to the middle, where the umpire was waiting. Cyril gave him the news, and the umpire nodded. 'I've warned that clever young bugger Whitehead about short-pitched bowlin', he said.

Cyril took guard and saw out the current over and the next, leaving Maurice to face Whitehead, who seemed to have learned nothing from the incident. The first ball of the new over was short-pitched again, but Maurice hooked it past deep fine leg for four runs, to the delight of the visiting side. He played the next two deliveries defensively, but drove the fourth ball through the covers for another four. The last two balls went for one and two runs respectively, with Maurice answering Whitehead's livid scowl with a straight face. He was there to play cricket, after all, not to pull silly faces.

After two more expensive overs, Northcoate's captain took Whitehead off and replaced him with a bowler known for his economy, although Maurice and Cyril still managed to score quite heavily.

By tea, West Stoke had made a hundred and thirty-one. It was a comfortable total to defend, even though it had cost them an injured man. Meanwhile, tea was served.

Iris told him, 'Bill Staveley's gone to the infirmary. I think his elbow's broken, but I can't be sure.'

'It's as well you were here,' said Maurice. 'No one else had a clue what to do, so well done you.' He underlined the point by kissing her on the cheek.

'You did well,' she said, only a little embarrassed at being kissed in public. 'Fifty-three not out.'

'What did I say? You're obviously my lucky mascot. Not only do you bring me runs, you patch up the casualties as well.'

'I hope he'll be all right. Elbows can be tricky.'

'I'll let you know, Iris. I'll be seeing him next week.'

She looked at him in horror. 'Surely he won't be playing next Sunday.'

'No, I'll see him at his office. He's a client.'

'Ah. Let me know, won't you?'

'Of course. Meanwhile, I have to take some wickets. Keep up the good work, lucky mascot.'

In the event, Maurice wasn't quite so lucky with his bowling, taking only two wickets, but he had the satisfaction of dismissing Whitehead, catching him off his own bowling.

Later, they called at Maurice's flat, where he had a quick bath and changed into a suit.

'Thanks for waiting,' he said.

'You were less than fifteen minutes.'

'Good, I hate to be a nuisance.' He opened the door of the flat and waited for her to go ahead of him.

'How did you manage to do all that?'

'Early training, I suppose. First, my mother trained me to undress and jump into the bath. It was a while before she got me to do it without splashing water all over the—'

She rolled her eyes. 'I meant so quickly.'

'Oh, that was down to the Kriegsmarine.'

'The what?'

'The German Navy. The E-boats had a way of interrupting bath time. It was most uncivilised of them, but what else could we expect from a nation that doesn't play cricket?'

She took her place in the car and asked, 'What are E-boats?'

He hadn't wanted to remind her of Malaya, however fleetingly, but it was necessary. 'Do you remember seeing ML Six-Five-Seven, my ship?'

'Yes.'

'Try to imagine something more streamlined, with more guns, torpedo tubes and very much faster, and you have an E-boat. At least, that was our name for it, but the Jerries called it *Das Schnellboot*, and anywhere the blighters could reach in the North Sea was known as E-boat Alley. They thought they owned it, but we showed 'em.' To steer the conversation away from the war, he asked, 'Do you like dancing?'

Taken aback by the change of topic, she said, 'I... did. I haven't danced since before the war.'

'It's easier to take up again than swimming. There's a band where we're going for dinner, and it's very good. Whether we dance or not is entirely up to you. I shan't sulk or drag my feet if you don't feel comfortable dancing with me, because all I want to do is see to it that you have an enjoyable, relaxing time.'

As he drew into the hotel carpark, she said, 'You know, I'd like that.' She hesitated and said, 'You mustn't take the touching thing too literally. I'm improving, you see. I don't think I'll ever be rid of it altogether, but I'd like to dance with you.'

'Then so you shall,' he said, switching off the engine. 'You'll find that the old boys in there play music from a bygone age, in fact, from before the war, which suits me down to the ground.'

'Me too,' she said enthusiastically, 'as I've been out of touch since then.'

They went in and were shown to their table. The band were playing, and a few couples had taken to the modest dance floor. The number ended, and the band began the old standard 'Yours', revived more latterly by Vera Lynn.

Maurice asked, 'Shall we?'

'Yes, let's.'

He felt her flinch momentarily when he took her in hold, but then she relaxed. He asked, 'Are you all right?'

'Yes, I'm fine. Everything's fine.'

The foxtrot was an intimate dance, but he tried not to crowd her. If she were ever to overcome her inhibition, he felt, it had to happen gradually and naturally.

They followed the line of dance, with Iris taking his lead like a shadow. Only her features betrayed her uncertainty.

'You haven't danced for several years,' he said, 'but no one would have known it.'

'Thank you, but I think you're being too kind.'

'Not a bit of it,' he assured her. 'You put me to shame.'

She laughed lightly. 'You're not that bad.'

'I'm not brilliant, either. Shall I let you into a secret? I'm also pretty hopeless as an accountant. In fact, if I hadn't made fifty-three with the bat this afternoon, I'd have died of shame, because that's the one thing I can do tolerably well.'

'You do talk the most awful nonsense, Maurice.'

'That's another of my failings,' he agreed, noticing with satisfaction that the light-hearted exchange had relaxed her to the extent that the gap he'd sensitively allowed between them was now closed. It seemed that, in a very short time, she'd found the confidence to dance closely with him.

Their courses were punctuated by dances, of which the foxtrot turned out to be Iris's favourite. In fact, the difference Maurice could now see in her composure made that evening at the restaurant unmistakably the highlight of the day.

17

Complaint and Conjecture

Jill arrived late at the football match, guiltily aware that it was her second offence since Liam was given a place in the Under-13s. He would have noticed her absence, and she was preparing her defence as she stood with Jessica on one side and Maggie on the other, the latter ensuring that the referee-abusing, effing-and-blinding dads, uncles and droppers-by all kept their distance.

'I don't understand it,' said Jessica in a bored tone. 'Do you, Mum?'

'No, and neither does Maggie.' As ever, Maggie looked up when she heard her name, but looked away again when nothing worthy of her attention seemed to be happening.

The final whistle went, with the home side winning by two goals to one.

'It shoulda been three-one,' said one of the spectators, glowering at Mr Emsley, who had refereed the match, although not to everyone's approval.

'Some people are just never satisfied,' said Jill to Jessica.

The dissident looked sharply at her and then saw Maggie and kept his feelings unspoken. Jill simply smiled and waited for Liam to join them.

When he did, he was predictably peeved. 'When did you come, Mum? I looked for you on the touchline and you weren't there.'

'I came as soon as I could, darling. I'll explain it to you later, but first, I have to get Maggie back to her owner before she thinks I've absconded with her. That would leave two of you out of sorts.' She opened the hatch to let Maggie in, and took out a dog rug.

Liam asked, 'What's that for?'

'It's for you to sit on, because you're filthy.' She ignored the 'Huh' and fastened Maggie in.

Jessica asked, 'What does "absconded" mean, Mum?'

' "Done a runner", "legged it" or "cleared off". In English, we say, "Escaped" or "bolted", but it's easy to forget proper English when you've been standing on a touchline, albeit during the second half of a match.' She spread the dog rug over the front passenger seat and then fastened Jessica into hers.

'They always say swear-words, don't they?' Jessica had only been to two matches, but her observation was nonetheless accurate. Liam continued to sulk.

Jill drew up outside Maggie's house, hugging and kissing her before letting her out of the car. When she returned, Liam said, 'You think more of that dog than you do of me.'

'And there are absolutely no prizes for guessing where that accusation originated.' Before she strapped herself in again, she said, 'Anyway, it's not true. Everybody knows I love you, even when you're covered in mud.' She proceeded to kiss him extravagantly, all over his dirty face.

'Mum,' he protested, 'somebody'll see us!'

'You can't have it both ways, Liam.' She fastened her belt and said, 'Right, breaded haddock beckons, and I may just stretch a point and give you oven chips, as well, with your peas.'

'Great!'

'Great!'

Suddenly she was popular again. It didn't take much.

After dinner, she had a grown-up talk with Liam, beginning with the question, 'What did you have to do after school?'

'Play in the match. You know that.'

'Yes, and that must have kept you quite busy, but I want you to put yourself in my position. At about the time you were kicking off, or whatever the proper term is, I was walking Maggie in order to earn the money that keeps the roof over your heads. I realised it was going to be a rush, to I put Maggie in the car and went to Jessica's school to pick her up. Having done that, I drove to your school playing field to be a dutiful mum, only to be accused by my ungrateful son of wanton neglect.'

'What does "wanton" mean, Mum?'

'I'll tell you later, Jessica, when I've finished making Liam see the error of his judgemental ways.'

Determined to make his case, Liam said, 'My dad says it's one of the basic duties of being a parent to turn up for matches.'

'That's funny,' said Jill. 'I didn't see him there. Did you, Jessica?'

'No.'

'When did he say that, Liam? Was it after the first time you told him I was late for your match?'

'Yes.'

'I thought it might have been.' As if it had only just occurred to her, she said, 'I've had a splendid idea. As I'm so unreliable, and your dad is so pious, why don't we arrange for him to go to matches instead of me? I've got plenty to do, and he knows things about football that I never will.'

'What does "pious" mean, Mum?'

'It means it's high time I taught you how to use a dictionary, Jessica. Will you pass me that one, please?' She pointed to the Concise Oxford English Dictionary on the nearest bookshelf.

'He's even worse than you at turning up,' said Liam.

'Haven't you explained to him that it's one of a parent's basic duties?'

'It's not fair. You always twist things round to win arguments.'

'That's right, Liam. Being right is another parental duty, and don't forget to put your football kit to the wash.' Turning her attention to Jessica, who was waiting patiently with the dictionary on her lap, she said, 'Right, there's "pious" and, what was that other word? I remember, it was "wanton".' Both definitions called for judicial editing, but she felt equal to it. At least, it was easier than fitting three jobs into the time of one.

———

She'd just put Liam's PE and football kit into the washing machine on their own. Jessica's kit would go in with an ordinary wash. She was sorting whites from coloureds when her mobile rang.

' "No task too big, no dog too small. Six legs are better than crossed legs." Jill speaking.'

'Hello, Jill. Your slogans seem to breed by the day.'

'Hello, Steve.' She recognised his voice immediately. 'Have you a dog that needs walking?'

'No, but I need your help with another little matter. Helen tells me you used to be a teacher – I mean in school.'

'Guilty.'

'Why do you say that?'

'Teachers are widely unpopular. It's government policy whichever way you turn, right or left.'

'Actually, I wanted to ask you something about learning theory.'

'Oh, I dunno, but ask me and I'll have a go. In fact, let me pour a glass of wine and then ask me.'

'Of course.' He waited.

She poured the requisite number of glugs and said, 'I'm ready.'

'Okay. Do you know what it's called when someone has a fixed idea, and then something happens to challenge it, causing a clash between what they believe and what they know?'

'Yes, you're talking about cognitive dissonance.'

'Thank you, Jill. I remember now.'

'It's no trouble. What are you working on?'

I'm still working on the jewellery piece, but I'm planning one about prejudice.'

'Fascinating. Purely in the spirit of co-operation, why don't you come over and help me demolish a bottle of wine, and then I can ask your advice?' It would be innocent enough.

'That's a good idea. I hope I can help you as neatly as you just helped me.'

'It's all to be tried for.'

'Okay, I'll see you in twenty minutes or so. 'Bye.'

''Bye.'

She tidied up the room, although there wasn't much to do. One advantage in being out for most of the day was that it allowed little opportunity for making it untidy. She imagined the washing machine would have finished performing noisy tasks by the time Steve arrived.

In rather less than twenty minutes, she heard his car outside and went to the door to let him in.

He greeted her with a kiss on the cheek and handed her a bottle of Burgundy. 'I thought it would be a bit much to come over and drink your wine,' he said.

'How very thoughtful, Steve. Take a seat while I open this.' She took it to the kitchen and plied the corkscrew. It made a change, as she usually bought less-expensive wines with screw caps. She took the opened bottle and two glasses into the sitting room.

'Thank you,' said Steve, taking a glass of wine from her.

'You're very welcome.' She sat opposite him, in the armchair. 'After three years,' she said, 'I've started writing again.'

'Oh good. What are you writing?'

'Nothing deep and meaningful, just what some people call "a good read". At least, I hope it will be.'

'What's it about?'

'Oddly enough, it's about a woman going through the throes of a marriage break-up.'

He was quiet for a moment, and then he asked, 'Isn't that a bit close to home?'

'Not really. I've done all that and it's behind me. The funny thing is, I started it before there was even a hint that we were going to part, and then, when it happened, it really was too close. Since then, I've had to cope with everything, and selling and buying houses is, as I'm sure you know, very time-consuming, especially on top of a divorce.'

He smiled and nodded. 'The house thing is bad enough. I can't comment on the divorce.'

'Of course, but now that I've run out of excuses and various forms of displacement activity, I've decided to start again, quite literally. I've scrapped the original manuscript.'

He nodded again, evidently as ready to listen as to take part in the conversation.

'Being as rusty as I am, I'd like to ask you something.'

'Ask away.'

'I'm sure you know the principle of showing, rather than telling?'

'Yes.'

'My question is, if I'm to plant an idea, now, that bears fruit later, how big a hint does that idea have to be? I'm always divided between making it noticeable and making it too glaring.' Before he could answer, she said, 'All that time I spent studying English literature, and I get hung up on something like this.'

'It's not so surprising, when you consider that most great writers have defied every piece of the received wisdom we take for granted nowadays. Dickens, as I'm sure you know, wrote page upon page of narrative.'

'Agreed, and we love him for it.'

'Justly so.' He leaned against the back of the sofa and said, 'I'd say, make your hint as tiny as you like. Never underestimate your reader, because he'll seize on it and say to himself, "This is obviously important for her to have mentioned it." Then, when you go on to make the connection, he'll have the satisfaction of saying, "I *knew* it was important." Readers love to do that. As you said, the mistake is either to hammer the point home so that it's irritatingly obvious what you're doing, or to slip in something inadvertently that has no connection with anything in the story. A rogue red herring, in fact.'

She smiled awkwardly. 'It's awful that I'm doubting my own judgement. I can't help wondering if it's a hangover from the divorce.'

'Was it an awful blow to your self-confidence?'

'I suppose it must have been.' She broke off and said, 'I'm sorry, I shouldn't bore you with my personal problems.'

'I'm not at all bored. Is it still a problem?'

'It's certainly not the problem it was.' She hesitated, wondering where to begin and finally opting for the beginning. 'Things seemed to be all right. It wasn't a perfect relationship, but how many are?'

'Perfection is an ideal,' he agreed, 'and an ideal, by its very nature, is impossible to realise.'

'Right, so our marriage was chugging along, when suddenly, Tony announced that he was seeing someone else and that he wanted a divorce. Now, that was a shock in itself. I wondered about this woman, imagining her to be glamorous, alluring and skilled in the social graces. The prospect was too awful to describe, but then I met her.' She saw that she had his complete attention. It seemed she'd not lost her story-telling ability altogether.

'Tell me about her. What's her name?'

'Deborah. She's plain, ill-groomed, devoid of dress sense, abrupt and unmannerly.' She considered that assessment and found it lacking in at least one detail. 'Oh, and she's a devotee of folk music. I hope you're not, or I'll have lost your sympathy in one go.'

He laughed. 'No, I'm not. I'm a glutton for the kind of music we danced to at the Exchange Club.'

'Happy music,' she said, 'congenial music, music to forget things by, music for celebration. I'm with you there.'

Returning to the original topic, he asked, 'How old is your ex-husband?'

'A few years older than me. He's… let me think…. He'll be forty-two.' She picked up the bottle to top up his glass.

'Please. Yes, I have to say, he's young for a mid-life crisis.'

'That's true, but he always wanted to be the first to do everything. He'd have put his name down for it at school if he could. Mind you, he'd have grown tired of waiting, as he did with his applications to join the Exchange Club and the Golf Club.'

He smiled at the thought, and said, 'The only explanation I can deduce, why a man should leave an attractive, charming and fascinating woman such as you for the one you describe is the infamous mid-life crisis. I've had no experience of it, so I can only speak from observation. Otherwise, it defeats me.'

'It's not often that I'm showered with compliments. Thank you, Steve.'

'It's straight from the heart, Jill, and speaking of which, how's your family investigation proceeding?'

It seemed there really was no need for wariness where Steve was concerned. Whatever Helen thought, he'd never made overtures. Even after lavishing compliments on her, he'd changed the subject to a harmless one. 'I keep finding out details,' she said. 'It's quite fascinating.'

'What have you discovered?'

'I told you about the cricket match, didn't I?'

'Yes, I believe he played in it.'

'Well, according to my uncle's letter, the cricket club were full of praise for her, although I don't know exactly what she did. Then, that evening, she and my uncle had dinner somewhere, and she danced for the first time in years. Now, that seems important, because.... Let me show you the letter.' She got up to take the letter from her desk and hand it to him.

He scanned the first two paragraphs and then read aloud:

' "I can't tell you how delighted I am to know how much you enjoyed last Sunday. Certainly, everyone in the club is singing your praises. By the way, Bill Staveley is plastered up but otherwise okay. He sends his thanks.

"As for Sunday evening, I've never seen you so happy. Dancing really is your 'thing', evidently, and I'm only too ready to indulge you, because I enjoy it, too. You'll just have to make allowances for my technique, which isn't a patch on yours, even after your enforced abstention!

"Finally, I understand fully the point you make at the end of your letter. You've made remarkable progress in a short time, but let me say that I'd never dream of making you feel uncomfortable or threatened in any way.

"With that dealt with, I'll just say that I'm looking forward to seeing you again on your next day off, when, if nothing else, you'll have the satisfying experience of improving my foxtrot.

"Yours with great affection,

Maurice." '

Steve handed the letter back to Jill, saying, 'Isn't that a nice touch? "Yours with great affection." It's one of the gracious, eloquent expressions that have disappeared from our language for good.'

'I agree.'

After a little thought, he said, 'I'm sure dancing was important to them, and not just for the usual reason. I'm thinking more about my theory that her wariness in male company may have stemmed from abuse in the internment camp. As you know, ballroom dancing calls for close, physical proximity, but in a perfectly innocent context.'

'Do you think it might have had a healing effect on her?'

'It's quite possible. We've both experienced it in our different ways.'

Looking at the letter again, she asked, 'What do you make of the last paragraph, the remark about making her feel threatened?'

'It's anybody's guess. In any case, I've already gone out on a limb with my theory about physical abuse. I think it's possible to read too much into these things.'

'All the same,' said Jill, 'I'd give a lot to know what was going on.'

18

Tea and Sympathy

Iris surveyed the plates of sandwiches and cakes with amusement. 'I only ever have tea when I'm with you,' she remarked.

Maurice adopted a shocked expression and asked, 'Am I the only person in this city who's trying to build you up?'

Before she could answer, a waitress came to ask what kind of tea they preferred.

Maurice asked, 'What's the choice?' He suspected that, as usual, only one would be available, but the question was worth asking.

'Lapsang Souchong or English Breakfast, sir.'

Trying to avoid looking at Iris in case they both gave way to laughter, he said, 'Let's have English Breakfast, just for a change.'

'I'll bring you some, sir.'

'Thank you, and congratulations.'

'I beg your pardon, sir?'

'Laying hands on Lapsang Souchong. Well done.'

The waitress looked nonplussed. 'I can easily get you some of that, sir,' she said.

'No, thank you. We'll settle for English Breakfast.'

'Very good, sir.'

The band was playing 'Oh, What A Beautiful Mornin' from *Oklahoma!* 'I don't think I'll ever get used to this modern music,' said Maurice in the manner of someone twice his age.

'I'm sure you will. If it comes to that, I thought tea dances would have gone out of fashion by the time I came home.'

'They have, apparently, except in Nottingham.'

Iris's attention appeared to have strayed. She was studying the right side of Maurice's face. 'I've never noticed it until now,' she said, 'possibly because I've never looked at you closely enough.'

'You should compare notes with your mother. The first time I came to your house, she studied me from all angles.'

'I know,' she said uncomfortably, 'she's an awful matchmaker.'

'But she has excellent taste. You have to give her that. Anyway, I imagine you're talking about my scar.'

'Maybe I shouldn't have mentioned it.'

'But now you have, it's where they sewed the ear back on.'

She gave him a stern look and asked, 'Can't you be serious, just for a minute?'

'I'll have you know it was a highly serious matter. One minute I had two ears flapping in the North Sea breeze, and the next, one of them had taken evasive action and dived for cover.'

With sudden concern she asked, 'Why?'

'It was being shot at. You can't really blame it.'

'You were wounded. That's not funny.'

'It's a lot funnier than being killed, which is what happened to my skipper.' It was time to be serious. 'We were escorting a convoy, as usual, down the East Coast, and we had to defend it against a flotilla of E-boats. The captain was killed, so I was left in command, and then, when I was least expecting it, I was hit by a shell splinter.'

'What happened then?'

'I bled all over the bridge, but we got the convoy to Harwich, and I went to hospital.'

With a mixture of horror and fascination, she said, 'But you drove the ship all by yourself.'

'There was a crew of fourteen,' he told her modestly.

'Yes, but without a captain. They should have given you a medal.'

'They did. If you're very good, I'll let you see it one day.'

She gave him a look of hopelessness and said, 'I never know when you're serious or when you're joking.'

'Oddly enough, a man at the Inland Revenue said the same thing only last week. Mind you, if they ever discovered a sense of humour, they'd assess it for income tax, find it penniless, and then hand it over to Immigration as an undesirable alien.'

The waitress arrived with a pot of English Breakfast, thereby bringing the conversation to a close. Her departure coincided with a new number, which was 'Surrey With A Fringe On Top', prompting Maurice to request the pleasure of the dance.

'It's modern music, Maurice,' said Iris, 'but I think you'll manage, even in extreme old age.'

'I blame the war,' he said.

'For what?'

'For happening. Music was perfect before the war, but six years spent fighting the worst philistines in history have left us no better than them.'

She moved easily with him and with no hesitation, asked him, 'Are you keen on music? I mean classical music.'

'What other kind is there?'

'Will you be serious for once?'

'All right. I only became an accountant when I realised I could never be a concert pianist.'

She closed her eyes in a gesture of despair.

'Actually, I only had lessons for five years, so failure was always the most likely outcome.'

'Will you answer my question, please?'

'Yes, Sister, I'm keen on music.'

'I'm only a staff nurse.'

'You were a sister when I met you, and that's what matters.' He kissed her cheek to reinforce his point.

'I was only a staff nurse, even then. They made me a sister when I came home.'

'A mere detail.'

'You're impossible, Maurice, and what's more, you're leading with your toe.'

'I'm sorry. Do you know the song "The Very Thought of You"?'

'Yes,' she said, surprised, 'it's one of my favourites.'

'If you study the lyrics, you'll realise why I forget to do things.'

She sighed. 'Do you mean the simple, ordinary things you ought to do?'

'The everyday things. You've got it.'

'You're a smooth-talking rascal.' Nevertheless, she surprised him by pressing her cheek against his.

When they returned to their table, she said, 'That's something else we have in common. I'm talking about music, by the way.' She examined the tea, replaced the lid and poured for them both.

'We have lots in common, Iris. It was written in the stars that we should meet. I'm a great believer in that.'

'Look,' she said patiently, you know the score, that we can never be more than friends. I'm very fond of you, but more than that is impossible.'

'Who said anything about wedlock or, if it comes to that, carnal goings-on under any arrangement? I meant that we were destined to meet, and you can't say that our getting together hasn't done us both some good, can you?'

'No,' she conceded, 'you've certainly been good for me.'

'Likewise, so relax and have a sandwich. I think they're paste, but I suppose we should be thankful for that.'

'You'll never hear me complain.'

After a while, the band put *Oklahoma!* to bed and began 'Be Careful, It's My Heart.'

'Bing Crosby sang this to Marjorie Reynolds in *Holiday Inn*,' he said. 'Of course, it was made during the war, so you won't have seen it.'

'No, but it's lovely. Shall we dance?'

'Why not?' He led her on to the floor.

She asked, 'What was the film about?'

'Fred Astaire and Bing Crosby were entertainers. Bing was disillusioned with working every day of the year, and he opened a night club *cum* restaurant that opened only on public holidays. Now, even allowing for the fact that the USA has a lot more holidays then we have, I have to say, speaking as an accountant, that his business plan was unsound to the point of being downright reckless—'

'I'm sorry I asked. Remember to lead with your heel.'

When the number came to its close, Iris said, 'That was lovely.' She poured fresh tea and said, 'Actually, there's something I need to speak to you about.'

'Speak on, but with some regard for my feelings. In fact, to coin a phrase, "Be careful, it's my heart".'

'It's nothing like that. I've been sent an income tax return, and it's couched in gobbledegook. I wondered if you'd help me fill it in.'

'As it happens, I'm fluent in gobbledegook, and I'll help you with pleasure. Unless you have several sources of income, it'll be fairly straightforward. I imagine they'd send it because you've only recently become employed.'

'Thank you.' Like an encouraging aunt, she said, 'You're lovely when you're sensible.' Standing up, she said, 'I'll only be a minute.'

In her absence, he listened to the band playing 'The Last Time I Saw Paris', and decided that they had taste, after all. He also suspected that he might eventually come to accept the changing style of dance music. He'd been too busy over the past few years to notice the changes as they took place, and he concluded that he was right to blame the war. He stood up as Iris returned, and waited for her to take her seat.

'You wouldn't believe,' she said, 'what a luxury it was when we boarded the ship for Australia, to have bathrooms, as well as lavatories with doors.'

'I wondered about that.' He wasn't going to mention it, but it was she who'd introduced the subject.

'About what?'

'When we first met, you used the officers' heads to freshen up, and you washed yourself without closing the door.'

'Did I really?'

'Nothing more revealing than that,' he assured her.

'Thank goodness for that.' Satisfied that she'd not committed an embarrassing gaffe, she said, 'Honestly, there was no privacy in the camp, and openness, using the word literally, became a way of life.'

He could think of nothing to say, so he took her hand and gave it a squeeze.

'Maurice,' she said ruefully, 'I wish I could be more to you.'

'I'm not asking you for anything more.'

'I know that. I just feel that I'm denying you something… I don't know… something essential.'

Squeezing her hand again, he said, 'It's not essential, and if I don't ask you for it, by definition, there's no question of your denying it.'

147

She was quiet, and it was evident that the matter was still very much on her mind. Then she said, 'I had another of those daytime horrors, last week.'

'That's awful.' For want of something useful to say, he asked, 'Shouldn't you see someone about it? I mean, in your line of business, you must have access to the right people.'

'I don't know. I really don't know what good it would do.'

'It's your decision, obviously, but you won't know until you ask.' The band had just begun 'Full Moon and Empty Arms'. He wasn't keen on the song, as it was an abstraction from Rachmaninov's Second Piano Concerto, which had done absolutely nothing to deserve it, but he asked, 'Would you like to dance?'

'Mm,' she said. 'It's better than feeling sorry for myself.'

'That's not why I asked you,' he said, leading her on to the floor. 'When you tell me these things, I want to hold you close. I can't imagine it would do any good – it's just a reflex, really – but, when we're dancing is the only time I can put, well, one arm around you, and do that.'

'You're wrong, you know.'

'Am I?' He was on unfamiliar ground.

'I mean about it doing no good. It does more good than you can imagine.'

'I'm glad,' he said, holding her even closer.

'If you remember, I told you last week not to take the touching thing too literally.'

'I just don't want to offend you.'

'You couldn't offend me if you practised for half a lifetime.'

They danced very closely to the end of the number, when Iris said, 'Another good thing is that I'm not the only victim, and they say there's strength in numbers.'

'Who else is there?'

'Rachmaninov. He just got murdered. Didn't you notice?'

'I couldn't help but notice. Shall we have some fresh tea? This pot's almost empty.' He caught the eye of the waitress who'd served them, and she came over.

'Can I help you, sir?'

'Could we have another pot of tea, please?'

'Of course, sir. English Breakfast, wasn't it?'

'That's right. Well done.'

'I'll get it for you now, sir.'

Iris watched her go, and said, 'You're a charmer.'

'Not really, but I'd like to be.' He could see she had something on her mind and was about to ask her, when she confirmed it.

'On my next day off,' she said, 'I really should visit my parents. It's Sunday, so it'll be an opportunity to see them both. Do you mind? I'll see you the following week, if you like.'

'Of course I don't mind. It's quite a busy time for me, anyway, so soon after the tax-year end, so you do that, and I'll look forward to seeing you later.' As an afterthought, he said, 'Give me a ring at home in the evening, and tell me about your financial affairs. I'll tell you what to write, and then you can send off your tax return.'

'You know, you're so good to me, the last thing I'd ever want to do is hurt you.'

'You can't do that, now that I'm immune. When you gave me the heave, a few months ago, it was like being vaccinated. Do it again, and I shan't feel a thing.'

'I don't believe you.'

They chatted and then danced twice more, until the time came for them to leave. They stood in the almost-empty carpark, and Maurice asked, 'Do you have to buy your own uniform stockings?'

'I'm afraid so, and distressingly often, ladders being an occupational hazard.'

'I did wonder. We chaps just don't realise how hard it is, being a woman.'

'That's very true.'

'What kind do you wear?'

'Black, forty denier. Why do you ask?'

'Concern, basically. I don't understand the technicalities, but it's good to know these things.' He drew her into his arms and held her close.

She asked, 'Is this a vote of sympathy because I told you about laddered stockings?' Her voice was muffled by his coat.

'Yes, it was a touching story that made a bee-line for my heart, but I'm going into Bossington's next week. I'll see what I can do.'

149

'Maurice, you're amazing.'

'I know.' He kissed her twice on the cheek, and then very lightly on her neck. She made no demur, but said, 'Thank you for a lovely afternoon.'

'It's not over, yet. I have to drive you home.' He opened the car door for her.

19

Manners and Mystery

Jill had only just arrived home after dropping the children at school, when her mobile rang. She was expecting a call from Tony. He'd intimated the previous evening, when he brought the children home, that he needed to speak to her, and she hoped, as she pushed the green button, that it wouldn't take long.

'No task too large, no dog too small. Six legs are better than crossed legs. Jill speaking, How can I help you?' She knew the answering rigmarole would wind him up.

'Jill, you know perfectly well it's me.'

'So it is. What a treat.'

'The reason I'm calling,' he said in his officious, business-like tone, 'is to speak to you about something it's better the children didn't hear.'

'How unusually delicate of you, Antonio.'

He ignored her teasing for the moment and asked, 'What is all this about me going to Liam's football matches?'

'It's perfectly simple. By the way, that "me" should have been a "my". I only mention it so that you won't go through your whole life sounding ignorant. I was late arriving at the match because of the need both to earn a living and collect Liam's little sister from school.'

Tony brushed that part of the explanation aside, saying impatiently, 'He told me that.'

'Good, you've trained him well. When he took me to task for the offence, he said you'd told him it was a basic parental duty to attend sporting fixtures.'

'And your argument is?'

'Antonio, I thought we'd established long ago that I don't answer cloze questions.'

Quite deliberately, he asked, 'What, precisely, is your argument?'

'There's no argument. I simply expressed surprise that I hadn't seen you there, as you're such a model parent, and then I had my brainwave. As I was so remiss, and you're so punctilious, why didn't I ask you to attend those fixtures? You could converse with the effing-blinding, referee-abusing fathers as well as debriefing Liam on the way home. It makes perfect sense, and it would relieve me of the unpleasant business of standing with our nine-year-old daughter in a line of foul-mouthed low-life.'

'And how, exactly, am I supposed to find the time to do that?'

'How indeed? With that one question, you've hit the nail squarely on the head, because you've identified my problem also. Now, I can do my best to attend on time, and explain to Liam why I can't always work a miracle, but I do object to being criticised for my human frailty in my absence and through the medium of an innocent child.'

Almost through clenched teeth, or so it sounded, he said, 'But you criticised me.'

'What on earth gives you that idea? I made the suggestion that you might be better at the job. At no time did the children get the idea that I was holding you to account for being disloyal, fatuous, sanctimonious, disingenuous, mischievous, point-scoring and, worst of all, doing it through Liam instead of levelling your pathetic accusation directly at me. Now, if you've finished, will you please allow me to end this call so that I can go about my business?'

'You got custody. It's your job to go to fixtures,' he snapped.

'And, presumably, yours to snipe. Goodbye, Antonio.' She pushed the red button gratefully.

The conversation had taken less time than Jill had feared, so she got herself ready for the big task, which was to persuade Mabel, the yellow Labrador, that Maggie was just an old softie, who wanted more than anything to make friends with her.

One by one, she collected her charges and drove them round to Maggie's house. Then, hooking Maggie, via her lead, to the gatepost, she let the gang of four out of the Volvo. They were already on the path to the moor before Mabel even noticed the addition to the group of canine ramblers.

Happily, a distraction occurred, then, when a familiar, black BMW roared past them, making Jill smile, though not at its driver, who was equally unfriendly. Her amusement was at the personalised number plate. It was so typical of Tony Umberto Barstow and his impulsiveness to display his initials on his beloved BMW. It was also one occasion when his correct first initial would have been rather less embarrassing.

Returning to the task in hand, she said, 'Isn't it lovely to have a new walking mate, Mabel? You've been thinking of Maggie as a threat, and all this time she's wanted to be friends with you.'

Mabel merely continued to walk, looking anywhere but to her right, and telling herself repeatedly that the threat might be held at bay for as long as she could pretend the interloper didn't exist. Jill, on the other hand, was hopeful that the problem would be resolved by the end of the walk.

She pointed out various features to her companions: unusual cloud formations, the abundance of gorse flowers, and a miniature waterfall, knowing that her observations meant nothing to them, and that they were more than capable of noticing those things without her help, but also convinced that they found her voice friendly and reassuring. Steve had agreed that talking to dogs was a civilised thing to do, and civilised behaviour was always to be encouraged.

As usual, time seemed to pass quickly and, before long, they had to return. 'Time to go home, gang,' she told them.

Inevitably, the U-turn resulted in a disorganised 'maypole' effect as dogs exchanged places and leads became crossed, but there was no harm done; in fact, Jill was suddenly aware that the resultant confusion had led to a new and welcome development. Mabel was sniffing the ground, and Maggie had decided to investigate. The two dogs sniffed, first at the ground and then warily at each other. Before long, they were touching noses. Mabel wagged her tail and Maggie twitched her stump in a blissful *pas des queues*. Completely without incident, nature had intervened to eradicate fear and mistrust, leaving in its stead the unqualified friendship that is peculiar to animals.

Jill took them down the moor, stopping first to put the original four in the car while she let Maggie into her service room. On her return to the car, she found Mabel whining at being parted from her new-found friend.

———

Over the next week, she found that walking Maggie with the other four made it easier for her to pick up Jessica and get to Liam's match on time, even though the next one was to be played at Shawcroft High School, six miles away. For security, however, she still brought Maggie to the match.

In keeping with tradition and courtesy, the home side provided the referee, which meant that Mr Emsley could stand on the touchline. He naturally made his way, as soon as he could, to join Jill and Jessica, wincing at the first outburst of dissent.

'What's the f...in' ref f...in' fink he's f...in' doin'?'

'I really am sorry,' said Mr Emsley, leaving Jill's side to remonstrate with the speaker. 'Look,' he said, 'do you think you could moderate your language? There's a lady here and a little girl.'

'That's their f...in' fault for f...in comin' into a man's f...in' world. Who do you fink you're f...in' talkin' to, anyway? We're not kids at your f...in' school.'

The exchange might have developed into a full-scale altercation, had Jill not joined Mr Emsley with Maggie at her side. 'Tell him, Maggie,' she said.

Almost without warning, the sweet-natured Dobermann underwent a Jekyll and Hide transformation. She curled her lips back, showing her magnificent, white teeth, and emitted a snarl guaranteed to chill the marrow of the most determined touchline barracker.

He and his companions stepped back in alarm. With gratifying timidity, he asked, 'Why's your dog snarlin' at me?'

'You've upset her,' Jill told him. 'She can't abide foul language.'

The man stared at her, divided in his fear of the snarling beast and his disbelief that a dog could object to such a thing. He managed to ask, 'Does she bite?'

'Only when someone really upsets her or me, but control your temper and your language, and you'll probably leave this match in one piece.' Crouching beside Maggie, she said, 'It's all right, Maggie. He's going to behave himself and stop swearing.' The fact that he'd given no such undertaking mattered little, because Jill was confident of an abrupt change in his behaviour. Maggie responded by relaxing her curled lips and looking dotingly at Jill.

'I didn't mean nowt by it,' mumbled the man, moving down the line with his friends, who joined him in looking over their shoulders to convince themselves they weren't being followed.

'That was magnificent, Mrs Barstow,' said Mr Emsley. 'What a wonderful dog.'

'I'm Miss Warneford now.'

'I beg your pardon. I didn't know.'

'There's no need to apologise, You'd no way of knowing, and you're right. She's lovely, but she's not mine.'

'No?'

'No, I walk her when her mistress is at work. I just brought her today for insurance. I don't see why my little girl should have to hear that kind of language.'

'Neither do I, but does Maggie really object to swearing?' Clearly, he'd had little experience of dogs.

'I honestly don't think she can tell swearing from Shakespeare. She just does as I say. She's very docile, although, if someone tried to manhandle Jessica or me, she wouldn't wait for a word of command.'

Maggie might have needed reassurance, had she been at the dancing school that evening and seen Jill teaching the Ballroom Tango, with its staccato movements and unfamiliar figures. Steve was quite good, needing only a little help, but the others were learning it from scratch, so he partnered Jill in her demonstrations.

As they came to the end of the evening's session, she asked him, 'Do you really want to do this, Steve? I seem to spend more time with the beginners than with you.'

'Don't worry about me. I'm learning plenty, both from what you're teaching them and from dancing with you. In any case, I don't want to go next door and do Latin.'

'Don't you like Latin?' She preferred Ballroom, but she didn't want to influence him.

'Apart from the rhumba, not really. I'm more of a smoothie than a groovy.'

'Are you quite good at the rhumba? I mean, you're pretty good at everything we've tried so far.'

'That's kind of you. No, actually, I'm not very good at all. I suppose I should wait until Helen's doing the rhumba next door and join that one class.'

'You could do worse. Helen's superb at Latin.'

'Who's talking about me?' Helen's voice came from the passageway.

'Steve wants to do some work on his rhumba, and I told him you're the Latin queen around here.'

'In two weeks' time, Steve,' said Helen, switching off the light next door, 'we'll be doing the rhumba. Feel free to come and join us. Meanwhile, I have to kick you both out, because I need to lock up. I have to buy supper on the way home.'

Jill asked, 'Are you cooking take-away tonight?'

'How did you guess? Mike's working late, and he loves his Indian.' She locked the door. 'See you both next week. 'Bye.'

They stood on the path outside, and Steve said, 'Let me walk you to your car, Jill.'

'Thank you, Steve. I've never been better protected. I had Maggie looking out for me this afternoon.'

'What happened?'

'A minor disagreement at the football match.' She told him about the incident.

'Good old Maggie. It's shameful, though, that they behave like that.'

'It's the way they are, I'm afraid.' They stopped beside Jill's car.

'Jill,' he said quickly, as if he'd been nerving himself to mention something of importance, 'there's a dance at the Exchange on Easter Saturday. That's the twenty-second, I believe.'

'Yes, Easter's about as late as it can be, this year.' She knew what he was about to ask.

'It's a kind of ball to celebrate Easter time. I just wondered if you'd like to come.'

This time, she'd no need to hesitate. She knew he was trustworthy, so she said, 'Thank you, Steve. I'd love to come.'

'Wonderful. It's a black tie function, so you can wear your long gown.'

'Good, I need to get some wear out of it. Not too much, of course. I don't want people to think it's all I've got, but it was an investment, after all.' She unlocked her car and got in, noticing that Steve waited until she'd started her engine and was ready to set off. She waved as she left him, happy that she could accept an invitation without feeling uneasy.

When she arrived home, she found Gemma hard at work, as usual.

'Hi, Jill,' she said. 'Been teaching Steve again?'

'As it happens, yes.'

'Ooh.' The utterance was laced with innuendo.

'Don't tease, Gemma.'

'You can't afford to waste time at your age.'

'I'll have you know I haven't reached my sell-by date yet.'

Gemma saved her work and put the disc in her case. 'But has it crossed your mind,' she asked slyly, 'that you might have competition?'

'How can I have competition when I'm not making a play for him, or whatever you youngsters call it nowadays?'

She shook her head. 'No,' she said, 'we don't call it that.' She put her coat on and picked up her case.

Jill placed money on her palm and folded her fingers over it.

'It's too much, Jill,' she protested when she uncurled her fingers and saw the money.

'Not when you play a dual role.'

'What?'

'Childminder and matchmaker.'

Gemma grinned. 'It's a fair point. Thanks, Jill. 'Bye.'

''Bye, Gemma.'

A bottle of wine stood opened in the kitchen, so Jill unscrewed the cap and poured herself a glass.

Reading Uncle Maurice's letters had become a late-night habit, and she found her glasses and picked up the one she'd been reading. She studied it again to see if she could make sense of it.

As far as your parents are concerned, I really don't think you've any need to reproach yourself. When someone's experienced what you have, that sort of reaction is only natural. I really think you should put it behind you.

I'm glad you got the stuff all right. Of course I don't mind you sharing the booty with the others. There's plenty where they came from, anyway, and I can get you some more when I take Bossington's Tax Return to be signed. Incidentally, was the damage out of sight, as they'd described it? I hope so. As I told you earlier, being a humble male, I don't understand the technicalities.

Another thing I'm struggling with is getting you to accept that you're not denying me anything. It really is so low on my list of priorities as to be of no importance whatsoever, and no, I'm not waiting patiently, as you suspect, for everything to come together. Please disabuse yourself of that idea, and let's continue to meet on the same basis as we have in the past.

Speaking of meeting, are you free for the Cricket Club Dinner on the 27th, or does it clash with your shift rota? Don't worry if you can't do it, but if you can, it will be wonderful. The venue and the band are both excellent.

Please bear in mind all I've said. I don't dispense wisdom lightly!
I look forward, as always, to seeing you again.
Yours with very great affection,
Maurice.

It still made no sense. She'd had a disagreement with her parents. Well, who hadn't done that at some time? Also, he'd sent her something that she'd shared with, presumably, her fellow nurses. The reference to being a humble male possibly suggested feminine clothing of some kind. The next paragraph was more cryptic than the *Times* crossword, although she realised it was unintentional. Finally, he seemed to want her to join him at a dinner that involved dancing. She couldn't blame him for that. She just wished she could unravel the rest of the letter.

20

July 1946

Disclosure

The stockings, described as 'slight seconds', that Maurice had sent in the post proved to be a blessing. In addition to making life easier and less expensive for Iris and the others on her shift, they had been found to possess bargaining power. Now that the shift was on nights, they had enabled her to swap nights off with Gladys Fox and make arrangements to go to the Cricket Club dinner.

That was one difficulty averted. Another had already occurred, and Iris was feeling a mixture of guilt and resentment because of it. Her visit home should have been pleasant for them all, and she should have returned to the hospital satisfied that she'd left her parents assured that she was in good health and happy in her chosen profession. Instead, a moment of tension had led to a disclosure that had shocked both her parents and created the worst possible situation at home.

The incident had arisen, as usual, from her mother's inability to abandon the subject of matrimony in general, and Maurice in particular, despite several diplomatic attempts on her father's part to change the subject under discussion.

'For the umpteenth time,' said Iris, 'marriage is not on the cards, with Maurice or anyone else.'

'You keep saying that,' insisted her mother, 'but you won't say why. What is the matter with you, girl?'

'This is doing no good at all,' said her father. 'When Iris comes home, it should be a happy time, not an occasion for argument and unpleasantness.'

'I simply want to know why she's adopted this silly attitude.'

They'd gone over the same ground so many times that Iris felt herself about to explode. It was inconceivable that her mother was so blinkered that she was unable to form her own conclusion. 'Do I have to spell it out? Did you really expect me to return from the savagery and brutality of Malaya completely undamaged?'

With her voice now risen with anger, her mother demanded, 'What damage are you talking about, for goodness' sake? We know you were half-starved, but your weight's back to normal, now.'

Iris was controlling her temper with difficulty. She said levelly, 'I'm talking about gratuitous cruelty and bestial behaviour on the part of the guards, and the fact that I can never have an intimate relationship with a man.'

'And this,' said her father, 'is where the conversation really must end.'

'For heaven's sake,' said her mother, ignoring him completely, 'by all the laws, we should bear a grudge against the Japanese for holding you captive, but we've managed to get over that. Why can't you?'

'Oh, you've got over it, have you?' Iris could restrain herself no longer. 'Well done, you,' she shouted, with tears of anger now flowing unchecked, 'but then, they didn't bloody-well rape you, did they?'

Just for a moment, there was silence. Her father's eyes were closed tightly, registering pain and realisation, as if he'd suspected the worst for some time, as it was likely he had. Her mother's expression was simply one of horror. Eventually and as if in slow motion, her face crumpled, and she gave way to a series of great, tearing sobs. With two women in acute distress and himself in shock, her father was confused, divided and helpless.

Eventually, her mother was able to speak. 'You've... never said any...thing about it,' she said.

'I was trying to spare you the horror. Even so, I thought you might have worked it out for yourself.'

'I never... thought,' she sobbed. 'I mean, there are... rules of war....'

'For some reason, the Japanese weren't terribly impressed with the Geneva Convention. I really don't know why.' Having recovered from her outburst, Iris was feeling some remorse at having done what she'd tried for so long to avoid, and she also felt concern for her mother. Whilst her obtuseness had prompted the disclosure, it had naturally come to her as a colossal shock. 'I'm sorry,' she said. 'I really didn't mean to tell you about that, but you just wouldn't leave the subject alone, and the words were out before I could stop them.'

'Those *fiends*,' said her father in a strangled whisper. 'There's no punishment fit for them.'

'They were all barbaric, but my experience was with one officer in particular, and he was hanged for his crimes a few weeks ago. I read about it in the *Times*.' She'd actually cut out the report and put it in her Pahang box, although, in retrospect, she didn't know why.

'It was too good for him. I've wondered, sometimes,' said her father, 'about the bombing of Hiroshima and Nagasaki, and the only wrong I can see is that they bombed innocent civilians and not the evil savages who did that to you.'

'It was only one man, Dad, and I really have to disagree with you about the bombing.' As she spoke, she reached across to her mother and took her hand. 'I hated and despised the Japs and Koreans who guarded us, but revenge killing solves nothing in the long term, and that's all capital punishment amounts to.'

'We each have our own ideas,' said her father, moving to the sofa to sit beside her, 'and it's wonderful, in a way, that you can take that line, but I'm glad, speaking for myself, that they hanged him.'

'What a mercy,' said her mother, recovering from her initial shock.

'What was a mercy, Mum?'

'I was going to say what a mercy it was that you didn't become pregnant by that monster. If you'd had to bear his horrible—'

'That was never on the cards, although I spent far too long worrying about it before I realised I couldn't become pregnant. The fact is that hunger on the scale we knew it causes ovulation to stop, so I suppose it was a mercy, as you said.'

'I want you to know, Iris,' said her father, 'that, when you're ready to see a doctor about this business, one who can help you with the devastating long-term effects, cost won't be a problem.'

'I know, Dad, and I'm grateful, but what can a psychiatrist do? He can't change history so that it never happened, and he certainly can't turn me back into the virgin I was when I was interned. No, the healing has to come from inside, from me, and I think I've made a start with my work at the hospital.'

———

When Maurice arrived at the Nurses' Home, he found a friendly receptionist on duty. This was in stark contrast to the harridan he'd met the first time. Once he'd explained the nature of his visit, she was even welcoming, inviting him to take a seat while he waited.

Iris came downstairs in an emerald-green chiffon gown that found him temporarily and unusually stumped for an adequate compliment. In the end, he said, 'Iris, you look exquisite.'

'Thank you. You cut quite a dash, yourself.'

'It's only evening dress,' he told her.

'But very smart indeed.'

'Thank you, Iris.'

'Did I tell you,' she asked, taking his arm, 'that I have an extension tonight? I don't need to be back until midnight.'

'How very appropriate.' Leaning confidentially towards her, he asked, 'Will that wonderful gown turn back into rags if you're late?'

'No, but I'll turn into a nurse standing in Sister's office and receiving the wigging to put all previous ones to shame.'

'Good,' he said, unlocking the car. 'I'd be horrified to be left holding a glass slipper.'

'You do talk nonsense.' She gathered her skirts so that he could close the door. 'I'll let you into a secret,' she said when he joined her in the car. 'This gown is borrowed for the occasion. Suffice it to say that stockings changed hands as part of the transaction, so thank you for that.'

'I'm glad they've been useful.' He started the engine and drove off. 'Is the damage as superficial as I was told?'

'It's hardly noticeable and well out of sight. Most of them have an imperfection in the welt, that's all.'

'Oh, good.' He hadn't a clue what the welt was, but he felt it might be indelicate of him to ask, especially as it was a part that was out of sight and therefore most likely private. Instead, he asked, 'Have you heard from home recently?'

'I've had a reply to my letter. Needless to say, my mother's playing the victim. It seems to have escaped her notice that the part was cast some time ago. Still, it must have been horrible for them both.'

'I imagine your father would be as shocked as she was.'

'He was horrified, although he'd already guessed something of the kind.'

He reached across briefly to touch her hand. 'Poor Iris. It wasn't your fault.'

'I should have been able to control my temper.'

'The fact that I can't begin to imagine you losing your temper only demonstrates the kind of stress you must have been feeling.'

'Honestly, Maurice,' she said, laughing, 'with your ability to work up a defence at a moment's notice, you should have been a lawyer.'

'I can only do it for you. I'd be hopeless at representing anyone else. If you don't believe me, ask the Inspector of Taxes.'

'I don't believe a word of it, and I'd rather steer clear of the Tax Office.'

'Very wise, too.'

'Tell me about tonight,' she suggested.

'Okay.' He was happy to do that. 'We'll be entertained by the Sherwood Forest Minstrels under the leadership of Mark Ridgeway, and they're very good.'

'Couldn't Robin Hood make it?'

'No, he doesn't do gigs. Don't breathe a word, but I have it on good authority that he's tone deaf.'

'Really?'

'I'm told he can't carry a tune in a quiver,' he said, pulling into the carpark, which was already filling up.

'I've never been to a cricket club dinner,' she said, 'so I don't really know what to expect.'

'It's not the annual dinner,' he told her, 'so there won't be the usual things.'

'What are the usual things?'

He switched off the engine and gave her his full attention. 'At the annual bunfight, which takes place each summer, there's the presentation of trophies, usually by a guest player from the County Club, and then he gives a talk about what it's like to play alongside the likes of Bill Voce and Ramsay Cox – I don't suppose they talk about Harold Larwood, now he's retired – and then everyone carries on drinking and so on.'

'What makes this one different?'

'It's just a get-together with dinner and dancing.' He got out to open her door.

'I see. Do such functions happen often?'

'Before the war, we had three or four each year. I imagine it's much the same, now. Dance bands are expensive, of course, but Mark Ridgeway is very flexible. He's an old school chum of our chairman, who's a dedicated terpsichorean.'

'Wouldn't they have him in the Freemasons?'

'No,' he explained, 'terpsichorean—'

She laughed. 'I know what it means.'

'Your sense of humour's returning,' he observed, offering her his arm to take her into the hall.

'It's had a long rest, but it should soon be back to normal.' Her smile was encouraging.

Maurice showed the tickets to the man on the door and then introduced Iris to the Chairman and his wife.

'This is the lady who dispensed first aid when Bill Staveley was injured in the match against Northcoate,' the Chairman told his wife.

'It was a blessing you were there,' she said.

'I don't know. He had to go to hospital, anyway, so I didn't do an awful lot.'

'You used your knowledge and training,' said the Chairman, 'and they're invaluable.'

'I was glad to help,' she assured him. As they moved on, she said, 'I wonder if Bill Staveley will be here tonight. A plastered arm's quite an impediment where dancing's concerned.'

'It'll take more than a broken elbow to stop me.' Bill's voice came from behind her, and she turned to speak to him.

'Hello,' she said, 'how are you coping?' His plastered arm was in a sling, and the left sleeve of his dinner jacket had been pinned up neatly.

'I'll be all right, thanks, duck. You did well sending for t' ambulance. This lot were all for makin' me carry on.'

'That's right,' said Maurice, 'it's not a game for softies.'

'Don't be rotten.' Iris gave him a playful push.

'He'd better not be,' said Bill. 'Here's my other half come to stick up for me.' He introduced Iris to his wife, who was as grateful as he was for her intervention at the match.

Soon, it was time for them to go to their places. Iris already knew some of their neighbours from the match against Northcoate, and Maurice introduced the others. During this time, the band played soft, unintrusive music, leaving no one in any doubt about the ability of its musicians.

Towards the end of the meal, Iris said, 'I'm looking forward to the dancing. I wonder how many people can claim to have danced to a band named after Sherwood Forest.'

'It doesn't just take its name from the forest,' Maurice told her.

'Doesn't it?'

'Most of them have served in the Sherwood Foresters. It's the local army regiment.'

'I know. I came back from Australia in the hospital ship with some of them,' she said, 'the survivors.'

Maurice nodded but said nothing. It seemed that there were reminders everywhere, and he was relieved when the bandleader announced the waltz: 'Deep in my Heart, Dear'. It was an old standard that was unlikely to evoke unpleasant memories. He asked, 'Shall we?'

'Let's.' Keen as ever, Iris accompanied him on to the floor, and they joined the others in the first dance of the evening.

After a while, she said, 'You're getting quite good at the waltz.'

'Thank you.' He waited for her to add a qualifying comment, but her generosity continued.

'You're improving at everything.'

'Thank you, Iris, but are you surprised? It's all happened under your tutelage, when all's done and said.'

'I know, but I thought you'd like to hear it, all the same.'

'Keep whispering compliments in my ear. No, I'll change that. Just keep whispering in my ear.'

'You're daft, Maurice, but don't change, whatever you do.'

He responded by kissing her lightly on the curve where her neck met her shoulder. Conscious of a reaction, he asked, 'Are you all right?'

'Yes, I'm fine.' She laughed nervously. 'I wasn't expecting it, that's all.'

That seemingly insignificant moment was more important to her than he imagined, because she referred to it again as they sat down.

'You must think I'm like a frightened little girl,' she said.

'Why on earth would I think that?'

'The way I behaved just then. You see, believe it or not, for all my twenty-seven years, I've had very little experience of men.'

'It's hardly surprising.'

'No,' she said, touching his arm in her desire to be understood, 'not just because of the war. You see, between school and the war, all the time I was training I had very little social life. I worked hard to gain the best possible marks, and then, when I was shipped out to Malaya, I found myself over-faced by the whole thing and completely unequal to it.'

'Do you mean men?'

'Yes.'

It seemed that it was very important for him to understand, and then, when he thought about it, it occurred to him that it very likely was. 'I'm not conscious of anything untoward,' he told her honestly.

'You surprise me.'

'Even so.'

'As a nurse in Malaya,' she went on, 'I met civil servants, doctors and army officers, and I felt out of my depth with all of them. Parties and dances were a time of awkwardness, because, whilst I danced with men, I couldn't spend time with them elsewhere. At least, I did on one occasion, and it was quite embarrassing, probably for both of us.'

In the absence of anything to say, he took her hand and held it.

The bandleader announced a foxtrot: 'Embraceable You', and she seized the opportunity to change the subject, saying, 'This is one of my favourite songs. Shall we dance?'

As he took her in hold, she said, 'I'm sorry I bombarded you with all that. None of it's your fault, and I'd no right.'

'You've all the right in the world if something troubles you, as that obviously does.'

'I don't think I explained it very well.'

'All I can say is that I've never been conscious of the thing you mentioned, and I don't feel at all threatened, put off, short-changed or in any way denied, so please set your mind at rest and enjoy the music.'

She must have taken him at his word, because they danced the rest of the number without speaking.

In what seemed a very short time, Iris looked at her watch and grimaced.

'Time to go?'

'I'm afraid so.'

'Okay, let's race the magic spell.'

They took their leave of everyone around them and collected their hats and coats. Stepping out into the carpark, Iris said, 'I hope I didn't spoil your evening with my histrionics.'

'Don't be silly. You know you're watertight as far as I'm concerned.'

'What does that mean?'

'It means that you can do no wrong.' He unlocked the car and opened the door for her.

'You put up with an awful lot, Maurice,' she said, arranging her skirts.

They'd left the carpark and were on the main road when she said, 'The reason I told you all that was because I feel I'm somehow cheating you.'

'I'm sorry, I don't follow you.'

She hesitated, and said, 'We've already established that... the ultimate... isn't possible, but I feel as if I'm giving you nothing else.'

He was beginning to understand. 'Iris,' he said, 'would you mind telling me what happened on that occasion you found so embarrassing?'

'It's going to sound ridiculous.'

'We're talking about a serious matter, so I don't see how it can be ridiculous.'

'Okay, you asked me.' She seemed to brace herself and then she said, 'I met a man, a junior army officer, at a dance. He asked me to join him outside, on the veranda, to enjoy the scent of the bougainvillea, he said, and I agreed. I was very naïve.' Clearly embarrassed, she hesitated again.

'You're doing fine,' he said. 'Go on.'

'He tried to kiss me.'

'I thought he might.'

'Well, as I said, I was naïve.'

'There's nothing wrong with that.'

With an effort, she said, 'I didn't know what to do. I'd never been kissed on the mouth before, and I hadn't a clue how to respond. I suppose I'd kissed relations in the usual way, but that was all.' She stopped and said, 'I told you it was ridiculous.'

'You'll have to tell me again, because I don't find it at all ridiculous. If I feel anything, it's a sense of tragedy.'

'What do you mean?'

He negotiated a right-hand junction before answering. 'Basically,' he said, 'I'm referring to your inexperience, and I mean the kind you've just described as well as the terrible thing you suffered as an internee. That's the tragedy.' He took one hand off the wheel and reached for hers. 'There's nothing ridiculous about being a victim.' He felt a tear fall on to his hand. 'As we've time in hand,' he suggested, 'we'll stop at my place, and you can freshen up.'

She sniffed, so he passed her the handkerchief from his top pocket. 'Thank you.'

He drove the short distance to his flat and let her in, pointing the way to the bathroom.

Five minutes later, she emerged, washed and with her make-up re-applied. 'I must still look a sight,' she said.

'A sight for sore eyes, and you'll never be less than exquisite in mine,' he assured her.

She smiled weakly. 'We'd better be going.'

'Yes, we're okay for time, but let's go.'

She was quiet on the way to the hospital, and he respected her silence until they were one street away from their destination, when he drew up at the kerbside.

She asked, 'Why have we stopped here?'

Instead of replying, he kissed her cheek, moving gently and naturally to her lips. Her surprise was evident, although she made no objection, but allowed him to explore them softly and insistently until, almost of their own accord, they parted. In a very short time, he felt her respond freely, mirroring his movements with new eagerness. And so it went on until mundane considerations intervened, and she remembered the time.

'I must go now,' she said with discernible regret.

'Okay.' The dashboard clock showed that it was only a few minutes to midnight. 'I'll drive you round the corner.' He took her to the entrance by the cedar tree and, having parked, opened her door and offered her his hand to help her out. 'Goodnight,' he said.

'Goodnight, Maurice, and thank you for a lovely evening.' Quite unself-consciously, she kissed him and went inside. When he looked at the dashboard clock, it showed one minute to midnight.

21

Sacrifice

When Jill arrived at Maggie's house, there was a car in the drive. The door to the service room was unlocked, so she pushed it open and called, 'Anyone at home?'

Maggie was ready to greet whichever of her owners it was. Her ears were up and her stump was wagging. It wagged even harder when Clare came into the service room, visibly pregnant and very emotional.

'Clare,' said Jill, 'what's the matter?'

'It's Lee, my husband. He wants rid of Maggie because of the baby.' Quite unnecessarily, she stopped stroking Maggie to point to the evidence.

'But Maggie's harmless, Clare.' She hadn't told her about the touchline incident, or the fact that she'd just returned from the home playing field, where the language was now fit even for the most fastidious and sensitive company. Even so, she knew that Maggie would never hurt a child.

'It's not that, Jill. He just doesn't think it's healthy for a baby to grow up in a house where there's animals.' She took a tissue from her pocket and blew her nose. 'He was keen enough to pay a small fortune for Maggie, but now he wants her to go to the Dobermann rescue place.'

'Incredible.'

'He has these crazes, you see, and they never last. He left it to me to take her to training classes and arrange for you to look after her when we were both at work, but he lost interest in her long ago, when she turned out to be faithful and affectionate.' Bitterly, she said, 'He's like a child when it gets a new toy. His latest is his new Audi.'

'I see.' Not surprisingly, that last piece of information evoked further sympathy from Jill, who could only hope his enthusiasm for the baby would turn out to be more lasting. She asked, 'Is he determined to let her go?'

'Yes, he wants me to take her to the rescue home at the weekend.'

'Don't do that, Clare.' The decision was easy enough to make. 'If he lets me take her, she'll have a loving, responsible home with all the exercise she needs, and you'll be able to come and see her whenever she's around.'

The offer provoked further tears, but it was soon evident that they were the product of relief and surprise. 'Would you really do that, Jill? He's not asking anything for her. He's so hung up about the baby, he just wants her to go.'

'It's as well that he isn't. I'm not exactly rolling in cash.'

'I'll tell him tonight, when he comes home and before he goes to the pub.' Crouching again with some difficulty, she stroked Maggie. 'You're going to have a new mum,' she told her with a mixture of fondness and sadness.

'And that's not all.' Jill remembered that the children were waiting outside, although they wouldn't mind when she told them about Maggie. Meanwhile, good manners prompted her to ask, 'When's the baby due, Clare?'

'Two months. It's a boy. That's why Lee's making such a fuss. He can't wait to buy him his first pair of football boots.'

It was comforting to know that there was at least one man who made Tony look grown up and responsible. 'Well,' she said, 'I hope it all goes well. Give me a ring when you've spoken to him. I shan't tell the children until we're sure.'

It was almost six o' clock when Clare phoned.

'I've spoken to him,' she said, 'and he's okay with it.'

'Good. It's much better this way, Clare. I'm sure the rescue people would have found her a good home eventually, but it would have taken time, and she'd have been caged at night.'

'She would, and she already knows you, as well.' Clare was sounding more settled already.

'How do you want to do the handing over?' It had to be Clare's decision.

'If you don't mind, I'd like to bring her over to you and see her in her new home. It'll be better than you just taking her to your house after a walk, and then me coming home to find her gone. I couldn't bear that.'

'All right. When do you want to do it?'

'Is Saturday morning okay?'

'It's probably the best time for me, Clare. I take Jessica to her ballet class, and Liam's started football practice as well, so I'll drop them off and be back here for about nine-thirty.'

'That works well for me, too.'

'There's just one thing I'd ask, and that's for your husband's signature on a statement that he's transferring ownership of Maggie to me. I'll type it and drop it in tomorrow when I take her for a walk, and then you can bring it on Saturday.' In dealing with a capricious and childlike anomaly such as Lee, she couldn't be too careful.

'I'll see that he signs it.'

'Good. I'll get the children together and tell them.'

'That'll be nice. 'Bye, Jill.'

''Bye, Clare, and don't worry. She'll be fine with me.'

As she put her mobile down, she heard footsteps on the stairs. A second later, Liam came into the room. 'What was that about Maggie, Mum?'

'Were you eavesdropping, Liam?'

'I don't know.'

'Listening when you shouldn't,' she translated.

'Yes, but I couldn't understand what it was about.'

At least he was honest. 'Homework all done?'

'Yes.'

'Football kit in the basket?'

With a sigh, he turned again towards the stairs.

'While you're up there, will you ask Jessica to come down as well?'

'What for?'

'A family meeting. Off you go and ask her to come down.'

She waited until they were both down, and was about to speak, when Liam asked, 'Do you need us to help you decide about something?'

'No, thank you. I'm not quite as senile as that. I've called you both to ask you what you think would make this house an even happier home than it is.'

Without hesitation, Liam said, 'A telly with a four-foot screen.'

Jill shook her head. 'That would be far too big for this room,' she said, 'and it would the focus of disagreement.'

'Why?'

'Because you'd want to watch football all the time.' Turning to Jessica, she said, 'Your turn, Jessica.'

'A dog.'

Jill turned again to Liam with a look of enquiry. 'A dog, Liam. What do you think about that?'

'Is it about Maggie? Is that what you were talking about on the phone?'

'When you shouldn't have been listening, yes.' Trust an adolescent, she thought, to spoil the surprise. 'Maggie is coming to live with us.'

'Yay!'

'I thought you'd be pleased, Jessica.'

'I am, too, but why is she coming here?'

'Clare's going to have a baby—'

'Yergh!'

'You've just committed two offences in one, Liam.'

Indignantly, he asked, 'What have I done?'

'You interrupted me very rudely to rubbish the very essence of motherhood. Don't do it again. May I continue?'

'Yes, but—'

Jill held up her hand to forestall him. 'Clare's husband doesn't want his little boy to grow up with an animal in the house. He thinks it would be unhygienic, so Maggie has to move house.'

Liam raised his hand.

'Yes, Liam?'

'I'm doing this,' he said in his long-suffering way, 'so that I don't get done for interrupting.'

'I always knew there was hope for you. What do you want to say?'

'Why can't somebody invent a better way of having babies?'

The idea made Jill smile. 'I think a few women might have wondered that at various times, Liam, but mainly in the latter stages.' She pondered the question briefly. 'I suppose they could be delivered in large, cardboard boxes by Amazon, or maybe we could start breeding storks.' Suddenly, she patted the arm of her chair and said, 'I've got it. We could plant mulberry bushes everywhere and solve three problems in one go. It would combat global deforestation, increase silk production and, at the same time, make the dream of painless and hassle-free childbirth a reality.'

Jessica had found a book on dog training and was studying that as an alternative to listening to one of Liam's interminable arguments.

'You're just being daft, Mum. I'm only saying that birds lay eggs all the time, and you don't hear them complain.'

'Except pigeons.'

'What do pigeons do?'

'They grumble and moan from morning 'til night. Moan, moan, moan. They never stop.'

Liam looked doubtful. 'How do you know they're complaining? For all you know, they might be squawking about something completely different, like the weather or something.'

'You're forgetting,' said Jill with theatrical archness, 'that I studied English at university.'

'What's that got to do with it?'

'I studied Old English, Middle English, Modern English and Pidgin English. That's how I know what they're saying.'

Liam's expression changed from disbelief to disgust. 'You never argue properly, Mum,' he said. 'You always say something like that.'

'And I always win,' she said, smiling. 'Don't forget that.'

———

She was walking the gang of five when she met Steve. 'Hello, Steve,' she said. 'Are you formulating an argument or bringing everything together in a concise and telling conclusion?'

'Neither. I looked out of the window at this cloudless sky, and a little voice whispered, "Go out and enjoy it, Steve. That's what it's there for. Work can wait for a couple of hours." I couldn't very well argue with that, could I? What's new with you?'

'The pitter-patter of tiny footsteps, an addition to the household.'

He accepted the information with a straight face, saying simply, 'You've kept very quiet about it.'

'I didn't know until last evening. Shall we walk together?'

'Why not?'

'Maggie is coming to live with us. Her master, who is immature, fickle, fanciful and a man of scant intellect, wants her to find a new permanent address, thus leaving the house fit for his as-yet-unborn baby to inhabit, free from the menace of tapeworm, parvovirus and every other known canine disorder. She was to have gone to a place that rescues the unwanted waifs of her breed, but I wouldn't hear of it.'

'Oh, good for you, Jill.' It was clear that he meant it.

'Maggie knows nothing about it, you understand. It'll come as a surprise on Saturday morning, when she arrives at my house and her bed materialises in the....' She stopped and said, 'I really haven't given any thought to where her bed's going to go, and it's a tiny cottage, as you know.'

'I imagine you've been concentrating on the more abstract aspects of the development.'

She looked at him in genuine surprise. 'You know,' she said, 'you're absolutely right.'

'Someone has to ponder the psychological implications of re-homing a sensitive animal, and why not you, Jill?'

Recognising the name of one of her favourite people, Maggie turned to look at her human companions, and then, satisfied that Jill was still there, continued on her way.

'Speaking of psychological implications,' said Steve, 'how are you progressing with your Uncle's letters?'

'Not at all, really.'

'Oh?'

'I've reached another brain-teaser,' she confessed. 'If only he'd kept my aunt's letters, I might have had something approaching a full picture, but there's no sign of anything from her.'

'It's difficult,' he agreed. 'What's the latest conundrum?'

'What a lovely word.' It was one of those words that were seldom heard outside *Countdown*, which tended to specialise in dated and unusual language. 'I haven't got the letter with me, so I can't quote it *verbatim*,' she said, 'but it was something about a suggestion he'd put to her, that seemed not to have earned her total agreement. From his side of it, though, which is admittedly the only side I know, it must have been quite important.'

'At the risk of sounding like Sherlock Holmes,' he said, 'you could try listing the evidence, everything you know about their relationship. Then, if you list everything you want to know, you can compare the two and make what connections you can between them.' He added, 'As ever, I'm happy to offer what help I can.'

'You're very kind, Steve.'

'I just enjoy a mystery.' They walked a little further, and he asked, 'Did you arrive at any conclusion regarding the business of your aunt's mother and the reference to clothing?'

'Yes, I did.' It was a pleasant change to be able to talk about solutions, however hypothetical. 'I can only imagine that the disagreement with her mother was connected with her experience in Malaya. I remember my uncle describing her mother as insensitive and less than diplomatic.' Recalling the rest of the letter, she said, 'I looked up Bossington's and found that they used to manufacture nylon stockings. They were bought out in nineteen forty-eight, and the name disappeared, but I now know that he supplied her with stockings that were slight seconds. I imagine any stockings would be precious during clothes rationing.'

'Well done, Jill.'

'Thank you. I can only surmise that the other mystery was about her attitude towards men. To put it bluntly, I think she was saying that she could never have a full relationship with him.'

'Ah.'

'Yes, I'm inclined to agree with you that her experiences in Malaya left her with a horror of sexual intimacy.' She'd discovered something else, as well, among her aunt's bits and pieces. It was a newspaper cutting about some war crimes trials held in Tokyo, but the details were too awful to imagine, let alone discuss.

Clare arrived on Saturday morning with Maggie, her bed and the document typed by Jill and signed by Lee. For Clare, it was always bound to be a tearful parting, although Maggie seemed unfazed by the proceedings. The children were naturally excited and happy to help Jill take her for long walks on the moor, only being parted from her when they went to bed. Possibly thankful for the respite from the excitement, she lay contentedly beside Jill's feet while, for her part, Jill re-examined what Steve had called the conundrum.

Regarding my suggestion, which, I'll admit, must have come as a surprise to you, let's not react too hastily. I didn't intend to put you on the spot, but rather to offer it as something to consider. You feel that it would cause tension between us, but I disagree. There are far more important aspects to a relationship; in fact, as stumbling blocks go, it's positively insignificant. I shan't labour the point. Instead, I'll leave you to reflect on it in your own time.

The words, *There are far more important aspects to a relationship* seemed to stand out from the rest of the paragraph, and she wondered why it hadn't registered earlier. Unless she was missing something equally dramatic, he was offering her the ultimate act of generosity.

22

A Malignant Bond

Iris waited for Maurice to join Mansfield Road, and asked, 'Where are we going?'

'Newark Town Hall, to a piano recital.'

'Oh, good. Who's playing?'

'Moura Lympany. It's a programme of Romantic music, mainly Chopin, Schumann and Liszt.'

'Wonderful.' Eyeing him speculatively, she said, 'You sound very well-informed.'

'I've been reading the programme,' he admitted. Changing the subject, he said, 'You look very fetching in that dress. Green looks perfect on you.'

'Thank you. You've probably seen the extent of my wardrobe, now.'

'And highly impressed I am, too.' After a short spell, he said, 'It was good that you managed to change your night-off again.'

'Ah, this time I was the one doing it as a favour, but it worked out to our advantage, so I was happy to do it.'

He thought of recent events and said, 'Favours seem to abound in your job.'

'We're a close-knit society. I suppose we depend on each other's co-operation and goodwill.' She added as an afterthought, 'Moral support is important, as well.'

'That sounded as if it came straight from the soul.'

'You're very astute, Maurice.'

'Are you going to spill the beans?'

'All right.' She paused, possibly wondering how to start, and then she said, 'We try not to become emotionally involved with patients, but we're only human.'

'Fortunately.'

'I suppose so, but it's hard to see a child suffering.'

He said nothing, but waited for her to continue.

'A little girl was brought in with mastoiditis. That's caused by an infection of the mastoid bone behind the ear. Nowadays, we have penicillin, which is a big step forward, but it involves very painful injections, and it doesn't always work. Last night, one of the ear, nose and throat surgeons had to take away part of the mastoid bone to drain it.'

'Will she be all right?'

'I hope so.'

He reached for her hand and squeezed it, saying, 'You'd be a poor sort of human being if you didn't occasionally take things to heart.'

'Occasionally, yes.'

'Use this evening as a hiding place,' he suggested.

'Escapism?'

'That's right.' He shrugged. 'I just couldn't think of the word.'

'You're amazing, Maurice.'

'It's good to hear you say it, but what led you to that conclusion?'

Instead of answering immediately, she waited until they'd crossed a busy crossroads. It was as if she wanted to be sure he would hear what she had to tell him. 'It's the way you put your finger on things that are troubling me,' she said eventually. 'You don't need me to tell you anything. You just know these things.'

'It's not so surprising,' he said. 'It's because I care for you as much as I do, and I usually know how you're going to react. I say, "usually" because there have been times when I've been wrong, but there haven't been all that many.'

She made no reply, but what might have become an awkward silence was conveniently averted when Maurice parked at the roadside outside the Prior Inn. 'This is where we're eating,' he said. 'We've plenty of time.'

'You spoil me to death, Maurice,' she said as he opened her door and helped her out.

'I really don't know why you're complaining. Most women I've known would jump at a chance to be spoiled. Some have even been known to demand it.'

'I know the type,' she said, walking into the restaurant with him.

When they were seated at their table, she ran her fingers over the linen tablecloth and said, 'Every time I come to a place like this, I have to remind myself, just for a second, that it's real, and then everything falls into place.'

'Even now?'

'I can't imagine a time when I'll take it for granted.'

When they'd given the waiter their order, Maurice said, 'You need a bollard.'

'What on earth do you mean?'

'You once told me you'd taken part in a production of *Ruddigore*.'

'Yes, we did it at school. It was an all-girl production, and I was Mad Margaret.'

'I know. You told me, but do you remember the bit in Act Two, when she's recovering from her madness? Every now and again, she lapses into her old self and has to grasp reality by saying—'

' "Basingstoke". Yes, I remember it.'

'That was her bollard. I'm not saying you're bonkers – perish the thought – but you need a bollard to remind yourself that it's nineteen forty-six and the war's over.'

The idea seemed to amuse her, but then she said, 'I can't think of one. What brings you face-to-face with reality?'

Without hesitation, he said, 'Income Tax. It works for me in both personal and professional contexts.'

'No,' she said after some deliberation, 'it doesn't work for me. I'd be using one horror to escape another.'

'Agreed. Maybe you can think of one that works better.'

Stroking the tablecloth again, she said suddenly, 'Clean linen. Yes, it's a fact of everyday life and it's also a symbol of civilised behaviour.'

'Well done. If it works for you, that's all that matters.'

'Mm.' She looked at him strangely and asked, 'What made you call it a bollard? What is a bollard, anyway?'

'It's a mooring post for ships. It's fixed very solidly into the ground, so it's a safe thing to hang on to.'

She nodded. 'It works for me. Your ship was my first glimpse of freedom, and I couldn't believe it when you tied it to the wooden thing on the riverbank.' Uncertainly, she asked, 'Was that a bollard?'

Reluctant to spoil the memory, he stretched a point and said, 'It was a kind of bollard.'

———

The recital was all they'd expected. The programme was a mixture of the familiar and unfamiliar, and Moura Lympany played everything with her customary brilliance, ending her performance with two dazzling encores. In his capacity as an accountant, Maurice might have been expected to call it money well spent, but his values were set, as ever, on a higher plane, and Iris evidently shared them.

'That was truly wonderful,' she said as they returned to the car.

'And enjoyed in the right company.'

'Of course.' She said it without conviction.

As they drove off, she asked, 'Are you playing cricket tomorrow?'

'Weather permitting, and the forecast is good.'

'Where are you playing?'

'At home.' Unusually, he didn't want to talk about cricket. He had something entirely different on his mind, and she seemed to sense that, because she was obviously trying to encourage harmless conversation as a sidestepping tactic.

'Cricket's a big part of your life, isn't it?'

'Yes, it is, but so are you.' There, he'd managed to dodge the small-talk.

Her response was immediate. 'I mustn't be, Maurice,' she told him firmly.

'Too late. You already are.'

'But you know how things stand. We've spoken about it often enough.'

'Yes, I do, and I respect your feelings.'

In the darkened interior of the car, she was clearly shaking her head slowly in frustration. 'This conversation is going round in circles,' she said.

'No, it's not. Let me tell you something, Iris. There's a couple in the village where my parents live, who were married before the First War. He enlisted, like so many others, and he was badly injured in France. Against all the odds, he survived and returned to Blighty, but he was no longer able, because of his injury, to… well, to function in the bedroom.'

'How awful for him.' She corrected herself quickly. 'For them both.'

'Ah, well, that's the point, because they're still happily married. Nothing physical has happened between them since he was last able-bodied and on leave, but they're still as devoted to each other as they were before his injury.'

She appeared to digest the information, but then asked, 'What are you saying, Maurice? That it would be equally unimportant for us? You're forgetting one important thing. I mean, I imagine his injury ensures that he doesn't feel the normal urge. You would, and it wouldn't be long before you found yourself resenting the fact that…. You know what I'm saying, don't you? It would create tension between us that would destroy everything.'

'I don't agree, Iris. I'd be going into it with my eyes wide open, knowing that I'd waived any conjugal rights.'

Apparently baffled, she asked, 'But why, when you could marry someone else and have everything?'

'Because I don't love anyone else. I love you, and I want to marry you!'

She was silent, and it was impossible to gauge her feelings. Eventually, she said, 'I love you, too, Maurice, and that's what makes this whole thing so difficult, and why it's unfair to both of us to let it go on any longer.'

It was just like the day she'd told him about her violation by the Japanese officer, and brought their relationship to a temporary halt. It seemed that, just when things seemed to be proceeding smoothly, the awful spectre would re-enter her life and ruin everything. Now it seemed that she wanted to end their association permanently. 'You seem to think of me,' he said hopelessly, 'as a determined Lothario.'

'I don't, Maurice. It's not just you.'

'Now you've lost me.'

She took a breath and said, 'The last time you brought me home, you kissed me properly.'

'I remember.'

'I know why you did it, and I appreciated it. It was a wonderful experience, possibly more wonderful than you realise.'

'Oh?'

She was struggling to describe something she was simply unused to discussing. 'While it was happening, I felt… certain things. It all seemed so straightforward, and I felt as if a change had taken place. It was as if the problem no longer existed, but then, when I was back in my room, I thought about it, about the actual… business… and suddenly, all I could see was that evil Captain Hayashi. Even though he's dead, he can still give me the horrors.'

From the sounds she was making, he knew she was crying. 'I'm sorry,' he said. 'Here….' He passed her his handkerchief. 'Look, I don't see why we can't establish a completely non-physical relationship. We may need to live apart, but spend time together, as we do now. In that case, nothing would change, and we'd still have each other's company and friendship. Rather than do anything rash, please think about it.' He drew up under the cedar tree.

'Don't get out, Maurice,' she said. 'Thank you for the recital. It was wonderful.' She opened her door. 'Goodnight.'

'Before you go, Iris….'

'What?'

'Tell me you'll think about it.'

'All right, I'll think about it.' She accepted a chaste kiss on her cheek before leaving the car.

23

Provocation to Promise

The Easter holiday resulted in a break in ballet classes and football practice, so the children joined Jill regularly in taking Maggie for a walk on the moor. They returned on one occasion to find Tony's car parked outside the cottage. The children greeted him briefly before attending to matters affording better entertainment.

'Oh, what a surprise to find you here,' said Jill. Having made that neutral observation, she introduced him to Maggie. 'It's all right, Maggie. He's quite harmless... now. I think he's got it all out of his system, but I'll keep you posted.'

'Very funny. I assume this one of your charges.'

'She was, which makes you less of an ass, I suppose, for assuming. She's now one of the family.'

'Is she safe with the children?'

'I'd say she is. So far, they've been very gentle with her.'

Rolling his eyes upward, he said, 'You know what I mean.'

'English is a tricky bugger, isn't it? Do you imagine I would even consider bringing an unreliable dog into a house where there are children? I presume you'd like coffee. It's only—'

'Only instant, I know. Yes, if it's not too much trouble.' Returning to the subject of Maggie, he said, 'They do have a certain reputation, and they're not the cleanest things to have around children.'

She pushed down the switch on the electric kettle and addressed Tony's concerns in reverse order because she found it easier and more entertaining that way. 'Maggie is the cleanest of dogs and, although I

184

says it as shouldn't, she's immaculately groomed. Is your preoccupation with animal hygiene based on reasoned thinking or recent domestic influence?'

'As a matter of fact, both Deborah and I disapprove of animals being kept as pets.'

She smiled at him sweetly. 'As far as the Dobermann stereotype is concerned, let me tell you that Maggie's previous owner, a self-styled stud muffin, whose tattoos outnumber his brain cells by an embarrassing majority, bought her as a status symbol, also believing the breed to be aggressive. That's why he named her after the bellicose, domineering, misanthropic harridan he most admired, albeit eight or nine years after her downfall. Fortunately, as well as being a total dickhead, he's bone-idle, and he left Maggie's training to his wife, who brought her up to be loyal, loving, gentle and downright civilised.' She couldn't help adding mischievously, 'She's not over-keen on foul language, but she's not likely to hear it from our children, is she? Unfortunately, though, the aforementioned dickhead's wife is pregnant and, like you and Deborah, he's determined that his child will grow up in a spotless and sterile environment.' The view from the window reminded her of something else. 'You and he have even more in common,' she said, 'although his penis extension is an Audi.'

It was clear that she'd touched one nerve too many. 'I bought the BMW for its performance and handling qualities,' he protested. 'I don't need a penis extension, as you well know.'

'I don't suppose anyone does, but men of a certain persuasion find them irresistible, all the same.' She handed him a mug of coffee.

'As a matter of fact, I'm considering downsizing to something more practical.'

'Oh dear.' It seemed that there was no limit to Deborah's controlling influence. 'However, at the risk of sounding business-like on a Saturday morning, to what do I owe the pleasure of this visit?'

'I was in the area, so I called.'

'I see. You've just sold a house for one of my neighbours, and you wonder if I'd like a free estimate.'

'Damn it, Jill, do you have to take the...' He looked unsurely at Maggie and, mindful of Jill's warning, rephrased his question. 'Do you have to ridicule me all the time?'

'I don't have to, but the temptation is hard to resist.'

'I was about to say that I can't have the children tomorrow. We're going to something that's not really suitable for them.'

It was too much for Jill. 'Do you mean it's strictly hey, nonny-nonny no kids allowed?'

'If you must be childish, yes, as it happens, it is a folk gathering.'

'Will there be boisterous drinking and hearty, navvy-style swearing at this gathering?'

'It's just possible.'

'Don't worry, Maggie,' she said soothingly. 'He's not going to give us a demonstration.'

'Anyway,' said Tony, going on to the offensive, 'What's this I've heard about you seeing someone?'

'I see people all the time. I only wear glasses for close work, if you remember.'

'You know what I mean. I understand you've been seeing a man.'

Jill had to laugh at his sheer pomposity. 'If I were, would I need your approval? As I recall, your indiscretion came as rather a surprise, as in, "Oh, by the way, Jill, I've found someone else and I want a divorce." '

'Of course you don't need my approval, but the fact remains that we have to consider the children.'

'As you did? I missed that. I must have been distracted.'

'Oh, for goodness' sake.' He half-turned in the chair, but realised the impossibility of turning his back on her, and resumed his former position.

'People who live in glass houses, Antonio, should think twice before rushing into judgement. Anyway, if I were to find myself involved with someone, I'd make sure the children were the first to know and that they were happy for it to continue. Then, if you were around, and not roistering tunelessly somewhere, or swapping your BMW for an elderly campervan, I might just tell you, as well.'

Clearly, Tony felt he'd suffered enough, because he stood up to leave. 'I gather you're out again, tonight,' he said.

'I can't deny it.'

'Liam tells me you're going to the Wool Exchange Club.'

'He's doing a good job as your intelligence man. Mind you, he tells me things about you and What's-her-name.'

'Deborah,' he prompted.

'Oh, still with the same one, are you?'

'Of course.' Mustering his dignity again, he said, 'Presumably, the chap who's taking you to the Wool Exchange is the same.'

'Same as what?'

'The same man who took you last time.'

'As it happens, yes. If you're wondering, and I think I detect the signs of curiosity, he's a friend. More than that I can't tell you, except that he's extremely personable, a good dancer, and he doesn't possess a penis extension. It's pure guess-work on my part, but I can't imagine he needs one, either.'

'I'm going.' His hand was already on the doorknob.

'Are you going to tell Deborah I've got a dog named after your favourite politician?'

'As a matter of fact, I find myself readjusting my political alignment.'

That was a surprise. 'Is that since you discovered that "Phoney" Blair strums an out-of-tune guitar? Mind you, he's more into rock 'n' roll than folk. That's when he actually gives a "folk". Sorry, Maggie.'

———

Frank met them at the ballroom with a warm and sincere greeting. 'Will you join us again? It'll be cosy, as my sister and her husband are here, but you're most welcome.'

'Are you sure, Frank?' Steve looked around the ballroom and saw several empty tables. 'We don't want to barge into a family gathering, do we, Jill?'

'Certainly not.'

'Don't give it a second thought,' said Frank. 'They'll be more than happy to welcome you.'

'What are you saying about us, Frank?' The question came from an attractive woman of around Frank's age, in an apple-green gown.

'Penny,' he said, 'you already know Steve, but I'd like you to meet Jill and.... Where's Tim? Tim, come and meet Jill and welcome Steve back to the fold.'

A tall, serious-looking man joined them and shook hands with them.

'Steve and Jill were just saying they didn't want to intrude on a family gathering.'

'Nonsense,' said Penny. 'Come and join us. What would you like to drink?'

When they were settled at the table and Sarah had joined them, she said to Jill, 'It may interest you to know that Tim and Penny were on *Come Dancing* back in the sixties and seventies. In fact, they were Northern Area Quickstep Champions.'

'How marvellous.' Jill looked at Penny in a new light.

'How embarrassing,' said Penny. 'It was a long time ago.'

' "Tim and Penny Renshaw",' mimicked Frank, ' "are from Cullington in the West Riding. Tim is an electrical engineer, and Penny is an art student. Fortunately, Penny's mother is neither of those things. She's a dressmaker, and just *look* at that dress. Penny tells me she and her mother sewed on all those sequins by hand." '

'That,' said Penny, 'will be quite enough from you, little brother.'

'I only mentioned it,' said Sarah, because Jill teaches Ballroom at Helen Rawlinson's School of Dancing.'

'Embarrassment all round, I'd say,' said Jill.

'As I told you last time you were here,' said Sarah, laughing good-naturedly, 'we only dance for enjoyment.'

Tim nodded sagely, clearly happy to let his wife engage with everyone.

Frank looked at his watch and stood up, saying, 'I have to leave you all, just for a spell.'

As he set off for the band room, Sarah announced, 'We have two new vocalists, both students from the Northern College.'

'It's almost like old times,' said Penny. 'How did you manage this?'

'I just had a word with a few people at the college. I used to work there,' she told Jill. 'At least, I was at Beckworth before it was absorbed into everything else, and that's where I found Dan, our first singer.'

One by one, the musicians came on to the platform and took their places. Conversation around the ballroom dwindled, and then Frank appeared, he gave a downbeat, and the band played 'The Sun Has Got His Hat On' to enthusiastic applause. Frank welcomed the members and their guests, and said, 'Let's begin with a waltz: "Marcheta, a Love Song of Old Mexico".'

'Come on, Tim,' said Penny. 'I haven't come here to be a wallflower.'

'Go ahead, everyone,' Sarah told them.

Steve led Jill on to the floor and they joined the others. 'What a pair,' said Jill, watching Penny and Tim. 'They're absolutely as one.'

'They've danced together for thirty years or more,' said Steve. 'Frank told me it was a photo of those two at Blackpool that gave him the idea for the band.'

'Really? It's a marvellous story, although I'm sure I haven't heard the whole of it.'

'You must be fascinated,' said Steve, 'You haven't criticised me, yet.'

'Why should I? You're doing well. You obviously have a good teacher.'

'The very best,' he agreed.

Jill made no reply, and they simply enjoyed the rest of the number.

It reached its end, with the dancers applauding the band, and Frank spoke again. 'Here's a foxtrot, a very old favourite,' he said. 'It's "Love is the Sweetest Thing", and here to sing it for us is Carl. Put your hands together to give him an Exchange Club welcome, because you'll be hearing him again.'

Steve asked, 'Shall we dance?'

'You bet. It's one of my favourites.'

The number began, and Steve and Jill moved easily and naturally to the gentle beat. Sixteen bars later, the vocal began, and all heads turned towards the band, where Carl, the new vocalist, was singing for the first time. His voice was gentle and his style was intimate. He could be no more than twenty, but he was singing the song, written sixty-eight years earlier, as if it were the most natural thing for him. The applause at the end of the number must have given him a tremendous reward, and it was completely deserved.

Frank handed over to Geoff, the pianist, and left him to announce the next dance. When Steve and Jill returned to the table, all the talk was about Carl.

Penny said, 'Isn't he glorious?'

'He's a real find,' agreed Sarah, 'but wait until you hear Kelly, and then hear them together.'

Jill wondered if she could cope with so much excitement. Maybe it was better to be like Tim, who put all his enthusiasm into his dancing. Now, there was a man who could control his feet and himself as well.

Frank came to the table and lost no time in leading Sarah into 'Embraceable You.'

'You know,' said Penny, 'when Sarah first arrived, she taught modern dance and ballet at Beckworth, but she'd never done Ballroom or Latin, and now look at her.'

Jill asked, 'Who taught her?'

'Frank.'

'And who taught Frank?' She was equally impressed with his foxtrot.

'I did, when we were very young. I'm just a year older than him,' she explained. 'It wasn't easy in those days.'

'Teaching Frank?' It was difficult to believe.

'No, I meant that life wasn't easy. Our dad died when I was four, and our mum had a struggle to bring us up, but she was incredible. Not only did she send us both to college, she made all my dresses for dancing.'

'She's a lovely woman,' said Tim, placing his hand on Penny's, 'my favourite mother-in-law, in fact.'

'He's only ever had one,' said Penny, 'but he gets confused, poor thing.'

As Frank and Sarah returned, Geoff announced a quickstep. 'It's "De-Lovely",' he said. 'Everyone, please put your hands together for Kelly, who's going to sing it for us.'

'It's a band arrangement I've done so that a girl can sing it,' explained Frank. 'It was worth the effort, as you'll see.'

Penny and Tim were already on the floor, ready to take part in their trademark dance.

Eight bars into the dance, Jill said, 'She's amazing.'

Frank nodded. 'My sister's a show-off,' he said, 'and as for that extrovert of a husband....'

'Don't be awful,' said Sarah.

A moment later, no one spoke, because the music had reached the vocal refrain, and they heard Kelly for the first time in the Cole Porter classic, announcing that the night was young and the skies were clear. Her voice and delivery were instantly engaging, and Jill heard her as if in a kind of daze. Like Carl, Kelly could only have been about twenty, but she was completely at home with the music.

At the end of the number, Jill said, 'It seems too good to be true, but everything's right. It's right that a wonderful band should have a wonderful leader and two wonderful singers.' She shook her head in disbelief. 'You wouldn't think I used to teach English, because I can't find the words to describe all this without repeating myself.'

'Have a dance,' suggested Frank. 'It'll give you time to think of a few. In the meantime, thanks for the compliment.'

Still marvelling, Jill allowed Steve to lead her into 'Bewitched', which the band played without vocal refrain. For Jill, it was sheer enjoyment; the music was perfect, and Steve was proving to be an excellent partner. She suspected that a kind of inevitability was emerging, that might easily raise questions at some time, but that was all to come. For the moment, she simply allowed the mood to carry her along, because she felt no urgency to resist it.

She danced the next waltz 'Paradise' with Frank to show her gratitude to her host, because he was an excellent partner, and because he was such good company.

He said, 'I hope we're going to see you here often.'

'That all depends,' she said. 'I can only come if I'm invited.'

'Oh, I think Steve will invite you again.'

She made no response, but enjoyed the rest of the number before Frank had to disappear again.

He'd just left when Geoff announced a foxtrot. It was to be 'Cheek to Cheek', the Irving Berlin masterpiece made famous by Fred Astaire, and it was to be a special duet arrangement for Kelly and Carl. Frank had been busy again.

As Jill had said earlier, everything was right; the band, the vocalists and the number itself couldn't have pleased her better. Steve, too, was at his best. Through their Monday evening sessions, they were quickly forming a natural partnership that was as enjoyable for her as it apparently was for him.

Steve saw Jill to her doorstep, prompting a vociferous welcome from Maggie.

'Will you come in for coffee?'

'Maybe it's better if I don't excite Gemma's already fertile imagination,' he said. 'Having said that, I'll hang around until she's on the road, and then we'll know she's safe. I'll be following her, anyway.'

'You're very kind, Steve,' she said, opening the door.

'It's no trouble.'

Jill pushed open the inner door, greeting Maggie as she entered the room.

'Hello, you two,' said Gemma. 'What a glamorous couple you are. Did you have a good time?'

'Thank you, and yes, it was very special.' Jill took the money from the Doulton vase and gave it to her. 'Take it,' she said, forestalling the usual protest. 'It's worth it to know that the children are safe when I leave them.'

'That's down to Maggie, now,' said Gemma, 'and you can secure her services for the price of a dog biscuit.'

'You know what I mean.' She watched Gemma pick up her things, and said, 'Steve's going to hang on just until you're homeward bound, so that we know you're safe, too.'

'What a lovely fella. 'Bye, Jill. 'Bye, Steve. See you on Tuesday.'

They waited until Gemma had driven off, and Jill asked, 'Are you sure you won't stay for coffee, Steve?'

'Thanks, but I'll make sure Gemma gets home.'

'Of course. Thank you for a truly lovely evening.'

'Not at all. Thank you for coming.' He hesitated, and then asked, 'Do you think we might do it again?'

'I'd love to.' She inclined her head so that he could kiss her cheek. 'I'd love to do it again.'

24

August 1946

Shaming and Taming

Maurice was bored and resentful. He disliked being the bearer of bad tidings, but it was nevertheless part of his job to advise clients, often business people of modest means, of their tax liability. Doctors and nurses wore rubber gloves, whereas the only barriers available to the business world and those whose responsibility it was to advise, were foresight, provision and skilful management.

In the summer months, his respite was cricket, at least when he was allowed to play, having been dropped recently from the side after a temporary loss of form. For the remainder of the year, he went to concerts and, more latterly, to dances, although that diversion had suffered a hiatus. He was still waiting to hear from Iris, who had promised to consider his proposition, although that was the extent of her compliance. He'd already decided that there was nothing to be gained by prompting her in any way; in fact, to do so might easily be self-defeating. He reminded himself frequently that he wasn't dealing with the whim of an undecided woman, but one who was enduring a terrible and insistent torment, and that he must respect her suffering.

Largely out of guilt at the hurt she'd unintentionally inflicted during her last visit, Iris spent her day off again with her parents. Happily, it passed without unpleasantness or difficulty, although their private pain hung over the event like the smoke from a recently-extinguished fire, and it was difficult to imagine that it would ever be otherwise.

At one point, she went to her old room to retrieve her Pahang box and, in doing so, prompted an objection from her mother.

'I came across that when I was cleaning your room,' she told her, 'and I was about to throw it into the dustbin. I left it because I thought you might like to do it instead.'

'I'm glad you didn't.' Iris would actually have been horrified, although she kept that thought tactfully to herself. Things were going reasonably well, and she had no wish to provoke an argument.

'Why do you want those things, when all they do is remind you of Malaya?'

'I don't know,' she said honestly. 'Maybe I need them as a reminder that Pahang is in the past, to help me accept that the nightmare's finally over.'

Her mother shrugged dismissively. 'I just don't understand you,' she said.

'There are things we don't understand,' said her father, 'I imagine, because we never had Iris's experience.'

Iris nodded gratefully, hoping the conversation was over. She'd found the newspaper stories of the war crime trials in Tokyo and began to read, simply because she couldn't help herself. It was the second of the two reports that seized her attention, the first being about the trials themselves. She had no wish to read the details of the offences again. Neither did she take any satisfaction from the executions; she simply wondered if, as she'd told her mother, the report might help her see the horror in a less immediate and more manageable context.

Five Japanese officers convicted of crimes against humanity, and sentenced to death by hanging, were executed yesterday, at 6:00 a.m. at Sugamo Prison, Tokyo. They included the infamous Captain Akira Hayashi, Second Officer in Command of the internment camp at Kuala Rompin in Pahang, Malaya. Captain Hayashi was guilty of a number of offences, including that of wilful murder.

The bodies were cremated, and the ashes will be scattered at an undisclosed location, so as to prevent the creation of shrines by the impenitent minority.

Despite her earlier fear and detestation of Captain Hayashi, Iris's views on capital punishment had not changed since she'd last made them known to her parents. She still believed in a better way to banish cruelty and disregard for life. She believed totally in the ascendancy of love over hatred, and she pondered that for a while, until the merest hint of an idea presented itself. The more she thought about it, the more definitely it took shape, until she was convinced of its soundness.

Maurice was chatting with Mollie on the switchboard. Her nephew had just been given his first opportunity with the school's Under-Thirteen Cricket Eleven, an accomplishment Maurice was quick to applaud.

'Good lad,' he said. 'Is he a batsman or a bowler?'

'He's an all-rounder,' she told him proudly.

'And, as such, worth his weight in gold, I'll be bound.'

'You're very kind, Mr Warneford— Oh, please excuse me a minute. I have a caller on line one. Good morning. Warneford, Barnes and Company.' She listened. 'Mr Maurice Warneford? Who shall I say is calling? Miss Lennox.' Isolating the line, she asked, 'Will you take the call, Mr Warneford?'

'Yes, of course. I'll take it in my office.'

'I'll put you through, Miss Lennox.'

Picking up the phone, Maurice said eagerly, 'Hello, Iris.'

'Hello, Maurice. Can we meet? My next day off is Saturday.'

Iris asked her usual question as she got into the car. 'Where are we going? It all sounded very mysterious on the phone.'

'Not really. We're going to lunch, and then to the cinema—'

'Oh, good. What are we going to see?'

He turned into Mansfield Road and said, 'You don't like surprises, do you?'

'Of course I do. I'm just excited. I haven't seen a film since…
nineteen forty-one. It was in Singapore.'

'This one's got nothing to do with war,' he assured her. 'I think
we've all had enough of that.'

'Good. What's it called?'

Her childlike excitement made him smile. '*Blithe Spirit*,' he told
her. 'It's based on the play by Noel Coward.'

'It sounds like fun. Who's in it?'

'Rex Harrison, Constance Cummings and one or two others. I can't
remember them all off hand.'

'I remember Rex Harrison,' she said, 'and her name rings a distant
bell. At all events, I'm looking forward to it.' Suddenly remembering,
she said, 'You told me to bring something "eveningy" to change into.
What's that for?'

'Dinner with dancing.'

'Wonderful. Is this an all-out assault on my romantic susceptibilities?'

'Of course. As suitors go, I'm one of the more determined kind.'
He drew in to the kerbside as close to the restaurant as he could park.

'I'm glad to hear it. I mean, who wants a half-hearted suitor?' She
asked, 'Didn't suitors do a bunk around the end of the last century,
along with swains and paramours?'

'I can't speak for the swains and paramours,' he said, locking the
car, 'but we suitors never went out of date.' He offered her his arm and
took her into the restaurant.

When the waitress had taken their order, Iris said, 'It's a detail, I
know, but where am I going to change into my "eveningy" things?'

'My rooms will be at your disposal,' he told her grandly.

'Your rooms?'

He nodded. 'I'll wait patiently in the sitting room while you
alternate between the bathroom and bedroom, making yourself even
more engaging than ever.'

'You think of everything, Maurice.'

'I certainly try.' He leant forward and looked into her eyes to ask,
'Are you feeling quite well?'

'Quite well, thank you. Why do you ask?'

'You look well,' he said. 'I only wondered, because you're much
more relaxed than you were the last time we met.'

'I am more relaxed,' she agreed.

He nerved himself to ask, 'Have you thought any more about my suggestion?'

'Yes,' she said, 'I have. I still feel that I'm denying you something that's more important than you'll admit, but I don't see why we can't carry on being friends.' She added, 'Close friends, of course.'

———

The film was everything it promised to be, with superb performances by the cast, not least of whom was Rex Harrison.

'I saw him in nineteen forty-one, in *Night Train to Munich*,' she told Maurice excitedly. 'That was the film I told you about, the last one I saw, and he was wonderful in that as well, but to see this one in colour was just blissful.'

Maurice was simply happy that she'd enjoyed it. He pulled into the shared drive and took her case from the car. 'I'll make a cup of tea,' he said, 'and then you can change and do everything else you have to do at your leisure.'

'What about you?'

'I shan't take very long,' he said. 'I'll shave and have a quick bath. It's the work of a moment, honestly.'

He made tea and brought it into the sitting room, where she was examining a photograph of a motor launch flanked by its smiling crew. She asked, 'Where are you in this photo?'

'There,' he said, pointing. 'Next to the captain.'

'Oh, wasn't this your boat?'

'Ship,' he corrected her. 'No, I was a humble sub-lieutenant in those days, and poor old Ninety-Four was scrapped after being badly damaged in an action in the North Sea. Six-Five-Seven, the one you remember, is over here.' He showed her another photograph on the opposite wall.

'Was the action you mentioned the one in which you were injured?'

'There you go, mentioning my injury again, and just when I thought you'd forgotten it. I'm very sensitive about it, you know.'

'Nonsense.' She accepted a cup of tea from him and said, 'Did I tell you about next weekend?'

'No, you were too busy reminding me about my facial disfigurement.'

'Facial fiddlesticks, although we've spoken a lot about my experiences, and hardly mentioned yours. I feel quite selfish, really.'

'Just to take your mind off it,' he suggested, 'tell me about next weekend.'

'Oh, yes.' She put her cup and saucer on the occasional table so that they were safe. 'Next weekend, I've got Saturday and Sunday off. If you like, we can spend more time together. Things are usually so rushed. Just for once, though, they needn't be.'

Maurice hadn't been particularly aware of a rush, but he wasn't inclined to argue, except to ask, 'Won't your parents be expecting you?'

'No, I spent last Saturday with them.'

'In that case, let's be greedy and spend two days together.'

They chatted until Iris decided it was time for her to get ready.

'Help yourself to anything you need,' he told her. 'Feel free to use the bath and anything you like. I've put out towels for you on the bed.' He couldn't think of anything else, but he made the offer in good faith.

He heard the bath being run, and he settled down to read the morning paper, so far unopened, until he heard Iris's voice. From time to time, she would find something that surprised her or captured her imagination, and she would share the experience, albeit from the next room.

'Maurice, do you really use an open razor?'

'Yes, it doesn't work very well closed.'

'You know what I mean. My dad has a safety razor, and I thought you might have one, too.'

Rather than challenge feminine logic, he said, 'I prefer to live dangerously. Mind you, I don't use it when I'm feeling down in the dumps, temptation being the sneaky blighter it is.'

She emerged eventually to say, 'I'm terribly impressed with your bedroom furniture. It's not at all what I'd expect to find in a man's flat.'

'That's my mother's influence, you see. She can't imagine how anyone can manage without a dressing table and a huge wardrobe.'

'It's all terribly tidy, too.' She sounded like an archaeologist who had just discovered a previously-unknown civilisation.

'That's down to naval discipline,' he told her.

'Is it?'

'And the fact that I knew you were coming. I arranged for the cleaner to come in yesterday and do her stuff.'

'Anyway, I've finished with the bathroom and your bedroom.'

'And you look stunning.'

'Thank you. Now it's your turn.'

As he lathered himself up, he knew he would never look stunning, but he smiled at Iris's reaction to the razor. She had no way of knowing that he'd asked his parents to send him it when he was in basic training at HMS *Raleigh*, where hot water was the rarest of luxuries, and a safety razor was pathetically inadequate. Since then, it had simply become a matter of habit to use it, and it also had the advantage of obviating the need to procure razor blades, now so elusive in the current state of austerity.

After a very quick bath, he reappeared, shaven, suited and shod. 'My lady,' he announced, 'your carriage awaits.'

———

'I'm glad we've come here again,' she said, commenting favourably on his lack of imagination, as he saw it. 'I have such happy memories of dancing for the first time after the war.'

' "Clean linen",' he reminded her.

'Don't worry, I'm in a positive mood. I've had a wonderful day, and this evening promises to match it.'

'Dare I ask,' he said, 'what brought about this moderation, welcome though it is?'

'Of course. Only you could have suggested something as loving and generous as you did. It should have been obvious to me that you were totally committed to it. I just needed to realise that.'

'I'll drink to that. At least, I would, but we haven't yet ordered the wine.'

'Let's dance to it instead,' she suggested. The band was playing 'Smoke Gets in Your Eyes'.

'Let's,' he agreed, leading her on to the floor. 'It's a beautiful song, but it's very sad.'

'Let's enjoy the beauty and forget the sadness,' said Iris.

'I'm getting the idea.' He moved closer to her, earning a smile of compliance, and they danced to the end of the number, enjoying the irresistible music, as Iris had said, and also the sensation of moving together by unspoken accord.

At the end, they returned to their table and, with diplomatic timing, the waiter arrived to take their order. Maurice asked for a bottle of Nuits-Saint-Georges.

Suddenly, Iris gave a start. 'I just had an awful thought,' she said.

'I thought you'd declared a moratorium on horrible thoughts and suchlike.'

'Not that kind. I was talking about us spending Saturday and Sunday together, and I just remembered that you play cricket on Sundays.'

'Usually,' he said with the air of a neglected orphan, 'but I've been dropped, at least for the time being.'

'Why, for goodness' sake?'

'I'm out of form with the bat,' he explained. 'They dropped me from tomorrow's match and the next one, so don't worry. I'm looking forward to next weekend already.'

'But it was awful that they dropped you.'

'It happens, but it matters much more to me that you've had a change of heart about my suggestion.'

'That's sweet of you.' She cocked an ear towards the band, who were starting the waltz 'It's a Sin to Tell a Lie'. 'Shall we?'

'My word, you're keen.'

'So are you. Be honest. The lyrics demand it.'

He took her hand to lead her on to the floor and, in the safe anonymity of the dance, they moved closely and familiarly to the insistent, romantic pulse. It set the pattern for the remainder of the evening.

'It's a shame they treat us as children,' said Iris as she took her seat in the car, 'but, to be fair, I suppose the student nurses are very young.'

'Be that as it may,' he assured her, 'I'll have you back before Lights Out, or whatever they call it.'

'There is no official name for it. They just cut up rough if we're late.'

'It's almost like being in the services,' he said, joining the A17.

'Things were stricter in the QAs, but you're right.' As if it had just occurred to her, she said, 'You strike me as an independent soul. How did you cope with military discipline?'

'I survived it until I joined Coastal Forces, after which it ceased to exist, at least as far as we were concerned.'

'Surely not.'

She was an eager listener, like a child at bedtime, and he had to smile. 'Coastal Forces, or "Costly Farces", as the top brass called us, was a pirate outfit. Most of the time, we didn't even wear proper uniform, but we never overlooked the important things, and that applied to officers and ratings alike.'

'It sounds civilised,' she said.

'Far from it, but it worked.'

As they drew closer to Nottingham, she said, possibly for the second or third time, 'It's been a wonderful day. I really don't want it to end, but it must.'

Eventually, Maurice pulled in beside the high stone wall and the cedar. 'We made it by nine minutes,' he said, glancing at the dashboard clock. 'Thanks for coming. It's been a grand day, as you said.' He leaned sideways to kiss her cheek, but she turned her face towards him. The invitation was as unexpected as it was impossible to resist, and they kissed unhurriedly and with great feeling.

Several minutes later, she looked at the dashboard clock and said, 'I must go. Thank you again. Goodnight.'

'Goodnight.'

25

May 2000

Discretion

Jill dropped Jessica at school and continued towards Beckworth High School.

'Mum?'

'Yes, Liam?'

'Daniel Brewer's dad says you're scary.'

'Does he? He must be confusing me with Maggie.' Looking in the driving mirror, she said, 'Did you hear that, Maggie? You've got competition.'

'It's because of Maggie. He says he daren't say a word on the touchline, now, in case he gets growled at.'

'Oh, diddums.' After brief reflection, she said, 'He must be talking about Maggie. I never growl, do I? Have you ever heard me growl, Liam?'

'You're being daft again, Mum.'

'Oh, dear.' When she wasn't being scary, she was daft. Would she ever gain her son's approval?

'Mum?'

'I'm still here, darling. Can't you hear me growling?'

He ignored her silliness for once, and asked, 'Are you going out with the man in the black suit?'

'His name's Steve, he only wears a black suit when he goes to a ball, and no, I'm not. We're just friends.'

'My dad says you are. Going out with him, I mean.'

'Oh well, your dad knows lots of things I don't. It's an important part of a dad's job to know everything.'

'He was wearing waterproof gear when we met him on the moor. I'm talking about the man, not my dad.'

'His name's Steve, and I'm glad you cleared that one up. Rest assured, Liam, that if I ever start "going out" as you call it, with someone, even someone whose name you can't remember, you and Jessica will be the first to know.' She pulled into an empty space beside the school. 'Are you going to give me a kiss?'

'No.' He edged away from her and opened the car door. 'People can see us.'

'Oh well, it was worth a try.'

Obviously determined to make himself understood, he said quickly, 'I only mentioned it because the man in the black suit seems okay. I mean, he's civilised, so if you did fancy him, it would probably be okay, not like Deborah.'

'Isn't she okay?' She knew the answer, but she thought she'd like to hear it again.

'No, she's manky, and she's always arguing with my dad. She wants him to get rid of his BMW, and I wouldn't be surprised if he left her.'

'He could so easily,' agreed Jill. 'He's got previous for it.'

''Bye, Mum.'

''Bye, Liam. Have a good day.'

Jill's next job was to collect Maggie's companions. The gang of five had now become the Beckworth Six, and she looked forward to introducing the new member to Steve when she saw him. Her opportunity came that afternoon.

———

The other five had barely finished giving Malcolm a thorough sniffing when Steve showed up.

'Writer's block again, Steve?'

'No, it just seemed a waste of a fine day not to have a stroll.' Surveying the group of dogs, he said, 'I see a new member's joined the rambling club. A Scottie, I believe.'

'His name's Malcolm, and he prefers "Aberdeen terrier", although you'd think he had a big enough problem with his given name.'

'It's certainly unusual,' agreed Steve, crouching to tickle the new addition behind his ears.

'Unusual in canine circles, I have to agree. Malcom's owner has named all his Aberdeen terriers after characters in… *The Scottish Play*.' She uttered the soubriquet *sotto voce*.

'Ah.'

'After Duncan, not to mention the eponymous character himself, Malcolm must have been born with his medallion already engraved and waiting for him.'

'Is that such a good idea? I'm thinking of potential dog-theft.'

'Nowadays, the Kennel Club advise anonymity.'

'I quite agree. May I join you?'

'Please do.'

As he fell in beside her, he said conversationally, 'There's an ordinary dance on the twentieth of May.'

'Just an ordinary one?'

'Yes, the next ball is in June, the Midsummer Ball. Would you like to come?'

'To which one?' She was genuinely confused.

'I'm sorry. I meant the dance on the twentieth.'

'I'd love to.'

Visibly embarrassed, he said, 'It would be wonderful if you could come to the Midsummer Ball as well, or am I being greedy?'

'Truly gluttonous, but the answer's the same. I'd love to. Thank you for both invitations.'

'It all seems so formal,' he said uncomfortably.

The poor man needed encouragement, so she asked, 'Would you be happier with things on a less-formal footing?'

'I should, really. I'm afraid I'm very much out of practice at this kind of thing.'

'I suppose I am, too.' With five leads in her left hand, she took Steve's arm with her right. 'Would you like to come over again for a drink when the children have gone to bed?'

He looked relieved as well as pleased by her invitation. 'I'd like that very much,' he said. 'What time?'

'Liam's in bed by nine, so any time after that is fine.'

'That suits me.' They walked a little further, and he asked, 'How's the novel progressing?'

'It's not. I really must establish a routine.'

'It's the only way, especially for someone with your lifestyle.'

That suddenly made her think. 'I didn't know I had a lifestyle. I thought only celebrities and politician's wives had them. Don't they have lifestyle gurus as well?'

'If they do, they're wasting their money as well as being pretentious. When I said "lifestyle", I meant your responsibilities and commitments.'

'They go with the turf, Steve. Being a wife and mum is demanding enough, but being a lone parent can be hectic. Still, we're a determined bunch.'

'I admire you. Because of various operations, Hayley, my wife, wasn't able to have children, so I was never tested as a parent.'

'Oh, Steve.' Jill stopped, and the dogs stopped with her. 'I'm so sorry. That must have been horrible. I mean, the whole thing.'

'It was, but we get through these things, although it's fair to say that I owe my sanity to the Exchange Club, one way or another.'

'I can imagine so.' Jill now recalled certain things being said at the Daffodil Ball.

'You know,' he said, 'if word got around about the Club's remarkable properties, we wouldn't be able to move for pilgrims. It would be like Medieval Canterbury, or modern-day Lourdes, if it comes to that.' He was smiling, but clearly not joking.

'I think,' said Jill, stopping to rearrange the dogs for the walk home, 'it's what we said earlier, that the healing quality comes from the good feeling generated by the music, the dancing and the company. It's certainly worked for both you and me, hasn't it?'

'Do you really feel that it's helped you?'

'Absolutely.' She persuaded the last two dogs to re-join the others, and gave a sigh. 'I'm sure I don't resemble a maypole in any way, but they treat me as one.'

'Can I help at all?'

'No, thanks. They're all sorted, now. What were we talking about? Oh yes, the healing property of the Exchange Club. You know, when I moved into the cottage at the end of December, I was still wondering how I'd managed to lose out to the plain, boring, left-over hippie who'd pinched my husband.' She smiled at the memory of it. 'And now, I honestly couldn't care less.'

'I'm glad to hear it.'

'Having said all that, I gather all is not hearts and flowers at the alternative abode. She's even trying to persuade him to get rid of his beloved BMW because it doesn't suit her lifestyle.' She paused to say, 'She really has a lifestyle. In fact, she has a name for every aspect and event in her life, from "downsizing" to "upgrading", not that we're talking about material values, you understand. You'd never think my ex-husband was an estate agent.'

'It sounds like an unusual pairing,' he agreed. 'I believe you said he was with Wilkinson's.'

'He's a partner, too. That's bound to rankle with Deborah.'

'Would you consider taking him back?'

She laughed easily. 'Not even for a moment.'

<hr>

Jill lifted the hairdryer to feel Jessica's hair. 'There,' she said, switching it off, 'bone dry and ready for bed.'

'Mum?'

'Yes, I'm still here, and what happened to, "Thank you for drying my hair"?'

'I was just going to say it. Thank you for drying my hair.' As usual with Jessica, there was no hint of indignation, only a bland statement of the facts.

'You're welcome. What else can I do for you?'

'Liam says you're not going out with the man in the black suit.'

'His name's Steve, and that was the case this morning, when Liam asked me about it.'

Jessica considered her answer and asked, 'Are you going out with him now?'

'We shouldn't rule out the possibility.'

It was clear that a great deal was going on inside Jessica's head, and she confirmed it by saying, 'I'm confused.'

'You're not the only one, darling,' she said, brushing a stray lock of hair away from her daughter's eyes. 'There's been a lot of confusion, lately. Come and sit down with me, and I'll try to make things a bit clearer.' Stopping by the staircase, she called, 'Liam, will you come down, please?'

'What for?'

'A family meeting.'

Hurried footsteps on the stairs signalled his readiness to attend. As he reached the bottom step, he asked, 'Are we getting another dog?'

'Not this time. Come and sit down.' When all three were seated, she said, 'This morning, Liam asked me if I were going out with Steve.' For the sake of clarity, she added, 'The man in the black suit.'

Both children nodded, although Jessica had spotted a possible flaw in her mother's grammar. She asked, 'Shouldn't you say, "I *was* going out with Steve"?'

'Well spotted, Jessica, but no. The word "if" changes "was" to "were". I'll explain it properly to you later, when it's not bedtime and you're more alert. Just now, I want to explain that, when Liam asked me that question, I told him I wasn't, because that was the case at eight-thirty this morning. Now, I've seen Steve since then, and the signs are that things are going to develop. In fact, he's asked me to go with him to a dance and another ball.'

Jessica's mind was hard at work. 'What's the difference,' she asked, 'between a dance and a ball?'

'Oh well, I suppose a dance is quite ordinary, and people go to it in respectable clothes just to enjoy themselves, really. On the other hand, a ball is usually a celebration, and people go in evening dress, hence Steve's "black suit".'

Liam, who had been unusually quiet, asked, 'What are you going to celebrate?'

'Midsummer.'

'Is that all?' He seemed disappointed.

'Don't you think it's worth celebrating, Liam? Mid-Summer's Day is the longest day of the year, and it's usually the warmest time as well.'

'I suppose so.'

'It's hard to be impressed at your age, isn't it?' She stroked his hair, and he pretended not to notice.

'When we met Steve on the moor,' said Jessica, 'he was nice.'

'He's suave and sophisticated,' said Liam. 'That means he's probably okay.'

Jill couldn't help laughing. She asked, 'Where on earth did you find that description?'

'I read it in a book. Anyway, he's civilised, not like manky Deborah.'

'I hope you don't say things like that when either of them can hear you.'

'No.' Liam shook his head definitely. 'We have a secret code.'

'I hope it's very secret.'

They both nodded earnestly.

'As this is a family meeting,' said Liam, what we're actually saying is that if you want to start going out with Steve....' He looked towards Jessica, and she nodded, so he concluded, 'You have our blessing.'

Jill fought to maintain a straight face. 'Thank you, both,' she said. 'I appreciate your generosity of spirit.'

The evening continued along less formal lines until Jessica, and then Liam, went to bed. Almost half-an-hour passed before Maggie alerted Jill to the fact that a car had drawn up outside the cottage.

'It's all right, Maggie,' she said, going to the door. 'He's okay. The children have said so.' She opened the door to welcome him.

'I thought I'd leave time for the children to settle,' said Steve as he kissed her and handed her a bottle of Bordeaux.

'Don't be surprised if they come down for a sneaky look,' said Jill, 'but you've already earned their approval. Jessica says you're nice, and Liam reckons you're suave and sophisticated. Come in and take a seat while I open this bottle.'

He sat on the sofa, and Maggie delivered her verdict. She seemed to be of the opinion that he was nice and quite possibly suave and sophisticated, especially when he stroked her behind her ears.

'I've been trying to explain to Liam and Jessica the difference between a dance and a ball,' said Jill, putting the bottle and two glasses of wine on the low table, 'and both concepts are beyond their experience.'

'I'm sure Liam's too old to be impressed by allusions to fairy-tales, and I imagine Jessica's moving in that direction, too.'

'She steps in and out. Last year, when she was recovering from 'flu, she was quite happy for me to read her bedtime stories. I suppose she needed the comfort, as well, after her dad had done his disappearing act.'

He looked deeply into his glass and said, 'They're bound to suffer, aren't they?'

'You wouldn't have thought so if you'd heard them earlier. Apparently, they have their own secret code so that they can cast aspersions on "Manky Deborah" without risking either her or Tony's disapproval.'

'Good for them, and I'm glad you're feeling so much better about it,' he said, taking her free hand. 'It's awful that you doubted yourself, although I suppose it's quite natural in those circumstances.'

Leaning her head against his shoulder, she said, 'I used to talk to the dogs about it when we were out walking.'

'I know, but why not? They'd be sympathetic.' He put his arm around her, demonstrating that he shared their concern. 'When I was going through my bad patch,' he told her, 'I didn't even have a dog to confide in, so I used to go into the Exchange Club lounge occasionally – the dances were out of the question – and I'd chat with whoever was there. I didn't talk about my problem, because I didn't need to. Anyone who knew me was well aware of the way I was feeling. I just chatted with them, and it made me feel better. Chatting can do that.'

She squeezed his hand, unable to find anything useful to say.

'When Helen put me under your tutelage, I saw your wedding ring and I remember chatting with you very naturally and easily. I thought what a lucky chap your husband must be. Naturally, I didn't know then that you'd split up.'

'I was wearing it as camouflage. Some men confuse the dancing school with a dating agency,' she explained. 'It's difficult to understand, but I have it on good authority.'

'I just wanted to start dancing again.'

'So did I,' she said, laughing. 'We did that for each other.'

'It's a personal question, I know,' he said, 'but are you divorced yet, or just separated?'

'We're divorced. We passed the point of no return some time ago.' She picked up the bottle. ' "*Decree Absolute*" has a gloriously final ring to it. Can I top you up?'

'Yes, please. I'm glad I'm not being naughty.'

'I can't imagine you're capable of it. Being naughty, I mean.'

With no obvious sign of concern, he asked, 'Do you find me terribly bland?'

She laughed. 'Not in the least. If you want to know, I find you honest, straightforward and trustworthy, and they are all qualities I appreciate to the full, especially in the light of recent events.'

'That's quite a lot to live up to, but thank you for the accolade. I'll certainly do my best.'

'Not at all. I was thinking, only a few days ago, that some qualities are hard to find in this worldly society.'

'What made you think of that?'

Wincing with embarrassment, she said, 'Believe it or not, my uncle's letters.'

'Are you still struggling with them?'

'No, I seem to be getting the knack of reading between the lines. I think, as well, that I've discovered why they kept themselves apart from the rest of the family. I actually feel quite privileged that they accepted me as unstintingly as they did.'

'What's your theory?' As always, he was genuinely interested.

'They were dealing with something sensitive and intensely private. The family would have been an awful intrusion. My mum was quite resentful at being marginalised, as she saw it, but I can understand why they did it.'

He nodded in agreement. It was just one of his qualities that she appreciated, that he never tried to hijack the conversation.

'I've also found the most remarkable thing; at least, it's part of what I was saying, but remarkable in itself.' She got up to take a letter from the box on her desk, and said, 'I think you were spot on when you came up with the idea that my aunt had suffered the worst kind of violation at the hands of the Japanese. It's little wonder she was wary of men, and then, when I read this letter, I realised what a sacrifice my uncle was making. He was so devoted to her that, in proposing marriage, he was actually making a commitment to forego conjugal rights.'

'What a remarkable man.' Steve took the letter from her and studied it. ' "I meant every word", he read, "when I told you I would feel no less fulfilled in a life such as I was proposing, and that you would not be refusing me, simply because I should never make that demand on you." '

When he came to the end, he said, 'There's no doubt about it, Jill. That's what he's offering, and he has my fullest admiration. I imagine there are lots more letters?'

'Quite a few,' she said, 'but I've decided I'm not going to pursue it any further.'

'I thought you might do that. These things can reach a stage that seems intrusive, almost voyeuristic, can't they?'

She nodded. 'I don't know if they ever worked things out between them, but it was very much their affair. I'm just glad I learned what I did about them.' Remembering a particular discovery, she asked, 'Did I show you the order of service from her funeral?'

'No, I'd have remembered that.'

She opened the box again, replaced the letter and found the order of service. 'The details of the service tell us very little. The interesting thing is on the back of the cover.'

He turned it and read, ' "Hatred and brutality have no more powerful an adversary than love for our fellow human beings".'

'I'd quite forgotten until recently – you know how memories re-emerge after a while – but he referred to it in his tribute at the funeral. It obviously meant an awful lot to him.

Handing it back to her, he said, 'And so say all of us, but it meant a great deal more, coming from someone who'd suffered as much as she had.'

'I'm glad she had the last word,' she said, laying down the order of service, 'although I think she spoke for them both in the end.' She leaned forward so that he could put his arm round her again and draw her closer.

26

The Final Reckoning

On Saturday afternoon, they saw *I'll Be Your Sweetheart*, starring Margaret Lockwood and Michael Rennie.

'It's just wonderful to go to the cinema again,' said Iris when they returned to the flat. Then, she added thoughtfully, 'I remember Margaret Lockwood, of course. She was in the film I told you about, *Night Train to Munich*, but Michael Rennie's a new face, isn't he?'

'I suppose so.'

'You were too busy looking at Margaret Lockwood, to notice him,' she said. 'Mind you, in that respect, you're no different from most of the male population of this island.'

'Not in the least.' He couldn't let her accuse him of that. 'With you beside me, how could I possibly be distracted?'

'You're a smooth-talking scoundrel and, if I could find a cushion in this flat, I'd throw it at you.'

'I think we were talking about Michael Rennie.'

'I was, certainly.'

'He hasn't been around long,' he agreed, 'in films, at least. Interestingly, he's from the north. Yorkshire, I believe, although, to hear him, you'd never suspect it.' He reflected on that observation and said, 'That lot just have to get involved in everything.'

'Oh,' she said, 'are you feeling resentful because they're set fair to win the County Championship again?'

'Well, if I am, who can blame me?'

'Remind me. Where are Notts, currently?'

212

'Halfway down the… blooming… table.'

'It's too bad, Maurice.' She decided to stop teasing him. Instead, she picked up her case and asked, 'Do you mind if I use your bathroom now?'

'Not in the least. You know where everything is, and you're welcome to anything you need.'

'Yes, it's becoming a habit.'

Maurice certainly hoped so. Meanwhile, he prepared himself for disappointment in another field by reading the reports of the latest County Championship matches.

He'd been reading for a while, when Iris's voice seized his attention. She was singing in the bathroom.

'To a garden full of posies
Cometh one to gather flowers,
And he wanders through its bowers
Toying with the wanton roses,
The wanton roses,
Who, uprising from their beds,
Hold on high their shameless heads
With their pretty lips a-pouting,
Never doubting – never doubting
That for Cytherian posies
He would gather aught but roses….'

It was Mad Margaret's aria from *Ruddigore*. Iris had an appealing voice, and he recalled her telling him that she'd sung the part in a school production. That must have taken place sometime in the mid-thirties, when she was studying for the School Certificate that would eventually enable her to join the QAs. It must have seemed to her at the time, as it did to many, that life offered an abundance of opportunity. That was before the world descended into insanity and turned her mission of healing into a struggle for survival against disease, starvation and brutality. It hurt to think of it, and he deliberated about that until the sound of her singing happily in the bathroom set his thoughts in a more positive direction. She'd picked up her life in England and was trying her hardest to turn her back on the abhorrent events of the past. It seemed to him that, rather than rail at past deeds, he had a responsibility to help her in that recovery, and that involved following her example. It wouldn't be easy, but she'd demonstrated very ably that there was no better way.

He was still thinking about it when Iris came into the room, wearing his old rayon dressing gown that he'd worn under training at *HMS King Alfred* and later, at the coastal forces base at *HMS St Christopher*. Once at sea, it had quickly become a frivolous luxury, although Iris must have discovered it behind his bedroom door and found it convenient, so it still had a purpose.

'I hope you don't mind my wearing this,' she said. 'It was looking lost and uncared for.'

'You're more than welcome to it.'

'And you're too kind. I'll just wait until you're in the bathroom,' she said, 'and then I'll borrow your dressing table to do my make-up and get dressed.'

Standing up, he asked, 'Must you go so soon?'

'Yes, because beneath this rather modest gown of yours, I'm quite indecent.'

It was only partly true, because the outline of her underclothes was clearly evident through the flimsy fabric of the gown. 'Iris,' he said, still mindful of his self-imposed obligation, 'will you promise me just one thing?'

'Oh, that depends on what it is.'

'Promise me you'll never change.'

'I must change into my eveningy things, as you call them.'

'You know what I mean,' he said, drawing her into a lengthy kiss.

'I do, really,' she said when she could break free, 'but you've caught me at a disadvantage.'

'I love you, Iris.'

'I know, and I love you. Now, go and shave and do everything else you have to do, and I'll love you even more.'

He kissed her briefly and went to his room, emerging after a few minutes in his thick, woollen dressing gown, and disappearing into the bathroom.

'All the music I know is pre-war,' said Iris as they sat listening to the band.

'That's the best kind. Crimes have been committed during the last six or seven years in the sacred name of music, as I believe I've already said. Trumpets are made to squeal, and trombones routinely bray as if they've done it all their lives.' With an airy gesture intended to suggest that his argument was self-evident, he said, 'That's why we come here, where the band still embraces civilised music and plays it as the composers intended it to be played.'

'It means so much to you, doesn't it? Did you hear much music during the war?'

'No, we were kept quite busy on the East Coast. Coal was perpetually in demand, so dances were few and far between, at least as far as we were concerned.'

She wrinkled her nose in uncertainty and asked, 'What has coal to do with dancing?'

'The nation needed coal, so the convoys that brought it from Scotland and Northern England operated on a non-stop basis.'

'Do you mind talking about it?'

'No. Ask away.'

They were interrupted when the waiter brought the wine for Maurice's approval. He tasted it and nodded. 'That's good,' he said. The waiter poured some into their glasses and left them.

'What kind of thing did you do?'

'It was quite boring, really. We protected the convoys. It was routine stuff.'

'Except when you were injured.'

'There you go again. I'd forgotten about my scar until you mentioned it, just now.'

'Baloney.'

'Would you like to dance?' It was a convenient diversion.

'I'd love to.' The band were playing 'The More I See You'. She asked, 'It's not too modern for you, is it?'

'It's just about acceptable.' He led her out and they joined the dance. 'It's the Lindy-Hopping and Jitterbugging that upset me,' he confessed. 'They're both quite unseemly.'

'You poor old thing.'

'Did you know that this country has been invaded twice since ten sixty-six?'

'No one told me.'

'The first time was the Glorious Revolution of sixteen eighty-eight, when the English language almost gave way to Double-Dutch.'

'Now I think of it, I've heard about that.'

'The second time was in nineteen forty-two, when the Americans brought Swing music to this country. They were welcome, I seem to recall, but they might have left their music at home. I mean to say, "When in Rome", and all that sort of thing.'

They danced for a while without speaking, and then Iris said, 'Someone told me recently that Americans don't subscribe to the "When in Rome" custom. It seems they always bring their own culture with them.'

'That's certainly been my experience.'

'Ah, but you had that experience. I missed both their arrival and their departure.'

' "Clean linen",' he reminded her, kissing her on the cheek.

'I'm fine, honestly.'

The number ended, and they applauded the band and returned to their table. As they took their seats, Iris recognised someone a few tables away and returned her smile.

Maurice asked, 'Who's that?'

'A doctor, someone I hardly know.'

'She recognised you, though.'

'It's the redhead's burden. We stand out to the extent that anonymity is impossible.'

Their order arrived, prompting a change of subject. 'At the hospital, they call me "The Diner-Out",' Iris told him. 'It's all very good-natured, although they're quite envious. No one else is ever taken to nice places, apparently.'

'They should promote you to ward sister on the strength of that.'

'No, I'm afraid it takes a great deal more than that. I still have a lot of experience to gain in paediatric nursing before they'll even consider me for promotion.'

'You really love it, though, don't you?'

'I wouldn't do anything else,' she told him definitely.

As they finished their first course, the bandleader announced a waltz: 'I'll See You Again', and Maurice said, 'This one's old enough for me. Do you fancy it?'

'Yes, if it's not too lively for you.'

They danced for a while, and Iris said, 'I get the impression that you're more at home with the waltz than the foxtrot.'

'I like both, but the waltz is easier for me.'

'You're not bad at the foxtrot.'

He shook his head sadly. 'Faint praise indeed.'

'But you're wonderful in absolutely every other respect,' she assured him.

He could live with that, so they danced contentedly to the end of the number, when they left the dance floor.

'Is the curfew eleven o' clock tonight,' he asked, 'or have you got an extension?'

'I'm signed out for the weekend. I haven't to be back until eleven, tomorrow night.'

'Ah.' Either, she hadn't mentioned it, or she had and he'd not been listening. It was an even shot. A little embarrassed, he asked her, 'Have you booked a hotel?'

'No.'

It was possible that he was supposed to have done that when she told him about her weekend leave and he wasn't listening. 'I'm sorry,' he said, 'but don't worry. You can have my bed. I changed the sheets this morning. I'll take the sofa.'

'Are you sure you don't mind?'

'Not in the least. I've slept in hammocks and in bunks, on decks and... lots of places.' He was still trying to remember the original arrangement. There must have been one.

'You're the perfect host,' Iris told him, evidently sensing his unease. 'Don't give it another thought.'

A distraction came in the form of a foxtrot, which was 'As Time Goes By'.

'When this film comes round again, I'll take you to see it,' he said, taking her hand.

She frowned, bemused. 'What film is that? This song was popular years before the war, when I was at school.'

'The film was *Casablanca*, starring Humphrey Bogart and Ingrid Bergman, and they resurrected the song for it.' Attempting an impersonation of Bogart, he said, ' "Of all the gin joints in all the world, she has to come into mine." '

As they danced, she said, 'I remember Humphrey Bogart as a gangster, but I can't remember her. Does she really talk like that?'

He ignored the jibe and said, 'Bogie played a goodie in *Casablanca*, and Ingrid Bergman is a superb actress.' He kept deliberately quiet about the fact that she was also an acknowledged beauty. Women could be funny about that kind of thing.

'All right, I'll look forward to that.'

In view of Iris's weekend pass, they spent a leisurely evening dancing almost every dance. Eventually, however, the time came when they had to leave.

'I've enjoyed this evening so much,' said Iris, getting into the car. 'Thank you again.'

'As ever,' said Maurice, closing the driver's door and taking his seat, 'thank you for coming.'

They drove the short distance to Maurice's flat, where he said, 'I can't offer you coffee, because I haven't got any. It's all the fault of Rationing and Austerity, as you can imagine.'

'Don't worry, we had coffee at the restaurant, if you remember.' Picking up her bag, she said, 'I'll be back in a minute.'

'Take your time.' While she was in the bathroom, he dug out some bedding and laid it on the end of the sofa.

When she returned, she took the seat beside him, clearly in no hurry to retire.

He asked, 'Is there anything I've forgotten? Anything you need for tonight?'

She adopted a thoughtful pose and said, 'I can't think of anything.' She looked so appealing that he was tempted to put his arm around her, which he did. As he did so, she moved closer to him, and he said, 'It's getting easier, isn't it?'

'Much easier,' she agreed, raising no objection when he bent to kiss her. After the kind of evening they'd spent, it was a kiss that showed no sign of ending, and neither of them was inclined to hasten its conclusion. Maurice knew that, sooner or later, it would be necessary for them to part for the night, but Iris seemed happy for the moment. Eventually, however, she stirred.

He asked, 'Is it time for bed?'

She nodded.

'Okay.' He got up out of politeness and waited for her to leave him.

'Maurice,' she said, 'you don't have to sleep on the sofa.'

'I can't let you sleep on it.'

'No, I don't want to, either.' She smiled at his confusion. 'Not when there's room for both of us in there.' She inclined her head towards his bedroom.

He couldn't believe it. 'Are you absolutely sure?'

'Yes, I'm sure.' There was no doubt at all in her tone.

'That's....' Then he hesitated. 'There's just one tiny fly in the ointment.' It really was a bugger. 'You see, all this time I've been contemplating a life of celibacy, and I haven't got any... the necessary equipment.' It was too bad.

'It's all taken care of,' she assured him. 'Do you remember the woman who recognised me in the restaurant?'

'The doctor you hardly knew, yes.'

'She's the doctor I saw at the birth control place. They call it the Family Planning Clinic now. I told her we were going to get married, which is quite true, isn't it?'

'Yes.' He was too stunned to say more.

'She possibly recognised me because she knew I was at the hospital.'

'And from your auburn hair.' He realised he was talking nonsense. It had become like one of the Christmases he remembered from childhood, and he was just as excited as if the Christmas tree were there in the room. 'When did you go there?'

'Almost a week ago.' Sensing his bewilderment, she said, 'Do you remember last weekend, when I told you I felt much more relaxed about things?'

'You weren't joking, either.'

'I decided you'd never do anything to hurt me. If you remember, I said that everything you do is gentle and loving.'

'That's right.' It was finally beginning to make sense.

'There's more than a world of difference between what happened to me in the camp and the way things are between you and me.'

'Oh, there is.'

She stirred again. 'I'm a little bit shy, so will you give me a few minutes to get ready?'

'Of course.'

She made her way to the bedroom while he gathered his wits. Eventually, still scarcely believing the turn events had taken, he undressed down to his pants.

After a generous interval, he tapped on the bedroom door and heard the words he'd never expected to hear her say.

'Come in.'

Switching off the lights, he finished undressing and slipped into bed beside her, taking her into his arms. Ecstatically, he kissed her, delighting in the softness of her body through the flimsy cotton fabric of her nightdress, and the ready way that, in spite of her inexperience, she responded to his touch.

As if by unspoken agreement, she eased the garment up to her waist and then pulled it over her head, so that there was now no barrier between them.

After some time, she made room for him, giving a tiny, blissful gasp as she accepted him.

———

Iris stirred, opening her eyes minutely and then closing them against the sunlight that made its way into the room through the gap between the hastily-closed curtains. From beside her came the gentle clink of china against china being placed gently on the bedside table, and then she was conscious of the blissful aroma of tea. A few seconds later, she felt a dip in the mattress, followed unexpectedly by a kiss.

'Good morning,' she said, finally opening her eyes properly.

'Good morning. There's tea beside you.'

'You're truly wonderful.' She accepted another kiss before raising herself into a sitting position. As she did so, the sheet fell away, exposing her upper body, and she lifted it to cover herself again, but then let it fall, mindful that secrets, as well as emotional impediments, were now in the province of the past.

He kissed her again and said, 'I love you, Sister Lennox.'

'Why have you promoted me?'

'That's what I called you when we first met. Just now, it seemed appropriate.'

'In that case,' she said, 'I love you, too, Lieutenant Warneford.' She sipped her tea gratefully, and her memory returned, not unpleasantly for once, to that day on the River in Malaya. She said, 'Thank you for finding me and for putting me back together.'

'You were welcome to the lift up the river. As for the rest, I didn't do it alone. We owe that and our future together just as much to your own doing.' On reflection, he said, 'Between the two of us, though, we did a pretty remarkable job. Don't you agree?'

'That's not all we did.' She put her teacup down while she considered the extent of their achievement. 'We put the enemy to flight and, in doing that, I think we proved a point as well. Don't you?'

The End

Ingram Content Group UK Ltd.
Milton Keynes UK
UKHW010632110523
421582UK00001B/16